MW01504633

# SOULMARK

Blake M. Isles

# DISCLAIMER

This book is intended for mature audiences as it delves into adult topics such as, but not limited to, physical abuse/assault, consensual and non-consensual sexual situations, violent deaths, medical experimentation, and torture. If any of these topics are potential triggers, you are advised to proceed cautiously.

# PLAYLIST

*Through Glass* - Stone Sour
*The Sound of Silence* - Disturbed
*Voices In My Head* - Falling in Reverse
*CASTLE OF GLASS - Linkin Park*
*One More Light* - Linkin Park
*Waiting for the End* - Linkin Park
*Iridescent* - Linkin Park
*Battle Symphony* - Linkin Park
*Leader of Men (Acoustic Version)* - Nickelback
*Here Without Your (Cover Version)* - Felix Irwan
*Boulevard of Broken Dreams (Cover Version)*
- Nick Warner, Frank Moschetto
*When We Were Young (Acoustic Version)* - Felix Irwan
*Take Me to Church* - Hozier
*Song on Fire* - Nickelback
*Mind Of Mine* - Lo Spirit
*Miracle* - A Day To Remember

*I always listen to my playlists on shuffle so the order does not pertain to the storyline.*

# CONTENTS

*With your love, I'm surrounded.*
*Faith in you, I've never doubted.*
*Of all the things I could lose,*
*The worst of all would be you.*

*Standing tall through all the pain,*
*Thoughts of you keep me sane.*
*With every breath, I feel your soul.*
*The piece that's you, makes me whole.*

*There's nothing that I wouldn't give*
*If tomorrow, you could live.*
*So, lay me down to sacrifice,*
*Sever the root of my life.*

BLAKE M. ISLES

# CHAPTER ONE

## *Snatched*

"**W**ilson Medic twenty three to Ridgeview ER," the radio barked with emergency sirens blaring in the background. The chitter chatter around the nursing desk fell to a hushed silence at the sound.

"This is Ridgeview, Wilson twenty three. Go ahead," our secretary, Katie, replied as she picked up a pen to record the ambulance's incoming report.

"We are inbound status post multi-car MVC. The driver of vehicle one was found unconscious on scene. Patient appears to be a male in his mid-twenties. He was extricated from the vehicle with spinal precautions. He has been intubated. Bilateral eighteen gauge ACs. Obvious trauma to the left side of the head. Bleeding is controlled. Positive seatbelt sign. BP eighty over palp. Heart rate 124. Two liters of normal saline bolusing. ETA, two minutes."

"Ten-four. Room upon arrival. WPIS four-oh-six out," Katie replied, holding the report over her head for me to grab.

"Wilson Medic fourteen to Ridgeview ER," the radio blared again.

"This is Ridgeview, Wilson fourteen. Go ahead."

There were no sirens this time, so I began organizing the plan for the first ambulance while Katie took the report.

"Alright. Medic twenty three will come to trauma room two. I want eyes on the patient as the medics bring him in. If he's stable, take him straight to CT. If not, we will stabilize in the room before imaging. Claire, that's your room, so you'll accompany to CT. Brent, set up the room for an intubated trauma level one. OGT, catheters, suction, trauma cart, the works. Increase the temp in the room to at least eighty degrees, and page the blood blank to have an emergency release of two units O neg brought down," I ordered.

"You got it, boss," Brent answered as I turned to Katie to grab the second report. The second patient was a seven year old girl from the second car. She was restrained with no obvious injuries. Mom wanted her checked out as a precaution. *Good*, I thought, *pediatric traumas are the worst.*

"Let's put her in room ten with Brandy. When the mom gets here, have triage bring her back to bedside, please."

Katie nodded, picked up the phone and dialed the triage nurse. At that moment, both ambulances rolled into the bay. The man was brought in first, and I immediately moved to do an initial assessment. The cardiac monitor showed stable vital signs, but his head injury was concerning. I pulled back his eyelids one at a time to check his pupil reactivity.

"Did you give him anything besides the saline? Any narcs or paralytics?" I asked the medic.

"No ma'am. Just the saline. Scene was only a few minutes from y'all."

"Dr. Havin!" I called. "Left pupil is blown!"

She stood from her desk and headed toward the imaging department. "Let's get him scanned. I'll evaluate as they set up," she directed.

"Claire, you go. I'll eval the kid, and if she's okay, I'll meet you bedside when you get back."

"Sounds good," Claire answered as she grabbed the stretcher and led the medics down the hall to the CT machine. Katie had directed the second ambulance to room ten.

"And, Katie?" I called over my shoulder as I headed to meet the other medics.

"I already paged out the level one trauma. The neurosurgeon is headed down from the ICU, and the trauma doc will be here in ten," she responded, already knowing what I needed.

"You're the best!"

Katie really was the best secretary we ever had. Half the time she knew what we needed before we did, making my job exponentially easier. As I walked into room ten, the little girl was clambering onto the ER bed while EMS packed up their equipment.

"Hi, my name is Lacey. What's your name?" I asked the child as I sat down on the stool by her bed. She had her head tucked down and peaked out at me from underneath her dirty blonde hair.

"She hasn't said anything since we packed her up," Joe, a paramedic, said from behind me. "Mom said her name is Sarah."

"Well, that's okay, Sarah. Sometimes I don't like to talk to people either. Especially, when I don't know who they are," I smiled. A small grin spread across her face. "So," I said, redirecting my attention back to Joe and his partner, "tell me a love story." I logged into the computer to start Sarah's chart as I got the details.

Joe began, "Little Sarah here is seven years old. She was the backseat passenger on the driver's side. She has no sign of injury. She shakes her head 'no' when asked if she is in pain. Appears alert and oriented from what I can tell without her explicitly talking."

"She was restrained, correct?" I interjected.

"Yes, ma'am. she was. Vital signs were within normal limits. Pupils, equal and reactive. Her mom has a few scrapes and bruises. She denied immediate transport. Police will bring her over after they get her statement, but she wanted Sarah checked out just to be safe," he finished.

"Alrighty then. That sounds good to me."

"Any questions for me, Lacey?"

"Nope. I think I'm good. Thanks, Joe," I answered as he held his tablet out for me to sign as a receipt for the patient and report. Joe and his partner left, and I turned back to Sarah. She was looking at me with obvious fear in her eyes.

"Sarah," I said as I rolled my stool toward the bed. "Now that it's just us girls, would you be able to tell me what's wrong?" I was careful to keep my body positioning relaxed and open. Body language said a lot in cases like this, and I needed Sarah to think of me as her friend.

"I don't like hospitals," she whispered.

"That's okay. Most people don't like to come to the hospital. Have you ever been to one before?"

"Only once," Sarah replied, "when my granny died last year. She had lots of machines and stuff in her room."

"Oh, I'm so sorry. I wouldn't like coming back to the hospital either after that, but your mommy will be here real soon."

"Ms. Lacey, am I going to die like Granny?" she asked with tears in her eyes.

"Oh no way! I'm going to take good care of you. I promise. You look quite healthy to me, but just to make extra, super sure, I'm going to give you a good looksy. Is that okay with you?" *Poor child. No wonder she was scared*, I thought.

"That's okay," she answered. I had her recline on the bed as I began checking her pulses, capillary refill, hand and foot strength, and abdominal and lung sounds.

"Sarah, I'm going to push real gently on your belly. Can you tell me if it hurts?"

She nodded her head in answer. I began palpating her stomach, starting in the right lower quadrant and working my way around. I looked at her, and she was smiling.

"It doesn't hurt," she said, "but it does kinda tickle."

A big smile spread across my face. "Tickles are a good sign," I winked at her. "I tell you what. You look great to me, but just to get a second opinion, I'll get Dr. Lyles. She is the best doctor in the whole ER. We will look you over together and make sure you don't have any bruises I might've missed; and, if she says it's okay, I'll get you a popsicle after to celebrate. Does that sound okay to you?"

"That sounds awesome!" Sarah exclaimed.

As I opened the door to the hallway I saw people running down the corridor in a panic. A loud bang rang out from the triage room, and the door shot into the adjacent wall. Two men dressed in all black with masks and assault rifles filed through the entryway before splitting up.

"Find the target then get to the rendezvous point," one of them called to the other.

Screams erupted as the men barged into the patient rooms. Two shots rang through the air. *Hide Sarah*, the thought raced through my mind. I didn't know what the men were after, but it sounded like they were killing people. I turned to look at the little girl who had run to a corner of the room when she heard the shots. I strode over to her and grabbed her hand. "Sarah, I am going to keep you safe, but I need you to trust me and do everything I tell you. Okay?"

She nodded her head and gripped my hand tightly. I pulled her behind me as I peaked my head out the doorway. The hall was empty, so we sprinted across to the supply room. I quickly typed in the code, pulled Sarah in, and shut the door behind us. On the far side of the room, there was a sink with an empty cabinet below it. I opened the doors and instructed Sarah to get in and not to make a sound.

"No matter what happens, you are not to open this door. Do you understand?" I asked. She nodded as I shut the cabinet doors. My heart skipped a beat when I heard the handle jiggle on the door we came through. When the lock wouldn't give, hard pounding rattled the wood on its hinges.

"CODE GOLD, LEVEL TWO, ER," blared over the intercom, announcing the active shooters to the rest of the hospital. Our security guards weren't armed, and it would take at least three minutes for the police to arrive from the precinct. While three minutes didn't sound like much, a lot of people could die in that time frame, and these shooters seemed determined.

The banging continued at the door as someone attempted to break the lock. All staff knew the code, so it had to be the shooters. The sink concealing Sarah was the only closed-in area for the entire room. The remainder of the walls were lined with open shelving that housed a vast array of equipment and supplies. Lacking a hiding spot, I scanned the shelves looking for something to use as a weapon. My eyes quickly landed on the scalpels. Grabbing an eleven blade, I tore off its wrapper and pushed the blade up. It wasn't much, but it was better than nothing.

A loud bang filled the air as an explosive blew the keypad lock off the door, and a man entered. Staring directly at me, he lifted the radio off his shoulder. "Target located in the first supply room."

My heart was racing at the word "target." As far as he could see, I was the only one here. Adrenaline and fear shot through my whole body. He raised his rifle and slowly started forward. I reached my free hand out behind me feeling for the doorknob of the second exit as I backed up. When I found the handle, I swung the door open and sprinted down the hall. I could hear my pursuer chasing close behind as the other man rounded the corner at the end of the hall in front of me.

An emergency exit with the west wing staircase was on my right. I scanned my badge for entry and ran through the door, passed the stairs, and toward the outside exit. As soon as I reached to push the door open, another man stepped out from under the staircase and wrapped his arms around me from behind. He lifted me into the air as I kicked and thrashed. Without thinking, I spun the scalpel in my hand, positioning the blade pointing down in my fist. I kicked my legs out and leaned forward to unbalance my attacker with the counter weight. With the built up momentum, I stabbed the scalpel into his right thigh. He dropped me as he screamed from the unexpected pain. The first two men entered the stairwell with their guns aimed directly at me.

My attacker wrenched the scalpel out of his leg, causing blood to spurt into the air. He clamped his hand down on the wound, but I had hit his femoral artery. Blood gushed at an alarming rate from underneath his hands. "Goddammit!" he cussed.

The other men's eyes flickered to their comrade. With his distraction, I rushed out the door to the ambulance bay. A black SUV was parked underneath with all four doors open. A fourth man stepped out of the driver's seat and headed toward me. I ran up the hill toward the parking garage, but before I made it out from the bay, I was tackled from behind. I face planted into the asphalt as all the breath was knocked from my lungs.

*Get away! I have to get away! I can't go with them!* the panic riddled thoughts screamed internally.

The man who tackled me was on his feet. He grabbed one of my legs and began dragging me to the SUV. The rough concrete scratched my skin as my scrub top rode up from the friction. I twisted onto my back and kicked my free leg up, connecting with his groin. He doubled over in pain as he dropped my other leg. I quickly made it to my feet, but I felt a gun barrel press between my shoulder blades.

"Give me a reason," a man hissed in my ear.

"You might as well shoot me, because I am not going to go with you," I said, my breathing heavy.

"Oh, I think you will," he replied matter of factly, "because if you don't, I'm going to go back in there, find that little girl you hid, and put a bullet in her brain."

I clenched my jaw in frustration. "She has nothing to do with this."

"Collateral damage happens. Now, move," he ordered as he shoved me forward.

"You are threatening to murder an innocent, little girl to get your way. That's not collateral damage, you jackass," I spat as I walked toward the SUV. The man I stabbed was lying in the backseat with a tourniquet on his leg. Blood drenched his pants as more spilled from the wound. Police sirens were blaring in the distance as the local department responded.

"Get in," one of the men barked at me.

"Why? What's this about?" I asked, trying to delay leaving. *When the police arrive, I may be able to get away in the chaos*, I thought.

"You know exactly what it's about. Now, get in." My captor went to shove me again, but I spun on my heel and slammed my fist as hard as I could into his face.

"Stupid bitch!" he yelled.

Two men grabbed me under either arm and slammed me into the side of the SUV. They pulled my hands behind my back and bound them in place.

"Help!" I screamed as a last resort, but I knew no one would come. One of them shoved a gag in my mouth and taped it shut. Picking me up under my arms, they threw me in the vehicle's hatch. One man climbed in next to me as the last two took their seats.

The SUV lurched off before all the doors were shut. I desperately started kicking as hard as I could in an effort to make contact with my co-riders head. He caught my legs and tried to pin them down; however, I continued fighting with all the effort I could muster.

"For the love of God, someone sedate this bitch!" he yelled at the others, grunting in frustration.

A backseat passenger leaned over the seat with a syringe in hand. He stabbed the needle into my upper arm and depressed the plunger. My legs felt like they instantly turned to lead. I couldn't move, and my vision began to fade to darkness within seconds. The last thing I heard was someone say, "Sleep tight, princess."

# CHAPTER TWO

### *Intersected*

W hen I first saw Callen, my entire body lit up. Every move he made felt like it was directed toward me. Then, when he looked at me, it was as if the world stopped. I don't know how long our eyes held each other, but a smile crept across both our faces. Just like now as I lay here with a mere memory.

I went with my friend to a self defense class that day. It wasn't really my thing, but Claire really wanted some company.

*"Thank you so much for coming!" she said. "I think you'll really like the instructor. Janet is amazing."*

*"I've been looking forward to it. Thanks for inviting me," I lied, but I put on my best excited face for her. A self defense class wasn't my idea of fun. I'd much rather be at home in my pajamas and reading a book with a large glass of wine, but I'd do anything for Claire.*

*We walked into the studio to a group of a dozen or so men and women.* Leave it to Claire to find a co-ed class, *I thought.* She was always on the prowl.

*"Welcome, everyone," a voice from the front rang out. "I see a few new faces, so for those of you who don't know, I'm Janet, the lead instructor for Self Defense Basics."*

*Janet was tall and slender yet strikingly fit. Her brown hair was pulled up into a pony with soft curls in the tail. She had a pleasant, sweet smile that compelled you to like her. Even her eyes looked gentle.*

*"Everyone gather around, and let's get started," she called, motioning the class to the front of the room. "A surprise guest - my brother, Callen - has come to demonstrate basic escape techniques from an assault," Janet stated as a man stepped out from the crowd.*

*Like his sister, Callen was tall with brown hair; however, that was the end of their similarities. While Janet emitted a bubbly, inviting personality, he looked curt and stoney. I felt my whole body tense as I stared at this man. My eyes flitted to his broad shoulders and muscled arms, his black shirt slightly snug around his biceps. I felt my breath hitch as my gaze ran down his figure. Everything about him called to me.*

*"It's nice to meet everybody, and I thank you for having me," he said looking around the room, his voice deep and commanding. Perfectly straight, white teeth shown behind his full lips, and a strong jawline was visible through a soft five o'clock shadow. When his eyes met mine, it felt like my heart stopped. My gaze locked with the most beautiful green eyes I had ever seen. They shone like emeralds as they held onto mine. A slow smile spread across his face, and he looked away.*

*I took a deep breath trying to calm my nerves down as he continued his introduction.* You're fine, I thought. Your heart needs to get it together. He's good looking - well, more than good looking to be honest - but he's just a random guy.

*Claire nudged me with her elbow. I looked over to see her eyebrows raised in question.*

*"Sorry. Zoned out," I mouthed. She shrugged and returned her attention to Callen.*

*"If you would all pair up, one male and one female, please,"*

11

*Callen requested.*

*Claire was quickly approached by a man who was checking her out when we arrived. She was stunning with blonde hair that flowed down her back, a neat hourglass figure, and crystal clear, blue eyes. She winked at me as she sauntered off with her latest catch, and I couldn't help but laugh at her antics.*

*"It looks like we have an odd number," a voice rumbled behind me, causing goosebumps to ripple across my flesh. "I guess that leaves you with me."*

*I turned around and nearly walked straight into Callen standing there with a smirking smile on his face. "Oh, I, um, I can just watch," I stammered.*

*"Nonsense, you're here to learn, and it's way more beneficial to participate rather than watch from the sidelines," Callen said as he offered his hand to me. The watch on his left wrist glistened in the light as he turned his hand palm up.*

*"Well, if you insist," I sighed, letting out a breath I had apparently been holding. I placed my hand in his and tingles shot up my arm like little jolts of electricity dancing between our fingers. His eye caught mine and a smile spread across my face. He led me to the front of the class, only letting go when he called the group to attention. As soon as our contact was broken, my body cried out to touch him again.*

You have got to chill, *I thought.*

*Callen was giving instructions to the class on our first technique. Instead of listening to the directions though, I found myself watching his lips. The way his mouth moved when he spoke was hypnotic. All I could think about was how those lips would feel against mine as I ran my fingers through his hair.*

*"Ready?" Callen asked, pulling me out of my daydream.*

*"Oh, um, do you think you could walk me through it one more time?" I asked, trying to keep the blush from my cheeks. "I*

*was lost in thought I suppose."*

"Sure," Callen responded with a glint of humor flashing through his eyes.

God, he probably thinks I'm an idiot, *I thought.*

*"I'm going to grab your left forearm like I'm going to pull you forward. You are going to wrap your right hand around your fist, take a step back with your right leg, and pull your left arm back toward your body. Kind of like a snapping motion," Callen instructed.*

"Alright." *This was a basic maneuver. One that I've unfortunately had to use in the past. Most of the time patients in the emergency room maintained their manners, and if they didn't, verbal abuse was the usual run of the mill event. However, a patient that would rather throw fists always shows up eventually. The majority of those patients are drunk, high, or psychotic, but occasionally, they are just assholes.*

*When I nodded my head to signal I was ready, Callen reached out with his left hand and grabbed my arm. As much as I hated to break contact with him, I demonstrated the movement and tore my arm from his grasp.*

"Good job. Let's try it a few more times," *he praised. Callen and I repeated the steps as Janet walked through the room assisting others with their techniques and offering suggestions.*

"Alright, everyone," *Callen called out when he was satisfied with the practice.* "Now, let's try it when the attacker grabs you with their opposite arm. Guys, if you would, grab your partners' left arm with your right hand. And if my partner would be so kind as to do that, I'll show you the next part," *Callen said as he extended his arm out to me.*

*This was another defense I'd used, so I decided it was time to make up for my earlier distractions.* "Oh, that's okay," *I said as I lifted my arm up,* "you can go ahead and grab mine."

Callen laughed, "Well, okay, if you insist." He reached out and wrapped his hand around my forearm. In one swift motion, I twisted my arm, wrapped my hand around his, stepped forward while pulling him toward me, placed my left hand into the back of his shoulder, and shoved him forward. Callen's eyes bulged with the unexpected motion, and the class erupted with laughter.

"Yes, just like that," he said with a smirk. "Now, you all give it a try." Callen turned to look at me as I tried to keep the pleasure of shocking him from coming out in my smile, but that was impossible. I felt pleased with myself and oddly enough, he seemed pleased as well with a half crooked smile creeping onto his face.

Callen went over a few more methods before class ended. Every time we touched, the electricity flared to life between us. Goosebumps riddled my skin beneath his fingertips, and a solid blush crept over my cheeks when I would catch him staring at me. His piercing gaze drove me wild, and the lilt of his voice drew me in like nothing I had ever experienced.

All too soon, Janet called an end to the session, and all the participants began dispersing. Claire immediately came to my side with a giddy smile spread across her face. "Derek, the guy I partnered with, and his friend want to take us for drinks."

"Oh, I don't know, Claire. I have to work early tomorrow, and it's already nine o'clock," I said, glancing at the two men standing by the door.

"Please," she begged. "Just one drink. I'll owe you big."

"Alright. Alright. But, just one," I replied, holding a single finger in the air, knowing that would never be the case.

"Awesome!" she exclaimed as she linked arms with me and headed toward the door.

I looked back over my shoulder and saw Callen staring at me. His jaw was set with a look of irritation. His eyes met mine, but before I could react, Claire had me out the door headed to the bar.

A loud bang pulled me out of my reverie. Two men walked in dressed in all black: cargo pants, shirts, and shoes. They were both physically fit with buzzed hair, and an undeniable military vibe radiated from them. If this was any other time, I would even note them as fairly attractive; however, they currently wore serious faces with a look of hatred beaming out of their eyes, which was deeply unsettling.

"Get up. It's time to go," one of them barked at me. I sat appraising them both for a moment with a narrowed look, debating whether or not I could make a break for the open door.

The speaker rolled his eyes and puffed, "Don't even think about it. Either get up and come on, or we will drag you."

I stared a moment longer, and - as if to make his point - he took an aggressive step forward.

"Fine." I stood up from the concrete floor quickly to dissuade any additional threats of being manhandled. As I walked, one stuck his hand out to grab me by the upper arm.

"I do not need your assistance," I spat, jerking my arm out of his reach.

They looked at each other for a moment. The one that spoke nodded his head curtly toward the other, who promptly turned and headed to the door. "Follow him, and don't dottle."

Begrudgingly, I followed the first man out the door, the second closely behind me, so close that I could almost feel his chest brush against my back. I'm not sure if he was going for intimidation or simply ensuring I didn't try to run. Either way, both of those things were being accomplished.

We walked in a single file line down the hallway encased in concrete. Dim lights shown above, illuminating our path.

Left, right, right, left...there was no way I could find my way back. Not that I was interested in trying to get back to my dungeon, but I desperately needed to orient myself to my location if I had any hope of escaping. We passed several doors as we walked. All with keycard entry locks. Wherever we were was tightly secured, and if I planned on going anywhere, I would need one of those cards.

Eventually, we came to a grandly open, circular foyer. Windows were high on the walls allowing for the first sight of natural light I had seen since awakening. There were several hallways that branched off in different directions, but there was only one door which stood adjacent from us. We crossed to the other side of the room, and the lead man rapt on the door.

"Come in!" a male voice bellowed.

The first guard opened the door and ushered me inside. I stepped in to see a man sitting behind a large mahogany desk, toying with a pen in his hand. He was handsomely young - no more than thirty, clean shaven with a catching jawline, and dark hair neatly styled. He sat idly with eyes glimmering as they met mine.

"I have been anxiously awaiting your arrival my dear. I do hope you found your accommodations acceptable."

"Acceptable?" I asked in a sarcastic tone. "If you find a concrete floor accommodating, then I think we will have to disagree on the circumstance."

"Watch your tongue," one of the men behind me ordered.

The man behind the desk rose, allowing me to appreciate his towering height and overall domineering physique. He was wearing an elegant, black suit with a white button down and slender black tie - the ideal picturesque business man.

"Gentlemen, why don't you step in the hall for a spell. I think the lady and I can become better acquainted in privacy. I will call when I am ready for your return," he stated as a suggestion, but it was anything but.

"Yes, sir," the men answered in unison.

I turned my head to see them promptly exit the office and snap the door shut behind them. Returning my gaze back to the man who was clearly in charge, I took a step toward the window on my right. It was too high for me to reach even while standing, but I couldn't help myself.

"Please, my dear, do relax and take a seat," he said, gesturing to one of the chairs in front of his desk. I took a deep breath to settle myself before heading to the chair. Once I was seated, he returned to his plush office chair. "You'll have to forgive my soldiers. They are rather put off with you I am afraid; but, in their defense, you did stab one of their friends. I'll see to it you receive better arrangements if our chat proves fruitful."

"Maybe I wouldn't have stabbed him if he wasn't trying to abduct me," I hissed angrily. "I don't know who you think I am, but I am sure there must be a mistake. And, I don't believe we have much to chat about unless it involves an apology and directions to the exit."

He laughed, "Why, you are a little spicy, aren't you, sweetheart?" I gritted my teeth at the pet name, but before I could counter, he continued, "It's not who you are that peaks my interest. I, frankly, could care less about the 'who', darling. It's the 'what' I am concerned with."

"Excuse me?" Doing my best to look clueless, I lied, "I haven't the faintest idea of what you are talking about."

"Let's not beat around the bush. It is a waste of my time and yours," he said matter of factly. "You are a marked one."

My hand shot to my left wrist feeling for the bracelet I normally wore to cover my soulmark, but it was gone. Chills ran down my spine, and I bit my bottom lip trying to think how to deny what he clearly already knew.

"You see," he continued, "the entire existence of your kind utterly fascinates my colleagues and I. How a person can be born with a soulmate - a soulmate that bears an identical marking to his own and no one else  - is the question of the millennium." He stood and began pacing around the room with his hand casually pulling at the knot of his tie.

"There must be a genetic component, obviously. Everything stems from DNA. Eye color. Hair length. Skin tone. However, while those things are passed via parental heritage, the markings appear to happen randomly - as if it is a mutation." He slid his tie off and threw it on a sofa against a back wall, followed by his jacket. He then proceeded to cuff his sleeves as he continued pacing. "Yet, if that's the case, two people are born with the same mutation that is never repeated. As long as your kind has existed, there have been no studies identifying a marking appearing more than twice; although, the soulmarks are always in the same place - left wrist at the base of the thumb, parallel to the radial artery."

I watched as he turned to face me with that last statement and swallowed. "It sounds like you have given this some thought."

It was no secret that scientists had been trying to explain the evolution of the soulmark for centuries. Many of the studies started with volunteers who were anxious to explain the phenomenon thrust upon them. As test after test failed, the researchers became more aggressive in their searches and experiments. Many marked ones died during the studies, and some were outright slaughtered, their bodies dissected and examined for a physical indication.

When the volunteers stopped, they began forcefully

enrolling the new subjects. The marked ones that were fortunate enough to escape enrollment went into hiding, but there are only so many places to hide. It's been years since a marked one was found, at least according to the news. Multiple decades since a mated couple has been located. Rumors spread that the marked ones had gone extinct. When in all actuality, a few still remain, but we do our best to stay off the radar.

Personally, I never cared about finding my soulmate. My only concern was blending in as a background character in life, hiding in plain sight. I never drew unnecessary attention to myself, never maintained serious relationships with men. I watched my surroundings, and most importantly, I always covered my mark. So, when I found my mate, it was an utter accident.

"Oh, my dear, some thought is an understatement. I've devoted my life to discovering the truth," he replied, walking toward me. He leaned against his desk and wrapped the edge tightly in his hands. "I have had geneticists at my disposal for years. They have torn apart chromosome after chromosome, pulling the DNA spools from their histones and laying them flat. They have combed miles and miles of DNA and found nothing.

"Although," he sighed, "there are many traits about the body, besides soulmarks, we have yet to link to a particular chromosome. So, instead of solely focusing our efforts there, I thought it prudent to explore other avenues of detection. To do that, however, I need test subjects, and since a willing participant is unlikely, I decided a little encouragement would be necessary."

"You think kidnapping someone is an example of 'a little encouragement'?" I scoffed at him. "You may have brought me here, but that doesn't mean that I am going to participate in whatever it is you think you are going to do."

"Oh, I think you will, but there's no need to entertain the

ins and outs of what will happen just yet. We have other things to discuss first," he said as he crossed his arms over his chest. "I am particularly invested in you, but you would be much more interesting with your mate alongside you."

"Too bad I don't have a mate, then," I lied, keeping my facial features neutral. "I hate to disappoint you."

"My sources tell me otherwise. Where is he?"

"Well, your sources are sadly misinformed. I have never met my soulmate, nor do I have the intention. Perhaps, you should spend more time finding reliable help than abducting specimens."

A smile spread across his face. "My sources are quite reliable. I can assure you that. You've been careful, my dear. It took a rather long time to identify you. Years, in fact."

I clenched my jaw while making eye contact with him, careful not to blink. "As you can obviously tell from my wrist, I have a soulmark. Your informant is correct in that aspect, but he - whoever he is - is wrong about me having a mate. You can't find someone who you don't look for and, as you said, I'm careful. Searching for my mate would make me vulnerable, which is something that's never piqued my interest."

Suddenly, his hand came swinging down, slapping me hard across the face. My head whipped to the side with the impact.

"Fuck!" I yelled and brought my hand instinctively to my face. I wiped my palm across my mouth and felt something wet. Crimson blood smeared on my fingers from a split in my lower lip.

He bent down, grabbed a fist full of my hair, and yanked my head back. "You will tell me who your mate is. It is not up for debate," he snarled.

"I can't tell you who he is if I don't fucking know who he

is, you asshole!" I yelled back at him.

"That is no way for a lady to speak. Vulgarity is unbecoming, sweetheart. Don't you have any manners?" he questioned.

I winced as he tightened his hold in my hair and pulled. He glared at me, and I glared back. I would die before I told him about Callen. It didn't matter what he did to me. He let go of my hair and pinched my cheeks in one hand.

"You will answer me," he calmly stated.

Before he could react, I pushed my head forward, mouth open, and latched onto the web spacing between his pointer finger and thumb. As I dug my teeth into the tender skin, he screamed in pain. The two soldiers swung open his office door as he wrenched his hand from my bite and punched me so hard I fell out of my chair.

"The bitch bit me!" he yelled as he held his hand, blood running down his wrist. "She actually bit me."

I pulled myself up from the floor, grabbed a paper weight off the desk, and flung it at the oncoming soldiers. The first ducked, but the weight struck the second in the nose, causing blood to erupt. I skirted around the distracted soldiers and raced toward the door. I was a few feet from the exit when one of them tackled me from behind. I twisted in the air, and he landed on top of me, grappling for my hands as I tried to push him off. He pinned my arms to my chest and moved to straddle me, making my kicking futile.

The soldier with the bloody nose regained his composure and walked over to us, cussing me under his breath. The one restraining me rose at his approach. They each grabbed one of my arms and yanked me off the floor. I tried to pull free, but their grasps didn't budge. It was obvious our scrimmage was over, so I stopped resisting and stood between them.

The vision in my left eye was blurry, and I could feel the soft tissue swelling from the strike of the man's fist. Nothing felt broken, but there was sure to be a resultant bruise. I glowered as the head man walked toward me, bending so we were face to face before he spoke. "You will pay for this, but for now, I will see you in the morning. Bright and early, sweetheart." Straightening up, he barked at the soldiers, "Take her away."

Gruffly, the soldiers led me out of the office and back down one of the halls. I wasn't sure what was going to happen tomorrow, but tonight, I could try to make a plan. Unfortunately, it's hard to plan for the unknown. When we arrived back at my room, the soldier on my right opened the door and shoved me inside. The door slammed shut with a lock clicking in place.

# CHAPTER THREE

## *Connected*

I dreamed of Callen that night, but I don't know if you can call it a dream when you are reliving a memory. My unconscious thoughts took me back to the night we met.

*Claire and I had been at the bar for about thirty minutes with Derek and his friend Michael, and we were on our second round of drinks. Claire - being Claire - was laying on the charm thick. Derek had his arm wrapped around her as they sat across from Michael and I at the booth.*

*"Oh, I love this song," she cooed. "Let's go dance."*

*Derek led Claire onto the dance floor, spun her around, and pulled her in close to him. Slow, country music rang through the speakers as they became lost in each other's eyes.*

*"Would you like to dance?" Michael asked, pulling my attention back to him.*

*"Oh, no. I'm not much of a dancer. Thanks for asking though," I tacked onto the end trying not to sound rude. I actually loved to dance, but something about this man made me uneasy.*

*"So, tell me, how do you know Derek?" I asked to break the silence.*

*"We met in college. Freshmen roommates actually. Needless to say, we hit it off and have been friends ever since," Michael*

shrugged. *"How about you and Clarie?"*

*"Claire and I are nurses in the ER at Ridgeview. I've been there for a few years. Claire is closer to five I think."* Our conversation started to die out as the song ended and our companions rejoined us at the table.

*"Derek invited us to come back to his place and hangout since it's getting a bit crowded,"* Claire stated. *"I thought it was a great idea."*

Of course she did, *I thought. I plastered a fake smile on my face in an attempt to not look put off,* "Tonight isn't a good night. I have to work in the morning. Maybe some other time."

*Knowing Claire, her and Derek would be locked in his room most of the night which would leave Michael and I to our own devices, and while I did have to work early tomorrow, I didn't want to be alone with Michael. Besides, casual and random hook ups weren't my thing.*

*"Party pooper,"* Claire teased me, sticking her tongue out.

*I gave her a narrow look, but a smile creeped over my face nonetheless.* "Yeah, yeah, yeah," *I said,* "You kids go have fun though."

*The two of them said their goodbyes and left us alone in the booth. Michael was looking at me with a smile on his face. I politely smiled back, but I had a feeling he was not going to let me slide out of this booth anytime soon.*

*"Since you don't feel like going out, maybe we could just chill at your place for a bit,"* he said suggestively while sliding his hand over to my leg and resting his palm on my thigh.

*I looked down at his hand, gently set mine atop his, and slid it off.* "Look, Michael, you seem nice, and I don't know what Claire may have told the two of you, but I'm not really in the market for any kind of relationship right now," *I explained, going for the nice let down of* "it's not you, it's me" *which was not* untrue. I'm not opposed to dating, but starting something up with a person connected to anyone else in my life was not something I could ever do. Part of not drawing attention to yourself meant not intermingling circles of friends and "more than friends." The less drama, the better.

"Who said anything about starting a relationship?" Michael smirked, "One night for just a little bit of fun then." He reached his hand back out and grabbed my left wrist.

I jerked my arm from his hand, seething. "I said no. Now, if you will kindly get up, I would like to leave." My original misgivings about him echoed in my head. Instinct told me he was no good, and he was proving me right.

"Don't be in a hurry, hun. The night is young," he crooned at me.

Anger flashed in my eyes. He was starting to piss me off, but before I could respond, a man walked up to our table and drew our attention.

"Sorry, I am so late. Janet and I had a few questions from some students at the end of class," Callen said as he placed his hands on the table and leaned in, causing his arms to tense and flex his toned muscles.

"Oh, it's no problem, I'm so glad that you could make it after all," I replied, over exaggerating the flirty lilt in my voice. "Maybe we can catch up some other time though. I was just about to leave." I turned to Michael at the end of the pointed statement, leaving him no choice but to let me up.

"Right." Michael stood and moved slightly away from Callen, who was giving him a death glare. "I'll walk you out," Michael started to say as he reached his arm to put it around my waist; however, Callen stepped in between us before Michael had even finished his statement.

"That's okay," Callen said, "I'll be walking her home. Have a goodnight." He placed his hand lightly between my shoulder blades and motioned forward with his other hand. "After you of course."

I glanced back at Michael as I was ushered out the door. His expression of surprise quickly turned to one of irritation as we faded out of sight. Callen had dropped his hand from my back as soon as I started walking, which was courteous, but I really wished he had left it there. Goosebumps danced along my skin where his warm touch had grazed ever so lightly.

We started down the sidewalk toward my apartment in silence. Finally, I looked at him. "I would say you either have impeccable timing or you followed me after class." The bite on my lower lip released with a smile as I spoke.

Callen was smiling as well and replied, "Definitely the first one. Naturally." Even in the dark night, I swore I saw a slight blush pool into his cheeks.

"Well, either way, I believe I owe you a thank you."

"Men should behave themselves better than that asshole," Callen said, the smile fading and a glint of anger crossing into his eyes; however, it passed almost as quickly as it came. "So, how long do we have to walk before you tell me what your name is?"

"You know, that would probably be helpful information," I laughed. "I'm Lacey, Lacey Reynolds."

"Callen Davis."

"It's nice to officially meet you," I teased.

He laughed in response. I stopped when we reached my apartment building. He turned to me, and butterflies erupted in my stomach. The depth of his beautiful, green eyes was all consuming. I felt like I could stand there in that moment for the rest of my life.

"Would you want to come inside?" The question escaped my mouth before I had time to stop myself.

"I, unfortunately, should be going," he replied.

The words hit me like a sledgehammer to the gut. "Oh, sure." The rejection felt heavy, and I wasn't quite sure why.

"I am truly sorry. Trust me. I just have something I need to do," he tried to explain.

"You don't have to explain. It's okay. Um, well, goodnight, and thanks again." I turned to go inside the building before my disappointment showed too much. As I reached my hand up to open the door, I felt the air shift behind me.

"Lacey."

I turned and he fully pushed me up against the building. Taking my face in his hands, he pressed his lips urgently to mine like he was afraid I'd disappear. I kissed him back matching his passion and entwined my fingers in his hair. Our bodies were tight together, but I wanted him closer. A fire ignited across my skin where he touched me and spread throughout my body, the physical craving of him taking over. His tongue gently traced my lower lip seeking entry.

All too soon, he broke away, both of us breathless. That was definitely the last thing I expected to happen, yet it was the best kiss of my life. I bit my lip nervously trying to think of something to say.

"I'll pick you up after work tomorrow, shall I?" he half asked, half told.

"Y-yeah, okay," I replied. "Ridgeview ER. Seven o'clock. Don't be late."

"Wouldn't dream of it." He turned and headed back down the street toward the bar. With a smile I couldn't quite wipe from my face, I headed inside to my apartment, aching for tomorrow to arrive.

*I entered work that morning already counting down the hours until shift change. Twelve hours normally flies by in the ER, but I knew today would drag in anticipation. Everytime I walked past the desk, I couldn't help but to look at the clock. Thankfully, Claire wasn't scheduled to work today. I wasn't in the mood to discuss her latest conquest or what she had set up to be mine. I also didn't want her to know about Callen. Technically, seeing him was not breaking any of my rules...he was not part of the friend circle, nor was he friends with any of my friends. However, Claire did see his sister at her classes, and I was uncertain how often Callen was a surprise guest at those classes like the night before.*

*But, technically, he isn't off limites. Technically,* I thought.

*Thankfully, the department was very busy during the afternoon. An apparent stomach bug was sweeping through the community. Over twenty patients came in with excessive nausea, vomiting, and diarrhea. I lost track of how many bags of intravenous fluids I hung and how many doses of antiemetics I pushed. Before I knew it, the night shift nurses arrived ready to take over.*

*I only had two patients to give report on tonight since the other four were conveniently all put up for discharge ten minutes ago. Landon was taking over my assignment, and he would not be pleased with all the empty beds. That just meant he could expect four new patients in the first twenty minutes of his shift, if not sooner.*

*"Alright, girl. Lay it on me,"* Landon said as he walked up to my desk at the nurses station. *"Who's dying and in what order?"*

*"No one is dying today, Landon - at least not while I'm their nurse. Someone can reevaluate after you take over though,"* I teased.

*"Mmmm. You know I like it when you're mean."* He shot me a wink across the desk as he took a swig of his energy drink.

*I rolled my eyes at him before launching into report.*

"Beds seven, eight, nine, and fifteen have just been discharged. Housekeeping is here working on turning the rooms over. They are freshly stocked with supplies for you.

"Bed thirteen is a fifty year old woman who came in with the latest gastrointestinal virus. She had two liters of normal saline, four milligrams of Zofran IV push with the first bag, and twelve and a half milligrams of promethazine IV push about thirty minutes ago. She finally quit vomiting after that dose.

"Bed fourteen is an eight year old boy who fell at school on the playground earlier today. Since then, he has been able to move his left arm, but the pain has been getting worse. No bruising or swelling at the site. X-rays showed a hairline fracture to his ulna. Doc wants to do a plaster cast after the radiologist signs off on the report. I took the cart to the room already."

"Damn, I hate plaster casts," Landon complained. "They are so frickin' messy. Why can't we just do fiberglass? Who's the doc?"

"It's Dr. Whitts. You know he likes to play."

"True. True," Landon agreed. "Alright my friend, time for you to hit the road. Are you back tomorrow?"

"Not if the world depended on it."

I went to the time clock to punch out and grabbed my things from my locker. I stepped into the bathroom to change out of my germy scrubs and donned a pair of jeans and a navy, fitted t-shirt. I brushed the tangles from my hair and did my best to not look like I had just been at work for the last twelve hours.

Walking out the front entrance of the ER, I scanned the parking lot for Callen, unsure what I was looking for without knowing what kind of vehicle he owned. When nothing caught my eye, my stomach sank thinking he stood me up, but then, I saw him at the back of the lot leaning against the door of an old pickup. A smile swooped across my face, and my heart skipped when we made eye contact. I sauntered over to him where he immediately *wrapped his arms around me and kissed the top of my head. Despite it being brand new, it felt so right.*

# CHAPTER FOUR

### *Disputed*

**A**ll too soon, I awoke stiff on the floor. I wanted to return to my dreams of Callen, but reality was crashing in. I stood and stretched to relieve my joints. My vision was back to normal, but my face ached around my eye and down my cheek. I strode to the door and tried to open it even though I knew it was locked.

Besides the light hanging from the ceiling, there was nothing else in the room. I paced back and forth trying to come up with a plan. Under no circumstance would I admit Callen existed. If this guy had any concrete proof of who Callen was, he would not be asking. The only thing I can think to do is lie, and lie well; but, it's hard to play poker when you do not know the variation.

It felt like hours had passed when the same two soldiers came to retrieve me again. The one I hit with the paperweight definitely had a broken nose. I couldn't stop myself from smirking when his eyes met mine. He gritted his teeth and stiffened like he was going to hit me, but I didn't move. I refused to give him the satisfaction.

"Both of you get on with it," the other soldier ordered. Broken nose turned on his heel and headed down the hall. Lacking any better ideas, I followed with my second escort close behind.

Instead of taking me back to the office from yesterday, they led me into another fully concrete room with a light swinging from the ceiling. The only difference was the metal chair in the middle of the floor.

"Sit," the rear soldier barked.

"Pass. Thanks though," I replied with as much defiance as I could muster.

"It wasn't a suggestion," the one with the broken nose said, stepping forward to tower over me. "Sit, or I will make you sit."

I set my jaw and narrowed my gaze at him. Deciding this was not the time to fight, I took a deep breath and sat down. They both produced zip ties from their pockets and bound each of my limbs to the chair. The ties were heavy duty, industrial strength. There was no way I would be able to tear myself free.

"I'll stand guard. Go collect the supplies," the first guard said to the one with the broken nose. He seemed to call the shots between the two of them.

The second guard left the room without a word. I watched the remaining soldier carefully as I attempted to adjust my arms. The zip ties were uncomfortably tight, so I wasn't able to move a fraction, which, I supposed, was their goal.

"You won't be able to get out of those if that's what you are thinking," he called from the wall he had propped himself against.

"I highly doubt I need a guard then. Why don't you scurry on out of here and leave me alone," I said coolly as I tried to move my legs next to no effect.

"Probably not. Better safe than sorry though in my opinion."

"I didn't ask for your opinion."

He laughed at my brazenness which further infuriated me. There was nothing humorous about this situation.

"You should save your energy. I have a feeling this is going to be a long day with that attitude of yours." He straightened up and walked toward me.

"What's that supposed to mean?"

He stopped in front of me, leaned down, and placed a hand on each of my forearms so we were eye to eye. "It means the boss doesn't like women with an attitude or a smart ass mouth, and you happen to have both of those."

I rolled my eyes at him, "Good thing I'm not looking to make any friends then."

"Oh, come on, we could be friends."

"Friends don't kidnap one another." I felt completely helpless, unable to move, but I refused to let him know I was afraid.

He laughed as he stood back up, "That's fair. We could wipe the slate though. If you tell me who your mate is, then I'll cut those ties off. You help me, I'll help you. You know, like friends do."

"I don't have a mate."

"Yes, you do."

"Well, I guess I technically do. Everyone with a soulmark has a soulmate - it kinda comes with the territory. I don't know who he is though. I told your boss yesterday that I've never met him; nor, do I ever intend to."

"Why is that?"

"Why is what?"

"Why do you never intend to meet him?"

"I'm perfectly content on my own. Just because he exists

doesn't mean I want him."

"You can lie all you want. I know it's not true." He sauntered back over to the wall and leaned a shoulder against it.

"Where are we?" I asked.

"Nice subject change," he answered. "We are at our main headquarters."

"Which is where?" I prompted with another eye roll.

"Which is here. You know, for a nurse, you're not very smart," he mocked.

"You're not funny."

"I think I am. Maybe you don't have a sense of humor. Have you considered that?"

"Listen, I am not in the mood. I'm kind of in the middle of a shitty situation here, so if you aren't going to be helpful, please shut the fuck up." I yanked on my wrist restraints again. The plastic pinched my skin, but they didn't budge.

"Will you stop that? You're going to hurt yourself," he sighed in exasperation.

"I think a few cuts on my wrists will be the least of my worries here in a few minutes."

"It doesn't have to be. Offer still stands: I'll release you for the name of your soulmate. You don't even have to tell me a location, just a name."

"For the love of god, I don't know his name," I said in annoyance, looking up at the ceiling.

"Fine. Let's talk about something else." He moved in front of me and crossed his arms.

I sighed in response, closing my eyes for a moment before looking at him.

"Why'd you become a nurse?" he asked like we were new acquaintances having coffee in a cafe rather than a captive and captor having a standoff.

"You've got to be kidding me," I mumbled to myself.

"If you don't want to talk, we could just stare at each other and wait."

I took an exaggerated, deep breath and slowly let it out as I thought it over. Deciding bland conversation was better than sitting here dreading what was to come, I answered, "I became a nurse because I wanted to help people that needed it."

"And do you?"

"Sometimes. Other times not so much."

One of my patients from the critical care unit came to mind. Her heartbeat kept dropping into the twenties, and the cardiologist wouldn't allow my coworker and I to externally pace her - even though she was severely symptomatic - much less come and evaluate her in person. Finally, the other nurse and I decided to pace her anyway since the doctor hadn't shown up after being paged five times, but before we could get everything started, she coded. We restarted her heart, and the cardiologist put in a transvenous pacemaker to stabilize her.

Unfortunately, when he placed the access catheter in her groin, he damaged the vessels delivering blood to her lower extremity, so she lost her pulses from her knee down. Vascular said she was too unstable to take to surgery to repair the artery. Cardiology said she was too unstable for a permanent pacemaker. She was on life support for almost a week before the cardiologist took her back down. By then, her leg was dead and gangrenous. She ended up having her limb amputated and lived in constant pain afterward. She spent the next six months in and out of the hospital with complications before she finally died. She was only fifty four.

"What happens the other times?" he asked, pulling me back to the present.

"Let's just say, some things are worse than death."

He nodded as if he understood.

"What about you?"

"What about me?"

"Why did you become…" I trailed off trying to think of what to call him, this?"

He laughed, "I was a medic for a few years before. I was injured in combat and honorably discharged, so when I recovered, I went into the private sector."

"Why here?"

"Why not?"

"I just think there are probably more prosperous and legal careers out there."

"Yeah, well, I like the science here. It's interesting."

I snorted in response. "Please, don't tell me you're one of those."

"One of what?"

"One of those fascinated by the soulmark. One of those so utterly jealous they don't have a destined mate, they'd do anything to understand it."

He laughed, "Between you and me, I don't give a shit about soulmarks. I'm more interested in the other research that's being done here."

"Other research?"

He nodded.

"Care to elaborate?" I asked, raising an eyebrow. I wanted to know anything and everything about this place just in case it would lead to an escape aid.

"No, I don't," he smiled at me.

A small grin ticked across my face as I shook my head at him. "You want me to spill my deepest, darkest secrets, but you won't spill yours?"

"It's not mine to tell. Besides, there's no way I'm giving you any information about this place. You and I both know you'll bolt out of here if you see an opportunity."

"Wouldn't you?"

He shrugged, "Doesn't mean I'm going to let you."

The heaviness of the situation settled back over us, and we allowed silence to engulf the room. Shortly after our conversation died off, the man from the office walked in, cracking the knuckles of his fingers as he did. The other soldier returned as well. My two guards moved to the side wall, leaving their boss and me face to face. He had a bandage wrapped around the hand that I bit yesterday.

"How's your eye, sweetheart?" he asked as he leaned up against the wall in front of me. His nice suit had been replaced with khaki cargo pants and a black t-shirt. Clearly, he had plans beyond our previous conversation.

"Fine. How's your hand?" I curtly asked. He snorted and subconsciously rubbed his injured hand with the other.

"You'll have to excuse your accommodations. Seeing as in the last twenty four hours you have managed to stab one of my men, break another's nose, and bite me, I felt it was better to have you a little less...mobile," he said, gesturing to the ties around my limbs.

"You know. It's quite rude to tie a girl up without even asking. I can't say that I'm enjoying your manners." I knew he was trying to intimidate me into submission, and that was something I was not going to give him. I did not make it this far in life by being soft, and I certainly had no plans to start now.

"My dear, you have not begun to see my 'manners' as you say," he growled as he crossed the room toward me. Despite all the fury in his voice, there was a twinkle in his eye like he was enjoying himself. "You will tell me what I want to know. One way or another, I can assure you that," he continued as he began to pace around me.

I faced straight forward, not giving him the satisfaction of watching me pull on my restraints.

"Now, we can do this the easy way or the hard way. It's up to you. Why not save us all the time and effort and simply tell me who and where your mate is?"

"I don't have a mate. If you would open those damn ears of yours and listen, we could get on with whatever it is you think you will accomplish by holding me here."

"Tsk. Tsk. Always in such a rush. We have all the time in the world to get to know one another. I am just itching in my skin to unravel all the details, sweetheart," he said as he placed his hand on my shoulder.

I looked at his fingers as he drummed them against me.

"So, tell me, can I get a chair and sit down for a chat, or shall we begin with a little roughage?" He squeezed me tightly at the end of his rhetorical question, digging his fingers in hard enough to bruise the skin beneath my shirt.

We both knew what road this was going down. I looked over at the two soldiers, who were both staring at us. The one with the broken nose held a wicked glint in his eye as he watched. The other seemed almost impassive. I turned my head forward and glared at the cement wall, gritting my teeth in preparation.

As if sensing my resolve, the man let go and walked back around to face me. "Very well then." A vile smile spread across his face as he called to the soldiers, "Gentlemen, bring me the toys." Not only did he know where this was going, he wanted it to happen this way.

"Before you get too carried away in this little charade of yours," I said, "there's something you should know."

With his head tilted to the side, he asked, "And what would that be, my dear?"

"My safeword is apricot."

His laugh filled the room and a smile spread across his face. "My, my, you are a rather fascinating creature. I would think a person in your position would try to flatter her interrogator, not try and piss him off!" he yelled, his face flushed with fury.

"There are those manners again," I said, shaking my head with a feign of disappointment. "I think you were going for 'startlement' there, but I am afraid your performance fell flat. Why don't you try again?"

His nostrils flared in agitation. I had no way to defend myself. The only thing I could think to do was, frankly, piss him off. That way, he either knocked me out, killed me rather quickly, or left in frustration. His leaving would be my preference, but I would take the others if it meant not sitting for hours in this game of cat and mouse. Besides, the only sure way to keep Callen safe was for my memories to die and me along with them. The soldiers rolled in a cart carrying various needles, syringes, hammers, knives, and rope.

"I have to say, you and I have very different ideas of BDSM. You should really find a better outlet. I hear they have clubs for that kind of thing now," I cocked my head to the side as the words spewed forth. "I mean, I personally wouldn't know, but hey, to each their own I guess."

He closed his eyes, trying to rein in his temper. He took a

deep breath, opened his eyes, walked over to me, and slammed his fist into my stomach. All the air flew out of me, and I doubled over gasping for breath. Tears pricked my vision as I struggled to breathe. After what felt like ages, I was finally able to draw a breath and sit up straight in my chair. That strike caught me off guard, but the others wouldn't.

"Good thing you haven't fed me anything, or I probably would've thrown up on your shoes there," I said as I gathered myself. He grabbed a fistful of hair at the nape of my neck and yanked, causing me to wince involuntarily.

"You will tell me what his name is," he ordered as he pulled his hand tighter, the roots of my hair barely hanging on.

"I have nothing to tell you," I said through gritted teeth.

Relinquishing my hair, he slammed his fist into my already bruised eye. My head flew to the side, and my vision blurred instantly. Heat flooded my skin as more of the vessels broke beneath. It was by far the most painful strike since I'd been here, and I knew it was only going to get worse.

"If you could hit a different spot, that'd be great," I croaked out as I rapidly blinked my eyes to clear my vision.

"I am nothing but accommodating," he smirked as he strode toward the cart. He picked up a hammer and tossed it in the air, catching it in its free fall. Before I could tense, he slammed the hammer into my left hand. A scream erupted from me, my knuckles cracking and bowing from the force.

"What is his name?" he gritted through his teeth.

"I. Do. Not. Know. Who. My. Mate. Is." I enunciated every word, drawing in a shaky breath from the pain at the end.

"Garrett, hand me the knife," he instructed, sticking his hand out behind him. The soldier with the broken nose picked up a pocket knife from the cart and handed it over. He flicked the knife open in one slick swoosh, reached out, and swiped the blade down my left forearm. I gritted my teeth as blood sprang from the four inch cut. He dropped the knife on the floor between us, reached his hand behind him and called another order, "The compound."

Garrett passed him a ten milliliter syringe filled with a crystal, clear liquid. He pulled the skin apart at the wound, exposing the soft tissues, stabbed in the needle, and depressed the plunger. My flesh burned, and the muscles contracted in pain. I bit my tongue to keep from screaming, but I couldn't hold back the groans creeping from my lips. My entire arm was red from the burning tissues, and my hand began to tremble.

"Any smartass comments for me now, sweetheart?" he crooned, bending his head down to meet me face to face. When I didn't answer he pressed his thumb into the cut on my arm with all his strength.

I sucked in a deep breath as my eyes bulged in pain.

"Answer me when I speak to you."

"No," I managed to croak out.

He injected the substance into the wound twice more. Each time was more painful than the last as my endorphins faded away. After the third one, my entire body was shaking, red marks encircled the restraints from my pulling, and sweat drenched my body; but I refused to cry. He would not break me this easily.

"I ask again, who is your mate?"

"I fucking told you, I don't have a mate!" I screamed at him. "I don't know what is so hard for you to understand about that."

He reached back and slapped me across the face. My lip busted back open from the split he caused yesterday and blood seeped into my mouth.

"I told you not to speak like that. It is unbecoming."

"Oh, go fuck yourself already," I spat.

He wrapped his hands around my throat, compressing my trachea. I tried to pull away but there was nowhere for me to go. I could feel the blood pooling in my face, and my chest burned as I fought for air. Hatred was seething from him as he choked the life from me. As my vision grew black, I thought, *This is it.*

"Sir," the unnamed soldier called.

He loosened his grip as he turned his head. Seeing my opportunity, I quickly went limp and closed my eyes. Feigning unconsciousness would buy me a slight reprieve at least.

"Shit," he cursed. He grabbed my hair and pulled my head back. I let it lull backward and did my best to keep my breathing shallow but regular. He released my hair and kicked my chair, causing it to rock and tip over. My head collided with the ground first, and I let the chair pull me to the side, landing so the men were behind me. At least one of the soldiers must have moved to sit me up, because I heard the order for me to be left there followed by the noise of three sets of footsteps exiting the room.

Pain enveloped my head from the fall, but I did my best to stay still and quiet. When I was sure they were gone, I opened my eyes and looked around the floor. Only about a foot from me, the knife lay that he dropped. It took longer than I would have liked, but I was eventually able to scoot myself over to the blade and fumble the hilt into my left hand. After several failed attempts, I finally wedged the blade between my wrist and the chair. I grasped the hilt tightly and twisted my hand, digging the sharp edge into the tie. With a pop, it snapped in half. I made quick work of the other three restraints and stood. Transferring the knife to my right hand, I crept to the exit. Thankfully, the door hadn't been closed all the way, so the lock wasn't engaged.

I slightly pulled the door ajar to peer down the hallway. My guards were gone, but I doubted they felt like a bound, unconscious hostage needed supervision. A few doors were scattered down the hall, but they all required a keycard for entry. My only option was to continue forward and hope it led somewhere accessible. I gripped the knife tightly in my hand as I walked, hearing voices shouting at one another from one of the doors as I went past.

"I want her hooked up to that device," a male voice rang out - his voice.

"I am telling you it won't work. The only successful test subjects have been voluntary, unmarked individuals. I have no data to support the use of an unwilling participant," replied a woman.

"She can be your data. I want to know what she is hiding, and I want to know it today."

Before I could continue walking, someone came up behind me and shoved me to the ground. I fell on my stomach and carefully concealed the knife. My assailant grabbed me by my arm and pulled me up.

"Why, hello, Garrett," I said as I brought my other hand up with the blade. It scratched across his cheek before he could deflect. Grabbing my arm on the downswing, he twisted my wrist behind my back, forcing me to drop the knife. He shoved me face first into the wall and held me in place as he pressed his body up against mine.

"You cut me, you bitch."

"I thought it'd distract from that swollen nose of yours," I quipped while trying to pull free. He pulled my arm back tighter, and I winced in pain.

"I told the boss he would never break you like that. You like to fight too much," he said as he ran his nose down my neck, sending chills down my spine.

I tried to push off from the wall, but his weight was too heavy. "You know nothing about me."

"I know more than you think I do, princess. I can promise you that." I tried to pull my arm free again, but he just pressed his weight harder into me. A throaty growl ripped through his chest. "I told him you need to have the fight taken out of you. Playing around like that only fuels your fire." Dropping his voice to a whisper, he continued, "I want to put it out, and there's only one way to do that."

Garret slid his other hand over my ass and around my hip. He slowly brought it up over my abdomen and cupped my breast as I thrashed against him. Relinquishing my arm, he flipped me around to face him. A darkness clouded his eyes as a smile pulled at the corners of his mouth. I swallowed trying to think of a plan, but my mind came up empty. He was twice my size, and this time, I didn't have anything to use as a weapon at my disposal. The door swung open beside us as the boss and other soldier walked out of the room.

"Sir," Garrett greeted as he pushed off of me, "I was just about to bring her to you. I caught her trying to escape down the hall."

The boss's eyes flickered from me to the cut across Garrett's face and back. I swallowed hard not knowing what to expect. "Take her to a room with a shower, bed, and clean clothes. After that, take her dinner. She will need plenty of energy for tomorrow." He turned to walk up the hallway, but stopped after a step, spun around, and said, "Take Shane with you. No funny business."

He retreated down the hall as Garrett nodded. Shane stood there staring at the two of us. He gave Garrett a look of displeasure, shook his head, and led the way back down the hall. Relief flooded my system as I marched to my new room.

# CHAPTER FIVE

*Encouraged*

I stepped into the room without looking back, letting out a sigh of relief as the door slammed behind me. The room wasn't large but accommodated a bed with an open bathroom. Like all the others, the walls were solid concrete and windowless.

I closed my eyes and tilted my head back. I had no idea how I was going to get out of this. My best guess was that I had been here for two days. Callen would have started searching for me as soon as the news broke about the hospital raid. I desperately wanted to go home, but part of me hoped he would never find me. As long as he was safe, I'd be okay.

I took a cleansing, deep breath, opened my eyes, and walked to the shower. Stripping off my dirty, bloody scrubs while the water warmed, I stepped into the stream. As much as I hated the idea of someone walking in while I was washing, the desire to clean myself overcame the worry.

There bar of soap sitting on a shelf in the shower emitted a wisp of ivory as I lathered. Gently, I scrubbed the dried blood and sweat from my face and hair. Once the water ran clear, I focused on the cut to my arm. The tissues still burned constantly; however, a quick assessment showed no necrosis. Whatever compound he injected didn't appear to cause any damage, just irritation.

"Finally, something in my favor," I said aloud to myself.

My hand ached from the impact of the hammer. I slowly opened and closed my fist to assess the damage. The knuckle of my middle finger was too swollen to decide if it was fractured or not without an actual x-ray.

Standing under the water a moment longer, I enjoyed the warmth across my skin before begrudgingly switching it off and reaching for the towel on the sink to dry off. I wrapped the scratchy fabric around myself and walked to the bed to sit for a moment. I was desperately tired as the adrenaline drained from my body. A pair of plain, black pants and a matching shirt were lying on the bed. Dressing quickly, I ran my fingers through my hair as a makeshift brush.

As if on cue, the door swung open when I finished. My two guards came back with a tray of food, a fold out table, a chair, and a small, black box with a snap lid. The men set up the table and chair and laid the tray and box on top.

"Eat," Garrett barked as he left the room. Shane silently followed him to the door, but to my surprise, he didn't leave. Instead, he shut the door, turned, and strode back toward me. Defensively, I stood from the bed to ready myself.

Shane stopped and put his hands in the air. "Relax. I'm not going to do anything."

I eyed him carefully, not convinced by his admission.

"I expected that reaction. Look, I'll just sit here in the chair on the other side of the table, and you can sit on the bed and eat your dinner," he said as he sat, gesturing for me to do the same.

Reluctantly, I perched myself on the edge of the bed and glanced down at the food tray. It held a bottle of water, plain chips, and a peanut butter and jelly sandwich. As much as I didn't want to accept anything from these men, I was starving and desperately thirsty.

"You first." I shoved the tray forward.

He chuckled as he leaned in. "It's not poisoned, you know."

"Prove it."

With a grunt, Shane picked up the sandwich, tore a chunk off, and popped it into his mouth, followed by a chip. I looked at the water and raised an eyebrow at him in question. He rolled his eyes, opened the bottle, and took a large mouthful.

"Happy?" he asked, wiping his mouth.

"Happy? No. Satisfied? Yes," I answered as I grabbed the bottle and drank deeply.

"So, how are you?" he questioned, attempting to sound casual.

"Seriously?" I answered in an angry, disbelieving tone.

He nodded and waited expectantly.

"What can I say? I'm having the time of my life." My response rang out sardonically. I reached for a chip and popped it in my mouth. My jaw ached and the salt stung my split lip, but my stomach growled greedily wanting more.

"You don't have to do that, you know." Shane leaned back in his chair, watching me with peaked interest.

"And what is it that I am doing exactly?" I questioned, irritation filling my voice.

"Acting like you aren't afraid."

I swallowed and stared blankly at him. "How should I be acting? Crying? Screaming? Begging? What should I be doing right now then? What?" I yelled, outraged.

"I didn't mean it like that. Calm down. Gracious, you're

tumultuous," he said as he wiped his hand over his face. "I just meant that you could let your guard down for a minute."

I couldn't help the scoff that escaped as I rolled my eyes in disbelief at this man. "Cut the shit. What exactly is it that you want?" I asked as I took a large bite of the sandwich. He might be infuriating, but I was still hungry.

"There are several things I want, but what I have come here for is to help," he replied, leaning forward to rest his elbows on the table. "I thought I could start by stitching up the cut on your arm."

I looked down to examine the wound again. I agreed that it definitely needed stitches. I took a deep breath and bit my lower lip as I mulled over the idea of letting him suture me. I released the breath with a sigh, not really having any other option. "Fine, but no lidocaine injection. Just because I'm going to let you do the sutures doesn't mean I trust you to inject me with god knows what."

Shane laughed as he moved the food tray from the table to the bed and opened the black box. He took out a suture kit, thread, and topical spray lidocaine. "I had a feeling you would say that. Not that I don't believe you aren't tough enough to sit through a few stitches without numbing medication," he added to the end.

Despite myself, I laughed. He was right, of course. After all the injuries I had sustained in the last forty eight hours, a line of stitches would be easy sailing. "Well, it would be nice for something not to hurt for at least a few minutes I suppose," I replied as I stretched my arm out over the table.

"Yeah, I imagine there's not a part of you that isn't in pain right now. You've taken quite a beating to say the least." He sprayed the medication on my arm as he spoke. The initial contact stung slightly, but it immediately faded to numbness. Shane returned the bottle to the box, donned some gloves, and started to work on the first suture. "It would be easier, you know, if you just told him what he wanted to know."

"Is that why you are actually here? To try and reason with me again?" I asked as he pierced my skin for the second stitch.

"I can have more than one reason," he replied, looking up at me. "He will break you eventually. One way or another. You might as well save yourself some agony."

I set my mouth and held his gaze. He was being casual in his speech, but his eyes seemed to almost be pleading for me to listen to him.

"What's it matter to you what he does to me?" I asked in return.

He dropped his eyes down and continued working. "Let's just say I don't necessarily enjoy watching you get the shit beat out of you."

"Well, I don't really enjoy it either." Another laugh sprang forth, but this time I smiled. Shane reciprocated with a laugh of his own and shook his head. I had to be losing my mind. This was no situation to find funny, and in no fashion, should I be comfortable around this man. While he, himself, has only restrained me, he's stood by and allowed the other men to attack and assault me.

The smile faded from my face as I thought about the soldiers that brought me here. "Were you one of them? At the hospital?" I asked, not entirely sure why I wanted to know, but I did.

He sighed as he trimmed the last suture and began packing up the equipment. "Yeah, I was there," he replied. He kept his eyes pointed down as he continued, "Garrett and I searched inside. He's the one that found you in the supply room and chased you out of the building. I had stopped to tend to our partner that you stabbed."

"Oh," was the only word I managed to get out as he rummaged through the box. I could almost feel the scalpel still in my hand as I plunged it into that soldier. Unsure what to say, I asked, "Is he okay?"

"He's dead. He bled out on our way back. The wound was high in the leg, so the tourniquet wasn't effective. You completely severed his femoral artery," he answered casually as he pulled a tube of medicine from the box.

I don't know what I was expecting, but it definitely wasn't that. I never intended to kill the man, I was simply trying to escape. Tears threatened to prick my eyes. "I, um, I'm sorry. I didn't mean to - "

He held his hand up to stop me. "It's only obvious you weren't trying to kill him. I wouldn't have said anything if you wouldn't have asked."

He opened the tube and dispensed a white, creamy ointment onto one of his fingers. "This will help that lip heal so you quit splitting it back open," he said as he reached and gently dabbed my mouth. His hand lingered for a moment at my face with our eyes locked on one another.

A knock came from the door, shattering the fragile moment. Shane stood, removed the box from the table, and headed for the door as it swung open. Garrett was standing there with his fists clenched. "You're needed," he told Shane.

"Yes, I was just finishing up," he replied as he walked out and locked the door behind him.

I watched for a moment to ensure it wouldn't reopen. When it didn't, I returned to the partially eaten sandwich, but my appetite was gone. I moved the tray over to the table and crawled onto the bed. I kept playing the scene from the hospital over in my head. I knew I hit the artery by the blood spray when he pulled the scalpel from his leg. *Was he already dead when I saw him lying in the SUV?* I asked myself. It all happened so fast I couldn't be sure.

"He was abducting you. You had every right to defend yourself," I rationalized aloud, trying to convince myself it was true. I had spent my life trying to save lives, not take them. "You have nothing to feel guilty for." I sighed and closed my eyes letting the exhaustion take over.

*Callen grabbed my hand, led me to the passenger side of his truck, and opened the door. He moved to offer a hand to help me inside, but I pulled myself up into the lifted cab before he could.*

*"Well, alrighty then." He smiled as he shut my door. I caught his eye as he waltzed around to his side, and a smile crept across my face as well. My cheeks blushed with the eye contact, and I bit my lower lip as I looked away. Something about this man sent butterflies through my chest.*

*"So, what's on the agenda for the night?" I asked as the engine came to life and slid into gear.*

*"I thought we could start with dinner. I'm sure you're starving after working all day," he replied as he edged out of the parking lot.*

*"The lady in me wants to say no, but the rest of me really wants a burger, so I'm going to go with yes," I answered, peeking over at him.*

*He was still smiling and nodded as he replied, "A burger sounds great to me. Have you ever been to Dave's Diner?"*

*"Um, no, I've never heard of it."*

*"It's just on the edge of town. Great place to grab a bite."*

*The air felt charged in the cab, like electricity was flowing* between us. *I wrung my hands in my lap not quite sure what to say next. Something about this man had me all wound up. I was undeniably attracted to him, attracted to the point I couldn't think straight.*

*My eyes roamed over to his hands on the steering wheel. I could see the calluses on his palms from here. His knuckles were toughened from scratches and scars. My gaze traveled up his arm, inspecting his swollen muscles. I couldn't help but think of what those hands would feel like against mine, how it would feel to be wrapped in those arms with my head pressed to his chest. As if he could hear my thoughts, he looked over, practically smirking.*

*The blush crept up my face again, and I hurriedly looked out the window.* Why am I ogling this man like some school girl with a crush? What is happening to me? *I berated myself.*

*"You know, you are going to put a hole in that pretty lip of yours if you don't let it go soon," he said, winking at me.*

*My cheeks flushed red at the comment. Thankfully, I didn't have to come up with a retort as Callen pulled in front of a small diner and killed the engine. With a chuckle, he exited the truck. He made it around to my door as my feet hit the ground. I shut my door and pushed past him toward the building, mortified about him calling me out.*

*"Hey! Hey!" he called as he caught up to me. "I didn't mean to embarrass you. It's cute, honest. Here, let me get that." He reached out and opened the door, ushering me in.*

*I looked at him for a moment before walking inside. We sat down in a corner booth. I normally wouldn't sit with my back to the door, but Callen had motioned for me to take the first bench. When we were both seated, I blurted out, "I'm sorry. I'm not usually like this. Maybe, I'm just tired or something."*

*"What are you normally like then?" he asked, leaning toward me with his arms crossed and resting on the table.*

"Not a blubbering mess," I answered with a laugh and shake of the head.

The waitress walked over to take our order. "Callen, the usual?" she asked as she batted her eyelashes at him. She was tall, blonde, and beautiful, and clearly, she had a thing for Callen.

"Yeah, thanks," he said as he handed her the unopened menu without taking his eyes off of me. She grabbed the menu in a way that landed her thumb on Callen's hand. She lingered just a bit too long with the contact for it to be unintentional, but Callen didn't seem to notice.

"Would your friend like a minute, hun?" she asked him with a nod in my direction. Not only was she indirectly ignoring me, she was blatantly flirting with Callen.

Irritation flooded my body at her audacity. "His date can answer for herself, and she would like a cheeseburger and fries," I answered boldly, holding the menu up for her to grab.

The waitress's eyes popped out of her head with astonishment at my assertiveness. Her face reddened as she quickly took my menu and walked off. I scowled after her retreating figure, still irritated.

Looking over at Callen, I saw he was trying to wipe a smug grin off his face. "What?" I snapped.

He put his hands up in the air as if he was surrendering. Our waitress quickly returned with two sweet teas and set them in front of us before scurrying off.

"I hope you like tea," Callen said as he took a swig from his glass, trying not to laugh.

"I like tea," I replied with a laugh of my own. I've never been the jealous type either. I had to get a grip.

The waitress returned with our food, careful to avoid eye contact with me. The cheeseburger was delicious as we dug in.

"So do you go to Janet's class often?" he asked, breaking the silence.

"Oh, no," I replied with a slight shake of the head. "That was my first time. I went with my friend, Claire - the blonde I was with - on her insistence of needing company. What about you? Do you teach with her much?"

"No, that was my first time. I had a free day in my schedule, so I thought I'd give it a try. Glad I did," he ended with a smile and bit into his burger.

"So, what is it that you do then?" I asked curiously. "If it's not a regular instructor, that is."

"Research and logistics. It's really boring." He waved a hand in the air as if to dismiss the subject. "Tell me about the hospital. What do you do there?"

"I'm a charge nurse in the ER, and today involved a lot of vomit, so I doubt you really want to hear about that," I answered as I popped a fry into my mouth.

"I don't tend to be squeamish, but you're probably right," Callen laughed as he took his last bite. I picked up my napkin to wipe my mouth as the waitress approached.

"Can I get you anything else?" she asked while reaching for our plates.

Callen gestured to me, and I politely declined, my irritation from erlier vastly diminished; however, he waitress shuffled back to the kitchen with our dishes without another word.

Callen stood and held his hand out to me. "Ready?" he asked. I placed my hand in his for him to help me stand. Fireworks danced across my skin at his touch. I pulled my hand from his and risked a glance at his face to see if he felt it too; but if he had, he didn't let on.

"Just let me get some cash..." I trailed off, feeling in my back pocket for the money I kept there.

"Not necessary. It's like you said - you're my date, and I pay for my dates," he replied with a wink. Callen pulled out his wallet, dropped some money on the table, and led me to the exit with his hand placed lightly in the small of my back. He opened the door to his truck for me, and I climbed inside. Callen took his seat once I was settled and started the engine.

"Thank you for dinner. It was delicious," I said as he pulled out of the parking lot.

"Thank you for the company," he answered, reaching his hand over to mine and entwining our fingers. Tingles crept up my arm at his touch, my breath hitching. He slowly started rubbing small circles with his thumb on the back of my hand. I squeezed his in return as we drove down the road.

All too soon, we pulled up to my apartment complex. Callen released my hand to park and cut the engine. "Do you have plans this weekend?" he asked.

"Actually, no. I don't believe so," I replied.

"Good. Give me your phone," he commanded.

I pulled my phone from my pocket and handed it to him, asking, "Why?" I normally wouldn't let someone else touch my phone, but I didn't hesitate with Callen.

"I can't call you if I don't have your number," he answered as he programmed his into my phone. His own dinged in his pocket as he messaged himself before handing mine back to me.

Before I could pull my arm back, Callen grasped my wrist and pulled me toward him. His lips gently pressed into mine as he released my arm. I reached my hand out to rest on his chest and deepened the kiss. Wrapping his arm around me, he ran his hand up my back. Butterflies fluttered about my chest, and goosebumps spread across my skin under his touch. I wove my arms around his neck and pulled myself to him, parting my lips in the process. His tongue twirled in my mouth as I pressed against him. I caught *his bottom lip and softly bit down. He moaned into my mouth, entwining his fingers in my hair. Callen pulled me onto his lap and slid his hand under my shirt to rest on the small of my back. Lust was burning through me as he roughly took my mouth to his again.*

I awoke with a start and bolted up in bed. My breathing heavy as the dream left me. I glanced around the room almost expecting to be in Callen's truck, but I found myself in the cold, cement room from yesterday. I flung myself back down on the bed and tried to rein in my emotions. I could almost feel Callen's arms around me and tears began to brim in my eyes.

I took a deep breath to steady myself as I reached to wipe the tears away. Pain seared through my face as I rubbed, forgetting about the damage. My eye was partially swollen shut, and I knew bruises enveloped the majority of my face on that side. I ran my fingers over my neck and flinched from the ache under my touch. My throat felt swollen from the trauma. A throbbing pain tore through my left hand and up my arm as I moved, and deep purple and blue bruising enveloped my swollen knuckles.

My head was pounding as I lay on the bed. There wasn't a place on my body that didn't hurt. All my endorphins had receded during the night, and I was finally able to feel the full extent of my injuries. I rolled on my side and closed my eyes as the room started spinning. The door swung open and slammed against the wall. My eyes popped open at the intrusion. I tried to sit up, but my head began to swim, causing me to collapse back onto the bed.

"Get up," a voice growled at me. I groaned in response and squeezed my eyes shut. I could hear footsteps approaching the bed, but I couldn't bring myself to move. A hand roughly grabbed my left arm at my suture site and squeezed. My eyes flew open as a scream tore through the air.

"I said 'Get up'," Garret seethed as he pulled me from the bed. I tried to yank my arm free, but he tightened his hold. A strangled noise escaped as I ground my teeth in pain.

"Not so tough today, are you, princess?" he mocked. My eyes locked with his, an evil grin spreading across his face as he dug his fingers into my wound. Stars clouded my vision as my knees buckled.

"Enough!" Shane barked from the door as he marched into the room. Garrett released me, and I held my arm to my chest trying to ease the pain. "You were instructed to bring her to the lab not rip her arm off," Shane spat.

"She needed some encouragement."

The two men stared at each other unblinking. A silent battle waging between them. Finally, Shane broke his gaze. He gently grabbed me by my upper arm and helped me to my feet.

"Lets go," he said as he turned and led me toward the door with Garrett following behind us.

# CHAPTER SIX

*Assessed*

We walked down the corridor and stopped outside the door I eavesdropped at yesterday. Shane never released his hold on my arm as if he was afraid our predecessor would snatch me backward. He pressed his badge to the scanner, a small click sounded from the door, and he pushed inside.

The room was larger than I thought it would be. A pristine, long, white desk lined with computers and machines sat at the front of the room. In the center stood a chair like the one I was bound to yesterday except this one had a headrest adorning the top. The entirety of the far side wall was a display screen with static ripping across. The dancing gray light made me dizzy, causing me to sway back and forth with a groan. I clenched my eyes shut and took a deep breath in an effort to restore myself to full function.

Shane half guided, half pulled me to the chair in the center of the room. I slumped forward and put my head between my legs, waiting for the spinning to stop. My guards bound my limbs to the chair, and I winced as Garrett yanked on my left arm unnecessarily rough. I wasn't resisting. I knew it wouldn't make a difference, and I needed to preserve what little energy I had for whatever would come next.

A hand fisted in my hair and pulled me to sitting height.

My head slammed back into the metal headrest, and stars shot across my vision as I gasped. A band wrapped around my neck, holding me in place. It wasn't strangling, but if I tried to turn my head, I could feel my airway being compressed. Pain shot down my neck and throat. The internal bruising hurt just as much as the external.

"She isn't resisting, Garrett. There's no need for that, so cut the shit," Shane's voice seethed.

"I'm just reminding her what will happen if she does," Garrett snapped back.

"I think she remembers just fine. Look at her fucking face! She doesn't even look like the same girl."

"Stop bickering you two. You sound like an old married couple," a female voice called from the front of the room. I snapped my eyes open in her direction. She was tall, blonde, and strikingly beautiful. Her pale porcelain skin was flawless. Deep, brown eyes swept over me like she was inspecting a new specimen. A smile spread across her face, exposing glistening white teeth behind her red painted lips. "Welcome to my lab. My name is Dr. Samantha Reid. I'm the in-house biochemical neuroscientist." She spoke with pride as she gestured to the room around us.

I stared at her unmoving, not sure what was to come. She tilted her head as she looked me up and down. Sighing, she let the smile fall from her face. "Can you see out of that eye?"

I didn't want to talk to this woman. *How could she stand there and let these men handle me the way they had and smile? What if it was her? What if she had been bloodied and restrained, taken against her will?* I asked myself. I attempted to turn my head to look away from her, but the band tightened around my neck and threatened my airway again.

"I wouldn't move too much if I were you," she called. I looked back over to her with a questioning eye. She continued,

"The band is made of a retracting elastic. Every time it's stretched, it pulls back tighter. Kind of like when you pull a seatbelt out too far and it locks. So, your eye - can you see?"

I didn't answer her right away and saw Garrett shift toward me out of my peripheral vision. "Partially," I snapped out, stopping his movements.

"Do you feel that your sight itself is damaged or just the soft tissue around your eye?" she asked, cocking her head to the side.

"I think it's just swollen," I answered. "I can see my cheek and eyelid creeping into my line of sight. My vision isn't blurry though unless I move my head too fast. I think I have a concussion."

She walked toward me and placed her hand on my chin. Pulling a pin light from her coat pocket, she shined it across my eyes, checking my pupils. She gently pulled my eyelids open and told me to look in different directions, tutting as she examined me. "She has a severe subconjunctival hemorrhage, a moderate concussion, and a facial hematoma causing ocular compression. And, that's just her face." She frowned looking away from me to the men behind us. "He didn't tell me she had been this injured during her retrieval, or I would have tended to her at her arrival."

"This didn't happen during my abduction if that's what you mean. These two helped their boss beat me while I was defenselessly tied to a chair yesterday," I said angrily. Rage flooded through my veins as I regained my resolve to fight. I would not let these people break me.

"Is that so?" she asked, raising a questioning eyebrow at my guards behind me. They didn't answer her and instead let the silence engulf us all.

I clenched my jaw trying to fight the tears that pricked my eyes. I hated myself for it. I looked weak when in reality the tears were from hatred not sadness. I balled my hands into fists but quickly released them when the pain tore through my left hand from the movement.

The scientist turned around and walked to her computer. Without looking up from the screen, she instructed, "Take her to the medical bay. She can't undergo this kind of cognitive stimulation while in this condition."

"I think she is in better condition than you think," a man boomed from the back. A chill ran down my spine at the sound of his voice. "Don't let her fool you. She's tougher than she looks."

He strode forward to stand in front of me. He had returned to his business attire from before. A soft, blue, button-down shirt accented with navy slacks and tie adorned his person, his sleeves cuffed to his elbows and his hands in his pockets as if on a casual walk to break up his day.

"Good morning, sir," the woman spoke flatly as if his appearance greatly inconvenienced her.

He ignored her cordiality while he stared at me, a smirk on his face as he took in my appearance. "As I told you yesterday, I want her hooked up to that machine. Now," he ordered.

"I still stand by my points from yesterday as to why this is a bad idea; however, I can't physically do the test now. Her neurological system is too impaired. Her left arm and hand are too damaged for the monitoring probes, and not to mention, her face and eye are too swollen to attach the ocular device."

I didn't want to like this woman, but she was standing up to this vile man. She could make an argument I couldn't. They both glared at each other, sizing one another up.

"Make it attach," he commanded.

She closed her eyes and inhaled deeply as if it took

everything in her body to remain calm. "The results will be skewed, and there will be no point in the experiment. Besides, the stress could kill her. Then we will be back to square one with no specimen." She opened her eyes and set her jaw.

Garrett and Shane shifted behind me. The tension was palpable in the room. I looked between the two people in front of me. They were both tense and headstrong in their position on the situation.

Finally, he relented, "Fine. How long until you can run the test?"

"Five days. She needs rest and medical care."

"Three," he countered.

"Fine."

My captor turned on his heel and headed out the door, not sparing me a second glance. The door slammed behind him, and I let out a breath I didn't know I was holding.

"Take her to the infirmary," she barked as she sat down at her computer and directed her attention to the screen.

Shane and Garrett moved together to release me from the restraints. My hand shot to my throat and rubbed. It didn't feel any worse than it did before the band, but it was like I had to touch the skin to be sure.

Shane bent to grab my arm, positioning his head right by mine. Ever so quietly he whispered, "Stay down."

Before I had time to fully process what he said, he jerked me to a standing position. I took one step forward as something hard slammed into the side of my weight bearing leg. The nerve and muscle spasmed as they crushed into my femur. I toppled to the floor in a heap, careful not to move like he instructed.

"What did you do to her?" the woman asked in an

accusatory tone.

"Nothing." Garrett answered, sounding confused.

"She just fell over," Shane responded. "I'll carry her down to the bay. She's probably just fainted." He scooped me up with ease and positioned me so I was turned into his chest, covering my face.

Garrett moved to follow, but Shane called over his shoulder. "I don't need a shadow. Go make her a tray. She's going to need to eat when she wakes up."

I could feel the resentment rolling off of Garrett at Shane's orders, but Shane continued walking without a glance back.

"You can open your eyes now," Shane said as he carried me down the hall. "It's just us."

"I could've fainted on my own, you know. You didn't have to give me a dead leg. It's probably going to bruise," I said with a glare as I picked my head up off his chest.

A deep chuckle rumbled through his body, his muscles contracting as he carted me along. "I wanted to make sure it looked real," he replied. "And - as for the bruise - it'll match the rest of your body."

"Hmph," I puffed at him. "Put me down. I can walk."

"You should let your leg fully wake up. Besides, I don't mind giving you a lift. Doc said you need to rest anyway."

"Well, I mind. Put me down," I ordered as I pushed against his chest, trying to free myself from his hold; however, he didn't budge against my straining and wiggling.

"You are so damn stubborn. I'm not putting you down until we get to the infirmary, and if you keep fighting, I'll throw you over my shoulder like a child," he answered with a smirk.

"You wouldn't dare."

"Try me."

"Fine," I caved grumpily. "Will you at least tell me why all the theatrics instead of you two just escorting me about like the last few days?"

I'd been too busy trying to get down to pay attention to the route we took to the infirmary. Shane had stopped outside a large sliding glass door to scan his badge. Upon entering, the smell of antiseptic flooded around us. It looked like a large trauma bay in an emergency room. The white walls were adorned with suction and oxygen equipment, brown cabinets full of supplies, cardiac monitors, and red biohazard bins.

Shane sat me down on a stretcher with a light green sheet before moving to one of the cabinets. He gathered items for an intravenous drip and blood samples and headed back toward me.

"Let's get you some fluids and run some lab work," he said, pulling a stool along with him and plopping down next to me.

"You didn't answer my question," I said, crossing my arms over my chest. "And, like hell I'm letting you take my blood."

"I did not; and, yes you will," he said sternly.

"If you want my blood so badly, go scrape it off the floor from yesterday. I'm sure there's plenty," I seethed.

"Look, I'm either going to get some restraints and tie you down or you can just lay there. Either way, you're getting an IV, and I am drawing blood samples."

His jaw was set and his lips pursed. Shane was more tolerant than the other men, but I knew it wasn't an empty threat to restrain me. I needed him to believe I'd be cooperative if I was going to attempt an escape at some point; however, I couldn't make it too obvious if I wanted it to work. He'd be suspicious if I didn't put up some kind of resistance.

I stared at him with my arms still crossed, waiting for him to continue. He sighed and ran his hand through his hair. "I wanted Garrett to leave, and I knew he'd only go without argument if he thought you were unconscious. He doesn't trust you."

"And you do?" I asked.

"Not even a little bit," he laughed. Reaching his hand out, he gently grasped my right arm. I let him pull it away from my body and position it for an IV. Shane prepared his supplies and placed a rubber tourniquet around my arm. Without another word, he quickly started an access, drew several vials of blood and flushed the line clean. The taste of saline flooded my mouth, causing me to involuntarily crinkle my nose at the intrusive saltiness.

"Can you taste that?" he asked as he moved to hang a liter of IV fluids.

"Yeah. It tastes like the ocean."

He laughed, "I've never heard it put that way before, but I suppose you're right."

"What kind of fluids are those?"

"Lactated Ringer's. I'm willing to bet your lactic acid is pretty high right now. You'll get two bags of this while I attend to your other injuries."

"They will heal just fine in a few days. They don't need tending."

"If we leave them, your face won't be healed for several weeks, and, you heard the boss, you get three days to recuperate. I need to speed the process along."

"What do you mean 'speed the process along'?" I eyed him carefully. "It's deep bruising. Only time will take care of that."

"Our scientists have been experimenting on new methods that rapidly increase healing in the body from breaks to bruises to open wounds. Now that you're in the infirmary, I'll have access to utilize them."

"Absolutely not. You are in no way using me as a guinea pig to test out some hybrid medical crap," I said, moving to get out of the bed. As soon as I stood, my leg buckled beneath me. It still hadn't recovered from the earlier deadening.

"Damn it, Lacey! Get in the bed. I mean it about the restraints," Shane barked as he moved to help me up from the ground.

"You know my name?" I questioned, caught off guard.

"Of course, I know your name. Why wouldn't I?" he responded as he eased me back into the bed. He swung my legs up and reclined the head of the stretcher into a resting position.

"Well, no one has said it since I've been here."

"We haven't said a lot of things."

"Like what?"

Shane glanced at me, contemplating his next sentence. Just as he was about to answer, the glass doors slid open. Garrett walked in carrying a tray of food. His eyes snapped to mine when he realized I was awake.

"Looks like sleeping beauty recovered quickly," he said, holding my glare. He placed the tray on a side table and walked toward the bed. Shane turned and exited the room while muttering something about supplies.

I balled my fists as he approached, preparing myself for another fight I knew I wouldn't win. Pain shot through my left hand, but I ground my teeth in determination to not let it show.

Garrett whistled and laughed, "You are a tough little shit. I'll give you that." Leaning down so his mouth was by my ear, he whispered, "and stubborn."

He pressed his nose into my hair and inhaled me deeply. His mouth skimmed across my ear, his breath hot against my skin. "I like stubborn. It's much more fun."

I pulled my head away from him as I tried to fight my instincts to lash out. He gripped a handful of hair at the nape of my neck and pulled me back toward him.

"What? No fighting? No snide remark? Don't tell me we broke you already, baby," he continued before sucking my earlobe between his teeth and moaning. Instinct took over, and I swung my fist toward his head. He deflected, let go of my hair, and pressed both my forearms to the bed. Leaning over me, his face almost touched mine. "That's my girl," he said as he dug his thumb into the wound on my left arm again.

Desperate for escape, I slammed my head forward and made contact with his nose. An audible crunch filled the room, and blood gushed from his nostrils. Stars lit across my vision from the impact on top of the concussion. Garrett jumped back as his hand flew to his face, yelling out profanities. I knew I was in trouble and hurriedly clambered out of the bed to flee. My leg was partially awake now, and I limped as fast as I could toward the door, screaming for help.

A hand snatched the collar of my shirt and yanked me backward. I landed flat on my back on the concrete floor, the air knocked from my lungs. I gasped trying to pull in a breath. A slew of cusses flew from Garrett's mouth as he landed a kick into my side. I rolled away from him trying to escape. Kick after kick landed on my rib cage, back, and stomach as I tried to crawl away.

"Stupid!"

Kick.

"Fucking!"

Kick.

"Worthless!"

Kick.

"Bitch!"

Kick.

Hearing the door slide open. I looked up, praying to see Shane returning. Before I could register who entered, Garrett's foot slammed into my temple, and my world went instantly black.

# CHAPTER SEVEN

## *Courted*

*A* knock sounded against my door. Callen was standing there leaning on the frame when I opened it. My gaze stretched the length of his figure. A black t-shirt clung to his broad chest and torso, and faded bootcut cut jeans spread down his powerful legs. I snapped my eyes back to his, scolding myself for ogling him again. A knowing smirk swept across his face which sent a slight blush flitting across my cheeks.

"Come on in," I said, moving to the side to allow him entrance into the living room. "I just need to grab my phone from the charger, and I'll be ready."

"Take your time," he called to my retreating figure.

I slipped down the hall into my bedroom and stole a quick glance at myself in the mirror. Soft, golden, brown waves of hair danced across my shoulders as hazel eyes stared back at me, appraising my appearance. I wore a simple v-neck, black tee and dark jeggings. A typical outfit that blends into a crowd but still flatters. I tucked a strand of hair behind my ear, plucked my phone from the rapid charging pad, and headed back to the living room.

Callen was looking around my basic apartment. I didn't own very many decorations like the typical woman. My walls were plain taupe, simple navy curtains hung from the window leading to the balcony, and a gray sofa faced a tv on a small stand. I had no need for frills. I never let anyone into my apartment, not even

*Claire. In fact, she doesn't even know the location. We always meet up at her place. I don't know what possessed me to allow Callen knowledge of - much less access to - my home.*

Another cardinal rule broken, *I supposed.*

*This was the only place I didn't have to be guarded. The hospital didn't even have my real address. I gave them a fake in the next town and have all my mail sent to a P.O. box. I only deal in cash, load minutes on a prepaid cell phone, and never carry my real ID. While I choose to have an active presence in the world, I do my best to stay under the radar. Being a marked one is dangerous. A fate worse than death awaits a marked one if they're found.*

So, why have I broken almost every rule I have in place to keep myself safe? *I contemplated.* I barely know this man, yet I've let him into my home.

*Tingles went up my spine as I watched him. I looked to my left wrist to ensure my black, leather bracelet was securely fastened and covering my soulmark. I'd tried everything to remove the mark when it first appeared, but nothing worked. It's as much a part of me as the color of my eyes.*

"Okay. I'm ready," *I said to get his attention.*

"You sure? There's no hurry."

"Yeah. I'm good. Let's head out." *I opened the door and exited my apartment. Callen followed behind as I pulled the key from my pocket and locked the deadbolt before heading down the stairs.*

*When we reached the bottom, Callen took my hand, sending bolts of electricity through me. His calloused fingers felt rough against mine. My mind strayed to thoughts of those fingers running over my body...him cupping my breast, rolling my nipples under his fingers...his body pinning mine against a wall...his hips grinding into me...*

"Lacey?" *he asked, ripping me from my lustful thoughts.*

"Ugh, sorry, I must've spaced out," I answered sheepishly.

"What were you thinking about?"

"Just…work," I lied poorly. "So, where are we headed?"

"I thought we could grab a drink at the bar. Then, go back to my place after and watch a movie?"

"A movie, huh?" I asked with raised eyebrows. I'd like to believe I'd given him the wrong impression with our intense make out session on our first date, but my body wanted this man. Lust filled me when I looked at him. My core clenched when our eyes locked. Never had I had such a visceral reaction. And god, I think he wants me too, I thought.

"Yeah, a movie." Callen shrugged his shoulders nonchalantly, but I couldn't miss the coy curl of his lips and the fire blazing in his emerald eyes.

When we reached the bar, Callen dropped my hand to open the door. He guided me with a palm on the small of my back to a high-top table and pulled the chair out for me to sit down.

"I'll get us some drinks. Do you know what you want?"

"Vodka water sour, please."

Every woman turned their head to get a second glance at him as he strode to the bar. Even the bartender skipped several customers to attend to him first. She batted her lashes and giggled while she made the drinks. I clenched my jaw as jealousy filled me. Pretty soon I'd have to beat these women off with a stick.

"Aw, baby, you look upset. Come dance with me, and I'll make it better," a male voice sounded behind me. I turned my head to see a tall, handsome blonde resting his arm on the back of my chair. His blue eyes raked me up and down as his tongue licked across his bottom lip.

"I'm actually here with somebody. Thanks though." I did my best to sound polite yet dismissive.

*"Don't be like that, beautiful. One little dance won't hurt."
He grabbed my hand on the table and gently tugged to lead me
away.*

*I yanked free from his grasp and scowled up at him. "I said
no."*

*"Your mouth may have said 'no' but those eyes are saying
'yes'," he argued, gripping my upper arm in a tight squeeze. We had
attracted a few onlookers at this point. Having overindulged at the
bar, he was oblivious to the scene developing.*

*I narrowed my eyes at him, my fist balled, preparing to
strike. "Look, buddy. You're drunk, and I'm not interested. Now,
let go of me." Feeling the air thicken behind me with his presence, I
knew Callen had returned.*

*"I think the lady said she wasn't interested, and I know
you should take your hand off her before I take it off for you." The
anger practically vibrated off of him as he set our drinks down.*

*The man released my arm and raised his hand to point a
finger in Callen's face. "What are you going to—" He broke off mid
sentence as Callen threw a right hook to his jaw. The man fell on the
floor, his hand rubbing his face instinctively. "Fuck, man," he said
with an already red and swollen jaw.*

*Two bouncers came over, pulled the guy off the floor, and
threw him out of the bar. Callen nodded at them in thanks
when they looked back. Everyone slowly returned to their own
conversations as the drama came to an end. Callen looked down at
me and tucked a stray lock of hair behind my ear.*

*"Are you okay?" he asked, worry stretched across his face.*

*"I'm fine," I said a bit too sharply. Sighing, I tried to let go
of my misplaced anger with Callen. "You didn't have to do that. I
think he was going to leave."*

*He snorted, "Yes, I did. He was practically undressing you
with his eyes. Besides, I protect what's mine." He leaned and*

whispered in my ear, "And, you, Lacey, are all mine."

My breath caught with his blatant possessiveness. My mouth went dry as I turned my head to look at him. Did he seriously just say that? Before I could respond, Callen moved away and took his seat across from me at the table. He picked his glass up and took a large slug of the double whisky, neat.

Following suit, I grabbed my drink and took a sip. "Do you know those guys or something?" I asked in an attempt to settle the electricity in the air.

"What guys?"

"The bouncers. They didn't seem to mind you punching another customer."

"He deserved it. They knew it," he deflected.

I thought about pushing the subject but decided it really didn't matter. I took a large drink from my glass as his words echoed in my mind: You, Lacey, are all mine. If only he knew, I could never be his. Fate had already selected my soulmate. A soulmate I didn't want; one I would never look for, never find. It's too risky. I'm better off alone. I know that, so I had no idea what I was doing with Callen. I feel pulled to him in a way I can't understand. I admit to finding myself lonesome at times, but lonely is better than dead. I rarely date and when I do, it's casual and never goes on long. My heart ached at how quickly this would have to end. I slammed the rest of my drink to push the thoughts from my mind. Live in the present, I told myself.

Callen raised an eyebrow at me in question.

"Let's dance," I said, jumping from my chair.

Callen chuckled, downed his whiskey, and offered his hand to me as he stood. I laced my fingers between his and let him pull me onto the dance floor. He spun me around and pulled my back to his chest. His nose nuzzled into my hair as his hands found my hips, pulling them in a circular motion to grind *against him to the beat. His left hand slid across my hip and onto my thigh, permitting his thumb to graze gently between my legs. My breathing caught and a moan slipped through my lips. Embarrassed by my audible reaction, my hand shifted to his and pulled his touch back to my hip.*

What is wrong with me? Well, two can play that game, *I thought as he snickered, undoubtedly pleased with himself.*

*I arched my back and grinded into him while lifting my arms behind my head to lock my fingers in his hair. I moved to the beat, firmly rubbing against him as I felt his excitement grow and press into me.*

*"Christ," he mumbled under his breath as he matched my movement and pulled me firmer into him. The longer we danced, the higher the sexual tension grew. "If you keep doing that, I might just have to take you right here in front of everyone," he breathed in my ear.*

*I gasped and turned to look at him. He pulled me to his chest and pressed his mouth to mine. The music transitioned to a slow song as I placed my left hand on his chest, bracing myself to deepen the kiss. Cupping his hand over mine, we swayed to the new rhythm. He ran his hand down my arm and back up to my wrist. Before I realized what was happening, his thumb slid under my bracelet and pressed into my mark. Pleasure shot through every nerve of my body, and the word "mate" flashed in my mind.*

Fuck! *I screamed internally as I ripped my arm from his grasp and pushed away.* This can't be happening.

*Callen looked shocked at my reaction.*

Hopefully, that meant he didn't feel it too, *I thought. My eyes shot to the watch around his wrist and back to his face. He took a breath and reached his hand out to me.*

*"I have to go," I said barely over a whisper as I turned and ran from the bar.* Stupid. Stupid. Stupid. No wonder I'm so

drawn to him. He's my fucking soulmate. You idiot woman! *I silently berated myself as I half jogged down the street.*

*"Lacey! Wait!" I heard Callen call from behind me. I stopped to allow him to catch up but took several deep breaths before I turned around to face him.*

*"What happened back there?" he asked.*

*"I'm sorry, but I can't see you anymore."* So he didn't feel it then? Good. It's better if he doesn't know. Safer, *I thought.*

*"What do you mean you can't see me anymore?" Confusion flooded his face.*

*"I mean that this has been great, but it's best if we go our separate ways."*

*"Give me a reason," he demanded, his confused expression shifting to frustration. "Give me one damn reason why you ran out of there like a bat out of hell. One reason why we can't be together."*

*"I don't have to give you a reason," I snapped back at him. He stepped forward, pulled my face to his, and crashed his lips into mine. He kissed me with such passion I couldn't help but kiss him back. His tongue twirled in my mouth, and I pressed myself to him.*

Stop it! *I chided myself, pushing against his chest and tearing his mouth from mine. I could already feel my lips swelling from the mutually aggressive kiss. His eyes bore into me as he panted for air. He reached for me, but I moved further away.*

*"Damnit, Lacey. Just talk to me. Please."*

*"Goodbye, Callen." I bounded down the street before he could grab me again. Folding my arms across my chest, I tried to hold myself together. It felt like I ripped out my own heart.*

My head pounded when I stirred. I tried to open my eyes, but they were too heavy. Faint beeping noises sounded in the background.

"Why is she still asleep?" a male voice asked.

"Well, outside of the general bodily trauma she has had inflicted upon her, she's sustained several intense blows to the head. Additional impacts while recovering from a concussion can cause irreparable damage," a woman explained, coolly.

"Are you telling me that jackass gave her brain damage?"

"I am saying it's possible; however, I don't think that's the case here. Her pupils are reactive. Her brain waves are normal. I think she just needs rest."

I knew the voices. I recognized them, but in my grogginess I couldn't place them through the darkness pulling me back under. I tried to fight against it. I tried to wake, but the abyss surrounded me again.

*It'd been a week since I walked away from Callen, and a gaping hole filled my chest. I had a good life - a safe life - but my body ached for him. I had spent my entire life content being half a soul. I didn't need the other half.* So why does it hurt so fucking much? *I asked myself. I never planned for what I would do if I found my soulmate, because I never thought it would happen.*

*I pulled the pillow over my face, fighting the urge to suffocate myself. I heard my phone ring and moved to grab it. Callen's name lit up on the screen. I groaned and flipped the pillow over my face again. He was making it so hard. That was the fifth time he'd called. It took every fiber of my being not to answer the phone just to hear his voice one more time. I groaned as I thought of his lips on mine and the pleasure that shot through me when he touched my mark.*

*My phone rang again. I grabbed it, prepared to chuck it against the wall, but the name "Claire " displayed on the screen.*

*Reluctantly, I answered, "Hey."*

*"'Hey' yourself stranger. What are you doing?"*

*"Laying in the bed with the pillow over my face, trying to smother out the world."*

*"Someone is in a sour mood." I could practically hear her eyes roll over the phone. "What's going on?"*

*I sighed. I normally told Claire a lot, but this wasn't something I could share with anyone. "Nothing. It's not important. What's up?"*

*"Well, I was wanting to see if you were interested in going out tonight."*

*"Not tonight, Claire."*

*"Oh, come on! I haven't seen you since we went to that self-defense class."*

*"Yeah, I know. I've been busy," I lied.*

*"Derek and Michael want to take us out again."*

*"You're still seeing Derek? I thought you were going to - and I quote - 'shag and bag his ass'?"*

*"Well, if you must know, I decided on a few more shaggings."*

*"That good, huh?" I teased.*

*"You have no idea. So, are you game?"*

*"I don't think so."*

*"Come on! Michael has asked about you a couple times. He said y'all's night got cut short."*

*"What exactly did he tell you?" I sat bolt upright, heart racing in my chest.* Michael knew Callen and I left together. What if he told Claire? *My thoughts ran wild with panic.*

*"He didn't elaborate, just said you left."*

*I let out the breath I was holding as silence filled in around us. When I didn't reply, she asked, "Did something happen?"*

*"No. Nothing happened. I was just tired and had to work the next morning. So, where are you and Derek going tonight?" I asked to change the subject.*

*"The guys are taking us to Club Vega. They will be here at ten so you better get moving. It's already eight thirty."*

*"Claire—"*

*"I'm not taking no for an answer. So, get all dolled up and come over. You need to get out. You lock yourself up too much."*

Maybe she's right. It would give me something to do besides wallow in this bed. The idea of spending more time with Michael wasn't on my top things to do. However, Claire would be there, and he wasn't the worst, *I supposed.*

*"Lacey?"*

*"Okay. Give me an hour."*

*"Yay! See you soon!" she squealed into the phone before hanging up.*

*I stared at the ceiling for a few minutes before I pried myself out of the bed, heading to the bathroom to get ready. I sprayed my hair down with some water, massaged some mousse into my locks, grabbed the diffuser, and styled the waves. My hair never would hold a full curl, and it never remained straight for more than a few hours when flatironed. Makeup wasn't really my thing, so I settled on some mascara and a soft lip gloss. I really should put in a bit more effort, but I didn't have anyone to impress.*

*When I finished in the bathroom, I headed to the closet to find an outfit. I'd much rather wear jeans, but Claire would kill me if I tried to go clubbing in denim. I pulled a strappy, black dress from the back of the closet. I'd never worn it. In fact, I only had it because of Claire. She insisted every woman needed a little black dress. It fit snugly over the bodice and torso but fluttered freely at the hips to disguise the built-in pockets with the hem hitting mid-thigh. I slid on a pair of black boho sandals and went to check out the ensemble in the mirror.*

*I had to admit that I did look nice.* Maybe going out won't be so bad; maybe, it'll even be fun. *With that thought, I grabbed my phone, some cash, and my key and headed out the door. It was only a twenty minute walk to Claire's house. I normally would Uber, but the night air was warm and inviting. I'd be there by ten til. Later than I said, but still before the men were due.*

*As I walked, my phone rang again. I pulled it out of my pocket and immediately sent it to voicemail when I saw Callen's name on the screen. I knew if I heard his voice, I'd want to see him - which was something that utterly couldn't happen.* Rejecting the bond is the right thing to do. You know it is, *I repeated to myself for the millionth time.*

*Claire lived in a quaint two bedroom house with a beautiful flower garden landscaped out front that popped against the baby blue siding. She must've been waiting, because she slung the door open before I could knock.*

*"About time! I was just about to call you."*

*"Sorry, I walked. It's nice out tonight," I explained as I entered the house. I looked Claire up and down and let out a wolf whistle. "Damn, girl. Are you trying to give Derek a heart attack?"*

*Her laughter filled the room. "Is it too much?"*

*"No way! You look hot!" I grinned at her. Claire was beautiful and loved to show off her body. I wouldn't be caught dead in her skin tight, strapless, silver dress, but it suited her perfectly. The skirt ended about an inch shorter than her finger tips, and she wore matching high heels.*

*"Thanks," she beamed. "You look gorgeous yourself. You really should wear dresses more. You have killer legs."*

*"Oh, stop it." I couldn't help but smile though. Claire always*

*puts me in a better mood, her happiness contagious.*

*A knock sounded at the door, cutting our conversation. Claire opened it and ushered in our dates. Derek eyed Claire from head to toe, saying, "Damn, am I one lucky guy," before pulling her in for a heated kiss.*

*Michael and I made eye contact, and I smiled at him in greeting. I knew this would be awkward with how our last date ended.*

*"Come on, let's get out of here," Claire called as she took Derek by the hand and led him out the door.*

*Michael and I followed behind them and hopped in the back of Derek's car while Claire took the front passenger seat. Music rang through the sound system when the car came to life. We were halfway to the club, and Michael and I still hadn't spoken a word to each other. Thinking things would be awkward was evidently an understatement. Feeling his eyes on me, I looked in his direction.*

*"Listen," he began, "I think I owe you an apology."*

*"You think?"*

*"Okay. I know I owe you an apology. I was being an ass that night."*

*"Yes, you were." I pursed my lips at him.*

*"Can we maybe start over?"*

*"I don't think I heard an apology in there."*

*"I'm sorry, Lacey."*

*I smiled at him, "Alright. You're forgiven." I've never been a grudgeful person and had no plans to start now.*

*"You look stunning by the way," he said with a wide grin.*

*A light blush crept over my cheeks.* Maybe this is what I needed, *I thought,* a nice distraction.

*Derek parked the car in a garage, and we funneled out to the street. People were everywhere, and a queue had formed for entrance to the club. Derek and Claire were wrapped around each other while we waited, leaving Michael and I to converse alone.*

*"So, um, not to be rude or anything...but, that guy...the one from the bar...are you guys involved?"*

*"We aren't dating if that's what you're asking."*

*"Oh, great. I just want to make sure. He seemed pretty into you. Possessive even." Michael regarded me with a look of suspicion as he spoke.*

He's my soulmate. Of course he's possessive. Even if he didn't realize it when he touched my mark. *I did my best to push the thoughts from my mind and groped for an answer that sounded dismissive. "If you must know, he has taken me out twice, but I assure you, nothing is going on any longer."*

*He nodded his head and did his best to fight the grin sliding over his face. Thankfully, the line moved fast, and we headed into the club. The music was raging, so I didn't have to worry about any additional Callen questions. Derek and Michael went up to the bar to grab us some drinks once inside, returning with double tequila shots for us all.*

*"Y'all trying to get us drunk?" Claire called to Derek over the music.*

*"Not trying to. Going to," Derek said, winking at her.*

*Michael passed me a shot he was carrying. I didn't normally do shots or get wasted. I swirled the glass while appraising the golden liquid sloshing around inside as I puffed out my cheeks in a sigh. When drunk, you lose control, which was something I never let happen.*

*"Just drink it, Lacey! We are here to unwind. What could happen?" Claire encouraged.*

*Suddenly, the air electrified, and I could feel eyes on me.*

*Looking over my shoulder, I found those deep, emerald eyes staring at me from across the room. Callen's jaw was clenched and strained. Outright ire and fury radiated off him. I swallowed hard as I took a breath. Even now, he was the most handsome man I have ever seen. I fought every muscle in my body from running to him, kissing him, and trailing my hands all over his body.*

*I looked down at the shot in my hands and back to Callen. He slightly shook his head as if telling me no. I set my jaw and glared back at him in defiance.* He might be my mate, but that means nothing. I don't want a mate, *I thought.*

*"Fuck it." I threw the shot back in one gulp. My tongue and throat burned as the alcohol filled my stomach. "Let's dance."*

*I grabbed Claire by the arm and headed to the dance floor in the opposite direction. I didn't think anyone saw what transpired between Callen and I, but I wanted more distance from him just in case. The music blared so loud I could feel the bass bumping in my bones. After a few songs, the guys joined us with more double shots. Claire and I cheersed and threw them back.*

*The alcohol flowed like a warmth through my veins. I could feel my control and inhibition lowering. Michael came up behind me and wrapped his hands around my waist as we danced. I whipped my head and slung my hair around seductively. I could feel Callen's eyes biting into me from across the room. If he insisted on watching, then I was going to give him a show.*

*A waitress came by with test tube shots. Claire plucked some off the tray and handed me one. I drank it without even thinking. Five shots in less than an hour. Drunken brazenness filled me. I put my hands in the air and circled my hips. Michael pressed up against me, his length pushing into the small of my back. I tilted my head to the side and closed my eyes as he nuzzled my neck. No sparks flew, no excitement fisted my stomach, but I kept dancing anyway. Michael's hands slightly hitched up my dress and skimmed my thighs. He kissed my neck and let out a deep moan as he thrusted himself forward.*

*My eyes snapped open as I realized where this was headed. I saw Callen push himself off the wall and head toward us. I immediately stopped dancing, turned to Michael, gestured toward the bathroom, and left before he had a chance to follow.*

*I made it to the hall where the bathrooms were when a hand wrapped around my upper arm and pulled me to the side. A firm body pressed me up against a wall with hands on either side of my head.*

*"What do you think you're doing?" Callen hissed in my ear.*

*"Going to the bathroom. Obviously."*

*A throaty growl rumbled from Callen. "You know what I mean. What are you doing* here? With *him?"*

*"What are you doing* here? Following me?" *I snapped back.*

*"You weren't answering my calls. I needed to know you were safe," he answered through clenched teeth.*

*"My safety isn't your concern."*

*"Everything about you is my concern."*

*I gritted my teeth as anger swept over me. I put my hands on Callen's chest and tried to push him off, but he only pressed against me tighter.*

*"I don't want you dancing with anyone like that but me."*

*"You don't get a vote. I'll dance with whoever the fuck I please." I shoved harder, yet Callen acted as if he wasn't fazed.*

*He grabbed my wrists in one of his hands and pulled them over my head. His other hand grabbed my chin and pulled my face an inch from his. "You are mine, Lacey."*

*Part of me longed to crush my mouth to his, to let him own me like he said, to wrap my arms around him and never let go. I smothered the urge, picked up my foot, and slammed it into his shin. Pain shot through my toes; however, it caught him off guard,* and I was able to pull my arms free and slide past him.

"I am mine!" I yelled as I dipped into the bathroom and slammed the door shut. I stood with my back to the door trying to catch my breath. Tingles lingered on my body from his touch. My vision swam from the liquor, so I splashed some cold water on my cheeks to try and sober up.

If he won't accept my verbal denial, then I'll have to show him with action, *I thought.*

*After drying my face, I ensured my bracelet was still in place, took a deep breath, and opened the door to find that Callen was gone. I returned to the dance floor, but my friends weren't there. Looking around the room, I quickly found them at the bar. When I approached, Michael shoved yet another shot in my hand. I knew I was drunk. I shouldn't have anymore, but the thought of Callen's hands on me lit my skin on fire. I took the shot without hesitation.*

*Michael grabbed my hand and took me back to the dance floor. He pulled me close to him and grinded the front of his hips into me. I could feel his excitement returning. I knew Callen was watching from somewhere in the club. This was my chance to make my point clear, so I pushed my hips forward. Michael fisted my hair and pulled my mouth to his.*

*The kiss was sloppy and wet and unreturned as I refused access to my mouth. I felt nothing for this man. Maybe before I had met Callen this would've been fine, but now, it made my stomach churn. I wanted no part of this. I broke the kiss and put my hands against his chest to push him away.*

*"I'm sorry. This is a mistake. I can't do this." I tried to take a step back, but Michael held me tight in his arms.*

*"Sure, you can. I know you want to."*

*"No. It's just the alcohol. I need to go."*

*"We can go back to my place, hun. It's not far."*

I tried to push him off again, but my arms felt like jello. "I... don't—" I broke off, words failing to come out. My eyes felt heavy. Something's not right, I thought.

I glanced around for Claire, but I didn't see her or Derek anywhere. Looking back at Michael, a knowing smirk spread across his face, his eyes full of lust. I hadn't been watching the shots after the bartender gave them over.

Stupid idiot, I scolded myself.

My knees buckled, and my peripheral vision flickered. I opened my eyes wider trying to steady my vision. Michael was holding me to his chest, supporting my weight. "Oh, baby, the drinks kicking in? I'll take care of you like I know you want."

He started dragging me toward the back exit of the club as I finally righted my footing and straightened up. Reluctantly, he released my waist but kept a death grip on my wrist.

"Lemme go," I slurred as a body pushed in between Michael and me, causing him to fumble my arm. I staggered to the side and braced myself against the wall.

"Hey—" Michael cut off as a fist connected with his jaw.

Taking the opportunity to flee, I stumbled out the back door without looking back. I could hear bodies slamming into one another and voices yelling underneath the drowning music. I stumbled into a wall in the alley as my vision swayed. An arm abruptly pushed my back into the wall. Michael held me with a forearm across my chest. Blood ran from his mouth, his breathing heavy.

"Let's go." He dropped his arm to grab mine and tugged. I dug the nails from my other hand into him as I tried to pull free, my mind too fuzzy to scream for help.

"For fuck sake, pass out already!" he yelled as he threw me back into the wall. His hand gripped around my throat as blood trickled down his arm where my nails tore into his hand.

*"Ssssstop, Michael…" I managed to croak out, my arms too heavy from the drugs to fight anymore. My vision became patchy blackness as he squeezed harder, choking me.*

*Suddenly, his grip relinquished, and I fell to the ground, gasping for air. I could hear the scuffle of another fight breaking out, but all my energy was too focused on breathing to pay attention to what was happening. A hard thud cracked through the air and silence fell around me. I tried to stand and run, but my legs wouldn't hold my weight. A dark figure loomed over as the air thickened. Strong arms cradled me to a male chest, and electric current spread across my skin from the contact.*

*"Callen," I sighed before losing the battle and falling into unconsciousness.*

Bright lights shown overhead. My head still pounded, but it wasn't all consuming like before. I tried to sit up, but the pain splintered. I layed back down with a groan. My stomach churned as bile crept up my throat. The woosh of a sliding door echoed through the room. I did my best to look like I was still asleep as footsteps approached.

"She should be awake." It was the same man from before.

"It's only been three days," the female replied.

"Yeah but the meds should've healed her."

"They did. Look at her. No bruising or swelling is left on her face, the x-rays show the fractured ribs and knuckles are whole, and the laceration on her arm is a thin pink scar."

"Then why isn't she awake?" he half yelled. The screeching of a chair rang out as it slid across the floor.

"She's in there. She just needs more time. The mind can be a fragile thing."

The man snorted in derision.

"The monitor shows she's been dreaming, so her brain is working. She's gone through a lot of trauma. Her brain is trying to process and protect itself."

"She's been dreaming?"

"Mmhmm."

"Do you know what about?"

"Unfortunately, no. If I could take her to my lab and hook her to the device, I may be able to display them, but I'm unsure. All the other participants were willing, awake, and memory projecting - not dreaming."

The silence was almost deafening. I could feel wires and stickers connected to me. The female broke the silence after what felt like an eternity, "You look angry."

"I am angry, Sam," he sighed. "I don't know why Garrett has such a hard-on for her. I never should have left them in that room."

*Shane. But, who's the woman...Sam? Sam?* I racked my brain trying to place the name. *The neuroscientist, Dr. Samantha Reid.*

"I don't think it's just Garrett that's overly interested in her."

"What's that supposed to mean?" he asked accusingly.

"Oh, I don't know...just an observation." I could almost hear the smile as she spoke.

"I'm just doing my job."

"If you say so."

I heard their footsteps retreating and the swish of the door. I didn't have the energy to try and get up again. My head pounded as I pulled for my memories, trying to remember what happened, but exhaustion quickly came for me with the mental effort. I did my best to fight the darkness closing in until sleep finally overwhelmed me.

*I sat upright, gasping. Looking around at my surroundings, I found myself laying in a soft, king sized bed. I flung the covers back and breathed a sigh of relief that I was still wearing my dress. The room was dark, but I could tell I was alone. I stood on two shaking legs. My whole body screamed with achiness. Bruises in the shape of handprints adorned my wrists and upper arms. My neck throbbed, and the skin smarted when I ran my fingers over it.*

*I could hear movement coming from outside the door. Quickly, I scanned the room for a weapon. I grabbed the lamp on the nightstand, flattened myself to the wall, and prepared to strike. The door creaked open as I held my breath. A shadowy, male figure appeared in the doorway. He took a step into the room, and I brought the lamp down as hard as I could.*

*"Woah!" he yelled as the lamp crashed into the arm he raised to protect his head. "It's me!"*

*Not waiting to listen, I made a break for the door, but two arms enveloped me from behind. "Lacey! Stop! It's me!" Sparks rained over my skin where he touched me as realization dawned, and I stilled.*

*"Callen?"*

*He let me go so I could turn around.*

*"It's you."*

*"Yeah. It's just me." A bruise shown on the left side of his jaw and his right eyebrow had a deep gash.*

*"You're hurt." On reflex, I reached my hand toward him and cupped his face. He closed his eyes and leaned into my palm.*

"I'm fine. Are you okay?" He reached out to me, opening his eyes, but I stepped back, withdrawing my hand from his face.

"Um, what...what happened? I remember being in the alley, then it's blank."

"By the time I made it outside, he was strangling you. I got him off, but you were in rough shape. You passed out right after I picked you up."

"Where is he?"

He shrugged. "Knocked him out and left him in the alley. I would've gone back to finish it, but I didn't want to leave you."

"I, um, I see. Thank you."

"I'd say anytime, but I'd prefer to not have a repeat of last night."

A blush went up my cheeks from embarrassment about my behavior, my mistakes, my helplessness. "I should probably be going."

"Have breakfast with me."

"I'm really not a breakfast person." I looked at him sheepishly. His beautiful face had been beaten because of me. How many times would this man have to fight for me? I questioned myself. He opened his mouth to argue, but I cut him off, "I like coffee though."

"Coffee it is then," he said with a smile.

I followed him out of the bedroom and into his kitchen. Callen's apartment was similar to mine in only having the essentials. The kitchen held a two seater table in the breakfast nook and no decorations on the walls. He pulled the coffee grounds from the fridge and set the pot up to percolate.

"I don't keep creamer or anything like that, but I probably have some milk if you want," he offered apologetically.

"I actually drink it black. Thanks though."

He poured us both a mug and gestured for me to have a seat at the table. I took a sip of my coffee, trying to think of something to say to break the silence.

"Where did you sleep last night?" The question spewed out before I could stop myself.

"Where did I sleep?" he asked as if caught off guard.

"It's just, I woke up in your bed, and I don't remember anything. So, I was just wondering..." I squirmed in my seat uncomfortably.

"I slept on the couch in the living room," he answered. "I carried you back here. You were completely out of it. I put you in the bed and covered you up so you could sleep off whatever it was he gave you."

"Right...I feel like such an idiot. I'm normally so much more careful." I ran my hand over my face trying to hide my mortification.

"Do you go clubbing often?"

"No." I shot a glare at him. "I don't normally do shots either if that's your next question."

"Then why were you?"

"Because—" I cut myself off. "That's none of your business. Why were you following me?" My temper swung in with full force.

"I think it is my business if you are going to be so reckless," he said pointedly, "and, I told you, you weren't answering my calls."

"That doesn't give you the right to stalk somebody. You had no business following me!"

"I think it's a damn good thing I did considering what happened."

My anger transcended into outright fury. "I appreciate what

*you did, but I can take care of myself. I've done it for this long. I can keep doing it." I got to my feet and stomped toward the door, but Callen stepped in front of me.*

*"Where do you think you're going?"*

*"Home."*

*"We aren't done talking about this," he snapped.*

*"Oh, yes we are." I moved to go around him, but he grabbed my arm and spun me into the wall.*

*"You aren't going anywhere."*

*He crushed his lips into mine and fireworks shot through me. I wrapped my hands around his head and pulled him into me. Longing for him took over all my senses as he lifted me into the air. I entwined my legs around his waist and parted my lips to grant him access. He moved his hands to cup my ass and grinded his hips into me. Need for him ripped through my chest and settled between my legs. He pushed into me hard, his need just as apparent. The rational part of my brain fought the primitive, sexual demands of my body. I broke the kiss and lowered my feet to the floor. I messed up enough last night. I couldn't continue the irresponsible streak of bad decisions.*

*"We can't do this. I have to go." I went to move, but Callen put his hand on the wall by my head to block me.*

*"Stop running from me, Lacey."*

*"I'm not running. It's just better if we aren't together, and deep down, I know you know that too."*

*"Hell no, I don't. I finally found you. I'm not allowing you to walk away. Not again."*

*"You won't allow me? You don't get a say in this. I'm leaving." I pushed his arm off the wall, but he grabbed my left arm and held me in place.*

*"I do get a say. You don't get to make this decision alone."*

"For the love of god. Just let me the fuck go, Callen! Please. This is hard enough." I wanted to strike him, and at the same time, I wanted to kiss him. Hate him, but love him.

"No," he said firmly.

"Why? Why can't you just let me go?" Tears pricked my eyes, frustration driving me toward the edge.

"You know why." He pulled my hand palm up. My breathing hitched as I stared at the fitted bracelet on my wrist. I jerked my arm, but he held on tight, his other hand moving to the clasp. "I'll show you mine if you show me yours."

I stopped fighting, unable to move as he took the bracelet off and let it clatter to the floor. His fingers caressed the half moon soulmark shining up at us. Pleasure shot through me again just like the first night he touched me there.

"I knew it from the first moment I saw you. It was like the earth stopped spinning when you looked at me. I never thought I would find you, and suddenly, there you were, right in front of me."

Callen unbuckled the watch adorning his wrist and turned his arm over. The same crescent moon glistened white across his skin. With trembling fingers, I softly reached for his wrist. I pressed my thumb on his mark and his whole body stiffened. The same electric current shot through my veins again, and now, I knew he could feel it too.

"Callen, I—" my sentence broke off as his lips found mine. He pressed me into the wall, and this time I didn't resist. Seeing the mark on his arm took all the fight out of me. I wanted him, all of him, in the most primal way. I shut off the voice in my head telling me it was too dangerous for us to be together, the one that insisted I was safest on my own.

Callen fisted my hair and rocked his hips into mine, his member pushing into my stomach. Warmth flooded my core from the feeling, and I plunged my tongue into his mouth as he pulled *my legs up to encircle him again. I ground myself down and moaned in pleasure. Pulling me from the wall, he headed toward his bedroom, our mouths never parting. Callen kicked the door shut behind him and threw me on the bed, eliciting a gasp from the sudden motion.*

*He pulled his white t-shirt over his head and stood over me, hunger flaring in his eyes, his chest heaving with desire. My panties dampened as I lay there looking him up and down. His muscles were tight over his torso, his abdomen lean and cut. My breasts heaved with my own rapid breathing as I ogled his body. I sat up on the bed and lifted my hands to the button of his jeans. We held eye contact as I pulled down his zipper and dropped his pants to the floor, his erection standing firm in his boxers. I slid off the bed onto my knees. He towered over me as I placed my hands on his hips and looped my fingers in the hem of his boxers. Grazing his covered tip with my nose, I inhaled his musk.*

*Callen groaned with the slight contact, flexing his hands at his sides as he tried to control himself. I angled my head as I pulled his boxers to the floor. He was huge in all aspects. My eyes widened at his impressive girth as I wrapped my hand around him. Guiding him toward my mouth, I licked his shaft from top to bottom.*

*He grabbed the hair at the nape of my neck and slightly pulled me backward to look at me. "Are you sure?"*

*"Do you not want me to?" After finally deciding to let go, the thought of him not wanting me stung.*

*"Oh, I want you to, but you don't have to. And once you start, I won't be able to stop myself from taking you." A darkness clouded his green eyes as he spoke those words. I wanted nothing more than for this man to devour me. He let go of my hair, nodded, and went to step away, thinking his warning had hit home; however, I dropped my head and plunged him deep in my mouth before he could move.*

*"Oh, fuck," he moaned as I took him in. I bobbed my head up*

and down as far as I could take him while stroking his remaining length with my hand. Both his hands fell into my hair this time as he thrust deeper into my mouth. He slapped against the back of my throat, causing me to gag.

"God, you are so sexy when you make that noise."

I took my other hand and started massaging his sack, rolling his balls in and out of my hand. Precum dribbled onto my tongue. A sweet, musky flavor ignited my taste buds, driving me to suck him harder. He tasted too good, and I wanted more.

Callen released my hair, grabbed me by my upper arms and threw me back on the bed. My dress fluttered up as I fell backward, barely touching the top of my thighs. Climbing on the bed, he shoved my legs apart with his. He pulled the hem of my dress up as I arched my back for him to remove it. I layed there bare in my black, lace panties with him on top of me. Callen sat up on his knees to look at me. A blush crept over my cheeks as he took in my nakedness. Feeling self conscious, I moved my hands to cover my breasts.

"Don't you dare," he said, grabbing my hands and pinning them over my head. "You are the most beautiful woman I have ever seen." Callen brought his lips to mine with a soft kiss. "Don't you ever be shy around me," he whispered against my mouth, his warm breath wrapping around me.

He then roughly took my mouth to his as I lay pinned beneath him. He thrust against me with only my panties blocking his entry. I moaned and writhed underneath him, begging him for more. He worked kisses down my jaw and throat until he reached my breasts. Sucking a nipple into his mouth, he twirled it with his tongue as he shifted my wrists into one hand, freeing his other to firmly cup my breast. I arched my back as he tugged and teased my nipples. The wetness between my legs increased with each pinch and swipe of his tongue.

Callen released my breast to skim his hand down the side of

my body, fondling each and every curve. When he reached my hips, he balled the lace fabric in his hand and tore the panties from my body, tossing them to the floor. Two fingers slid over my cleft and found my clit. I groaned in pleasure as he massaged me, bucking my hips toward him. Sliding his hand further down, he teased my entrance with a tip of a finger. He pulled his hand away from me, and I whimpered, craving for his touch to fill me.

"You are so wet."

"Callen, please, I—"

In one motion, he slammed himself into me. A stinging sensation ripped through me as I tore from his massive size. I sucked in a breath as I arched against him, my hands still pinned above my head.

"Fuck, Lacey. You're so tight," he said as he pulled out of me. Callen thrust back forward and entered me further. The full length of his shaft was buried deep inside. The burning pain morphed into undeniable pleasure as we moved. He collapsed onto me as I wrapped my legs around his hips. Releasing my wrists to wrap his arms around my head, he pulled me further into him. His slow thrusts picked up pace as I matched him stroke for stroke, stretching me further with each movement.

"Oh, god," I gasped under my breath as my climax built. A warm ball of pleasure formed in my lower stomach as I rocked against him. I ran my fingers through his hair and down his back, digging my nails into his skin as he rode me.

"Come for me, baby." Callen tugged on my left arm and pulled it down by our heads. He took his thumb and ground it into my soulmark. Stars flitted across my vision with the pressure, and I erupted around him. Wave after wave of ecstasy rolled over me until I was screaming his name and clenching around him. At that moment, he took me higher than I had ever been.

"God, yes," he breathed in my ear. He never stopped pumping into me as I writhed beneath him. Callen found his own release with the final quivers of my climax. His warmth flowed into me until our thrusts slowed together, both of us breathing heavily. He gently kissed me as we stilled with him buried inside me.

Slowly, Callen lifted himself off and rolled to the side. He pulled me over and draped me across his chest, our eyes never leaving each other's as he cupped my cheek in his hand and I nuzzled into it.

"You are amazing, Lacey."

I smiled at him and closed my eyes, feeling completely at peace. "You aren't so bad yourself," I quipped. He chuckled beneath me, moving his hand to stroke my hair. I pushed off his chest and sat up, letting out a slight wince with the movement. Soreness was setting in now that the pleasure had dissipated.

Callen cocked his head when he heard the noise and propped himself up on his elbows. "What's wrong? Did I hurt you?"

I laughed, "I'm fine. I promise. That was wonderful." My eyes trailed his body, admiring his physique. He was extraordinarily handsome. Watching him lay there made me want him all over again.

My eyes roamed down to his cock to see smeared blood down his shaft. I bit my lip as my cheeks lit up crimson. Simultaneously, Callen sat straight up in bed, the words, "Oh shit," ringing out of him when he took in the same sight. "You're bleeding."

I moved to get out of the bed, embarrassed. His hand grabbed mine and pulled me back down to him. "I'm so sorry. I should clean up. I don't want to ruin your sheets," I protested.

"I don't care about the sheets, Lacey. How could you let me do that to you? You should have told me!"

"Told you what?" I questioned him, taken aback by his response.

"If I would've known, I never would've...I should've been gentler." Worry filled his eyes as he looked at me.

*A small laugh escaped as I realized what his concern was. "Callen, you didn't take my virginity if that's what you're thinking right now, and I didn't want you to be gentle. You gave me exactly what I needed."*

*He looked at me, trying to decide if he believed me or not.*

*"Look, I just, um, haven't been with anyone in a long time and you, well, you are more well endowed than I was expecting," I said as the blush crept over my face again. "Besides, what good is all the pleasure without a little pain?"*

*Callen laughed, "Alright, I would have to agree with you on that, but you still should have told me."*

*"You didn't exactly ask."*

*"Well, I'm asking now."*

*"Asking what?"*

*"You said a long time. How long is a long time?"*

*I bit my lower lip as I eyed him, "That is none of your business."*

*"I told you, you are my business."*

*I continued chewing my lip as I thought my answer over. There really was no point in lying to him or keeping it a secret. I didn't know what he would think about my answer though, and it worried me.*

*"Lacey, answer the question."*

*"I just don't know what you are going to think..." I trailed off.*

*"You can either let go of that lip and answer the question or you can keep mulling it over while I take you again because you drive me crazy with wanting when you do that."*

*I gaped at him not knowing how to respond. He lifted his hand and shut my mouth as he smirked at me. "Now, answer the question."*

*"I haven't been with anyone since my mark appeared," I reluctantly admitted.*

*"The mark appears when you're eighteen though."*

*I nodded my head. "I was always afraid someone would see it if I let my guard down."*

*"So, it's been..?"*

*"Five years," I sighed.*

*"That is a long time."*

*"What about you?"*

*"Me?" he asked, raising an eyebrow.*

*"Fair is fair."*

*"It's been about a year."*

*I nodded again. I didn't know what I expected his answer to be. "How old are you, Callen?" I asked to change the subject.*

*"Thirty-two which makes me nine years your senior if my math is correct."*

*"That makes you sound old when you say it like that," I teased as I pushed off the bed and stood.*

*"Where are you going?" he asked.*

*"I think we should get cleaned up."*

*"We?"*

*"You don't expect me to shower alone, do you?" I called from over my shoulder as I headed to the bathroom.*

*"I sure don't," he replied with a smile.*

*After the shower, I put my dress back on and picked my torn*

*panties up off the floor. There was no saving them, so I tossed them in the trash. Callen walked out of the bedroom to see me pulling my shoes on by the door.*

*"Going somewhere?"*

*"I need to get home."*

*"Let me grab my keys. I'll drive you."*

*"You don't have to do that. I can walk or get a cab or something."*

*"First off, you don't even know where you are. Secondly, I know I don't have to, I want to," he answered as he strode toward me. He gently held my face in his hands and tenderly kissed me. Breaking the kiss, he walked into the kitchen, grabbed his keys, and returned to open the door for me.*

*"Thank you," I smiled at him as I walked outside.*

*Callen's apartment was on the third floor of the complex. We walked side by side, descending the stairs in silence. Like the gentleman he was, he opened the passenger door for me when we reached his truck. I climbed in and buckled up as he went around to his side. Pulling out of the complex, he headed down the road.*

*"So, is there a reason you were trying to sneak out the door?"*

*"I wasn't sneaking."*

*He shot me a look from the corner of his eye calling my bluff.*

*"Okay. Maybe I was," I relented.*

*"And?"*

*"And, I didn't know what to do, so I thought I'd just leave."*

*"What do you mean you didn't know what to do?"*

*"I mean, it's not like we can be together. I thought it would be easier if I just slipped out and disappeared."*

*"Why can't we be together?"*

"Callen, are you serious? We aren't supposed to exist anymore. There are people and companies out there combing the earth for marked ones despite not finding any in years."

"Whether we are together or not, they're still going to be looking."

"Yeah, but if they find one of us, then they'll find the other. Plus, I don't know what happens after two mates find each other. It's been decades since that's been known to happen."

"What happens is we can finally be happy and whole," he answered. "I've spent the last fourteen years knowing I had half a soul, and I'm not about to walk away from my other half."

"Exactly. It's been fourteen years that you've been safe. Fourteen years you've lived comfortably. I'm not worth risking all of that for." Callen's knuckles turned white as he clenched the steering wheel. I knew I was making him mad, but he had to see reason. "Why would you throw everything away for some girl you don't even know?"

"You're not just some girl. You're mine, and I'm not letting you go."

"Yes, you are. It's the smart thing to do."

"You don't get it, Lacey," he said, shaking his head.

"There's nothing to get. Our kind aren't meant for happily ever after."

"Bullshit. We were literally made for each other."

I crossed my arms over my chest. My frustration with his stubbornness was coming to a peak. Callen pulled into the parking lot of my apartment complex, cut the engine, and turned toward me. "Try and tell me you haven't walked around your entire life with a gaping hole in your chest. Tell me you haven't always known something was missing. You and I both know that life didn't make sense until you woke up one day and saw that mark on your arm. It was proof that you weren't complete." His voice was raised with his *own frustration.*

*"It doesn't matter, Callen."*

*"The hell it doesn't!"*

*I flung the door open and jumped out of his truck, careful to keep my dress pulled down. I slammed the door and stormed off toward my apartment.*

*"Lacey, get back here!"*

*"No!" I flung the door open to the building and headed for my apartment. Callen was closely following, but I ignored him. I quickly opened the door and tried to shut it behind me, but his foot wedged in at the last moment, pushing it further open to come inside.*

*"Get out," I barked at him.*

*"We aren't done talking about this."*

*"There's nothing to talk about."*

*"Lacey, I have been looking for you for years, and I'm not about to let you go after one night."*

*"Years, huh?"*

*"Yes. Years."*

*"Didn't stop you from fucking other people though, did it?"*

*He opened his mouth to argue, but shut it promptly. "Is that what's wrong? You're upset that I didn't wait for you?"*

*I rolled my eyes, "Of course not. I don't care who you've slept with. That's your business. We both made our choices, and we both had our reasons."*

*"They didn't mean anything to me, Lacey. They were mistakes. I have been looking for you."*

*"Well, I haven't been looking for you."*

*"You haven't?" He sounded surprised.*

*"Have you not been listening to me?"* My temper started rising again. *"We can't be together. I never asked for a soulmate, and I don't want one."*

*"You're saying you don't want this? You want to walk away and act like we never met? Act like today never happened?"* His voice softened as he looked at me.

*Tears began pricking my eyes as we stood staring at one another. "Yes," I whispered.*

*"You're lying. I can see it in your eyes. You're just scared."* He slowly stepped forward and wrapped me in his arms. *Pulling my head to his chest, he gently stroked my hair.*

*"I don't want to want you, Callen," I whispered, tears streaming down my cheeks as he held me.*

*"But, you do."*

*I shook my head. "It's more than that. I need you, and that's what scares me."*

*He kissed the top of my head and squeezed me tighter. "I need you too, Lacey. You're safe with me. I promise."*

*I lifted my head to look at him. His eyes were warm with emotion. I pulled his mouth to mine and kissed him. He gently kissed me back and ran his tongue across my bottom lip. I opened, allowing him entry. He picked me up, and I wrapped my legs around his waist. It'd only been a few hours, but I wanted him again - more than wanted - I needed to be with him.*

*Callen headed down the hallway toward my bedroom, and we toppled on the bed together. I grabbed the bottom of his shirt and pulled it over his head, running my hands over his sculpted body as he grinded his hips against mine. I reached down to undo his pants, desperate to be filled by him. Callen worked my dress off, exposing me completely. His hand went between my legs and started rubbing as he kicked his jeans and boxers to the floor. I moaned as he spread me open and found my clit.*

"My little mate is ready, and I've barely even touched you," he whispered. He nipped at my ear as he moved further down toward my entrance. I rolled my hips edging him closer, wet and desperate for him.

"Ah, not so fast," he said as he pulled his hand away. "I'm going to make love to you like I should have this morning. Like you deserve."

He kissed me with such passion, I melted into him. Butterflies tore through my stomach in anticipation. Callen's hand moved back between my legs, and he started rubbing again. I moaned into his mouth with his touch. Gently, he slid a finger inside me while he circled my clit with his thumb, my breath hitching from the intrusion.

"Are you okay?" he asked, worried. "I can stop if you're sore."

"No, please, don't stop," I begged as I lifted my hips forward, pushing into his hand. "God, I need you, Callen. I need all of you."

He pulled his hand away again and positioned himself between my legs. I grabbed his arm and pulled him down on top of me. Slowly, he pushed inside, his thick shaft filling me.

"Christ," he breathed as he thrust deeper. He stilled once he was completely buried and stared into my eyes. "You are so beautiful," he whispered as he placed a hand on my cheek. He lowered his mouth to mine and kissed me deeply as he began moving again. Rocking into him with each thrust, I matched his movements, urging him onward. Nothing had ever felt this good in my life.

Callen placed his forehead on mine and wrapped me completely in his arms, holding me tight as he loved me. The heat started building in my lower abdomen as he brought me closer to a release. His right hand pulled my left arm to lay beside our heads, his thumb gently circling around my soulmark. Tingles shot through me and settled in my core with his touch. I pulled his left arm out from around me and held his wrist. Bringing it to my mouth, I softly kissed his own mark. He moaned as the electricity ebbed through him. I grazed my thumb across his wrist as my orgasm threatened to unfold.

We locked eyes and pressed each other's soulmark together. A burning sensation started at my mark and exploded up my arm to the rest of my body. The current rippled through me stronger than ever before, and we toppled over the edge together. His release pulsed inside me as I clenched around him, our bodies writhing as we watched one another come apart.

Callen collapsed on top of me, our breathing ragged and chests heaving. He kissed me again before sliding to the side, pulling me to him, and wrapping himself around me from behind. A feeling of bliss enveloped me as I lay there in his arms. He nuzzled into the groove of my neck and placed delicate kisses on my skin. I laced my fingers with his and brought his hand to my mouth to kiss, but I stopped halfway when his soulmark caught my eye.

"Callen?"

"What's wrong?"

"Your mark. It's not white anymore. It's brown."

He pulled his arm back to inspect his wrist. The crescent moon showed a dark, chocolate brown against his skin. I turned my wrist over to examine my own mark to find the same thing.

"That's strange," I said as I ran my finger over my soulmark. It felt the same as before; the only difference was the color. "Do you think that happened with the burning?"

"Yeah, I believe so. It means our bond solidified."

"What do you mean?"

"When we held each other's soulmark at the same time, I think our souls bonded. It's a theory I heard about a few years ago."

"You've researched soulmarks?" I was surprised. While I

*had spent all this time fighting my fate, Callen seemed to have spent his time embracing it.*

*"You haven't?"*

*"No, I told you, I never wanted a mark. I've spent the last five years hiding."*

*"You don't have to hide anymore," he said as he wrapped his arms back around me. I rolled over and nuzzled into him. For the first time in my life, the hollowness in my chest was filled, and I knew I was finally home.*

# CHAPTER EIGHT

*Rejuvenated*

I woke to the beeping of the monitors, headache gone and thoughts clear. I layed there listening, trying to gauge if I was alone. This could be my chance to escape. Surely, they weren't guarding someone who had been unconscious for days. I slightly moved my arms to test for restraints and nothing pulled. As I formulated my plan, a voice softly spoke, "I know you're awake."

I sighed, "If you know I am awake, then you know I don't want company." I opened my eyes to see Shane leaning back in a chair with his arms crossed over his chest.

"We need to talk."

I snorted with derision. "There's a lot of things I need to do, but hanging out for a bonding experience isn't one of them."

I moved to sit up in bed, monitoring leads trailing from my chest and scalp. A thick brace was on my right wrist, and a new IV was in my left antecubital. After further examination, I saw the brace was to keep my wrist immobilized, not from an injury, but for the tubing snaked into the radial artery. Glancing up at the bedside monitor, a continuous blood pressure read out, the wave faltering with my movements. All my frustration bled away to confusion. "Why do I have an art line?"

"What's the last thing you remember?" he asked in turn.

I pursed my lips as I mulled over my answer. "I know you went to get something right after Garrett brought the food. He...well, ugh...it doesn't matter what he did. I remember headbutting him in the nose to get away. Then, he pulled me to the floor and beat me for it; but, after that, it's blank," I answered with a furrowed brow.

Shane looked furious as he watched me.

"Are you just going to sit there and glare, or are you going to fill in the blanks for me?" I asked impatiently.

"When I walked into the room, Garrett's foot connected with your head, and you went limp. I thought he killed you."

"I wish he had," I muttered while disconnecting the wires from my head. Gel matted my hair from their adhesion. *At least if I was dead, this would be over, and Callen would be safe,* I thought.

Shane rolled his eyes and leaned forward in the chair, his hands clasped together between his legs. "Well, personally, I'm glad you're not dead."

"Yeah, it would certainly suck for you to lose your test subject, I'm sure."

Shane clenched his hands together, turning his knuckles white. He took a deep breath and released them when he saw me staring. "Anyway, I got you put back on the gurney and took you to a more sophisticated exam suite. The ultrasound showed you miraculously didn't have any internal hemorrhaging or ruptured organs, but your concussion was upgraded to severe. You also had two broken ribs show up on x-ray and many additional contusions on top of the previous injuries."

I finished with the scalp leads and started on the ones adhered to my chest. That's when I noticed I was no longer in the clothes they had given me but a hospital gown. "You took off my clothes?" I raged at him, "How dare you! You had no right to—"

"I didn't do it. Dr. Reid did. Relax."

"You want me to relax? I've been unconscious for days, and anyone could have done who knows what to me while I was out! And, just to confirm that statement, I was fucking stripped naked for anyone in this godforsaken place to see."

"No one touched you. I made sure of it!" he yelled, jumping to his feet.

"Like you made sure I was taken care of in the infirmary? 'Cause that worked out great for me."

Shane grabbed his chair and flung it across the room. I was too angry to even be startled. Deep down I knew what happened with Garrett wasn't his fault, but I needed to be angry.

"Damnit, Lacey. The only time I've left you alone since then was when Dr. Reid was with you. Any other time, I've been right here or just on the other side of those doors."

"Why?" I asked, anger spewing out of me.

"Why what?"

"Why have you stayed? Do you feel guilty or something?"

We stared at each other for several moments. Shane's expression remained angry, but his eyes flickered with emotions. "I'm just doing my job," he finally answered.

I grit my teeth. I could tell this was the end of that conversation, and honestly, I didn't want to continue it. It didn't matter his reasoning, because it changed nothing. I was still here. I was still trapped.

"Well, continue doing your job and get me a suture

removal tray, sterile gloves, and some gauze. It's time for this to come out," I said with a gesture to my arm.

"You've lost your mind if you think you are removing that arterial line."

"Fine. You take it out then and the IV."

"No. You need to wait to be evaluated by Dr. Reid now that you are awake."

"Either you can get the stuff to take it out correctly, or I swear I will rip it out right now and hope I bleed to death or get an infection."

"You don't make the rules. You need to wait."

"Your choice." I shrugged and started unclasping the brace that kept my wrist straight for the arterial catheter.

"Fine! I'll take it out." He stomped to the cabinet and started pulling out supplies. Once the brace was off, I stopped fiddling with it. As angry as I was, I knew it was better for him to remove the line.

Shane settled himself next to my bed after he gathered all the necessary items and the chair he threw, mumbling under his breath. He set up his suture removal tray, discarded the bandage, and donned sterile gloves. With a quick snip, he cut the suture tethering the catheter in place. He balled up some gauze, placed it over the entrance site, and pressed it down right after he swiped the line from my arm. A slight sting caused my wrist to flex with its removal, but it was gone before I truly registered the discomfort. Shane held pressure on my wrist to staunch the bleeding. I watched him closely, but he was careful not to convey any emotion besides irritation.

"So, you said I had two fractured ribs?"

"I did."

"They don't feel broken though." I had absolutely no rib

pain. It felt completely normal to take a deep breath and move. I'd never had fractured ribs, but I had tended to plenty of patients with them and know they are miserable.

"They've already healed."

"Wait. How long was I out then?"

"Four days."

"That's not possible." I looked at him questioningly as he wrapped a pressure bandage around my wrist.

"All your injuries are healed. Check out your laceration I stitched up."

I looked down and saw a soft, white scar on my arm. It looked years old despite the injury occurring less than a week ago. "That doesn't make any sense," I said, shaking my head.

Shane moved around to the other side of the bed and started work to remove my IV. "Remember, when I told you our scientists had formulated medications to expedite healing?"

I nodded in response.

"Well, we gave it to you," he said with a shrug.

"You gave me experimental drugs?"

"Well, yeah. You were in horrible shape. We had to do something, and I told you about it beforehand."

"You said you had them. You didn't say what they were or how they worked."

He rolled his eyes again at me as he held pressure on my elbow where he had just removed the IV.

"It's called HyperStem-247. I am not aware of the nitty gritty. It's above my pay grade. All I know is it rapidly excels the body's natural processes by regulating the hyperproduction of cells, hormones, and proteins that range anywhere from white and stem cells to osteoblasts, parathyroid peptides, and any other thing needed to heal bones, absorb hematomas, or close a wound."

"How long does it take to wear off?"

"It's normally metabolized after forty eight hours."

"Normally?"

"It's only been given to a handful of people. You're the first marked one to ever receive it." Shane pulled the gauze away from my elbow. "I don't know if it'll make a difference or not. Not very much is known about your kind."

The spot from the IV was already gone, the skin completely healed like it had never been punctured. Without thinking, I ripped the pressure bandage off my wrist where the art line had been.

"Don't—" Shane's voice broke off as we looked at my wrist. The larger puncture site was already starting to scab over, appearing to be hours old rather than minutes. I ran my thumb over the spot in disbelief.

"I think it's safe to say it's still working for now," he said with a shrug. "I guess we will have to wait and see."

I scoffed, "Yeah, I'm sure we will know as soon as it wears off considering how the last week has gone."

Shane set his mouth in a grim line. He looked away from me and headed to another cabinet. Reaching in, he grabbed a stack of clothes and tossed them to the bed. "Might as well get dressed. There's a shower behind that curtain you can use to clean up first."

"I'm not showering with you here."

"Well, I'm not leaving."

I huffed while I tugged the remaining monitor leads off. "I swear if that curtain so much as ripples from movement, I'll —"

He cut me off, "Get in the damn shower. I'll guard the door." He turned around, and I stalked off to the shower with my new clothes in hand, careful to keep my gown closed in the back.

Once in the shower, I untied the gown and threw it out. A bench held a clean towel and amenities. Wanting this to be over as fast as possible, I started the hot water and lathered up. Despite the beating I remembered, there were no bruises on my body. My skin looked brand new, glistening under the water. My left hand was unscathed, and it no longer hurt to ball a fist. If anything, I felt much stronger than I would've suspected after being bedridden and not eating for so long.

I washed my hair twice trying to remove all the gel. It had hardened and crusted over since the electrodes had been placed several days ago. Hopefully, it was just a normal EEG to check brain activity and not some new-age tech like the medication they gave me. I remembered the neuroscientist saying something about projecting memories during one of my briefly conscious episodes, but the entire comment proved elusive.

*If she can project a memory, I wonder if I can block a memory or if she can select them?* I shuddered at the thought. The idea of someone sorting through my memories like a filing system sounded awful. Then, to top it off, the memories can be projected for anyone to see. I shuddered again thinking about these people watching my memories like a home movie.

I shut off the water, grabbed the towel, and dried myself. A black t-shirt and pants like before were in the stack of clothes, but this time a sports bra and underwear accompanied them. I dressed quickly, pulled the curtain, and padded barefoot back into the room. I was still drying my hair with the towel when Shane turned around.

"I feel much better," I said, looking for something to say.

"You smell better too," he teased.

I tried to scowl at him, but I couldn't fight a small smile. After all, I'm sure I didn't smell like roses since I only got to bathe one other time this week.

"It would've been nice to have a razor you know."

"Yeah, like I'm going to give you a razor. You'll just hide it and try to slit a throat or two later."

"You can't blame a girl for trying," I said as the door slid open. Garrett walked in with an exceptionally smug look on his face. Flashbacks popped in my mind from my unconscious dreams. The bar. The club. The drugs. Michael. Garrett. One in the same.

"Son of a bitch," I whispered. *Did he recognize me? Maybe not...he hadn't mentioned anything that happened...at least, not to me. But if he has?...he's seen Callen. He knows what he looks like. That doesn't mean he realizes Callen is my mate though. He could've just been another guy that I had dated.* The thoughts raced through my mind as Garrett and I stared at one another. Shane glanced between the two of us trying to read the tension. A smirk flicked across Garrett's face as he looked me up and down. My body was stiff with resentment and worry.

"I take it you finally remembered, princess."

Garrett strode casually into the room toward me. I took an involuntary step back as the memories flowed from that night. The movement looked weak - and I hated myself for it - but too many emotions flared inside me to stop myself.

"Remembered what?" Shane asked.

Neither of us answered him. I swallowed bile that crept up my throat as Garrett spoke, "I would've kicked you in the head sooner if I knew the recognition would freeze you up this much. It could've saved us a lot of time and energy fighting with you."

"This changes nothing. I still won't tell you anything, Garrett. Or do you prefer Michael?" I snapped at him, my nerve returning from the initial shock of recollection.

He tutted in response, wrapped his arms behind his back, and started pacing. "Michael is my first name. I prefer Garrett. I think it suits me better. What do you think?"

"I think you're a bastard. How long have you known?"

"Since the beginning. Imagine how surprised I was when we got the orders to collect a marked one and your pretty little face was attached to it?"

I took a deep breath to steady myself. I hadn't thought about the events of the club since it first happened. It was inconsequential when compared to the aftermath of waking in Callen's apartment.

"Think about it often do you? I've never given you a second thought."

Garrett dropped his arms and moved toward me. Shane blocked his path and shoved him backward. "That's enough. What the fuck is going on?"

"Go on, Garrett. Tell him what's going on. Tell him all about how you drug women so you can rape them when they don't want to fuck you!" I cursed. All self preservation had left me. The thoughts of pushing the conversation away to avoid the topic moving to Callen rescuing me disappeared. Anger overwhelmed my senses as I stood in front of this man. A man who wouldn't take no for an answer.

"Not women," he countered with a wink, "Just you, princess." Shane's fist pummeled into Garrett's jaw, causing him to stumble backward. A look of shock spread across his face. "What the hell, Shane?" he yelled.

Shane stood with his fists clenched at his sides, breathing heavily. "Is that true, Garrett? Did you rape her?"

"No. He fucking tried though!" Nothing but anger filled my body. I wanted to kill this man, to destroy him.

"When?" Shane looked between the two of us. Garrett stood massaging his jaw, glaring at me.

"It's been a few years. I didn't even recognize him until now. What happened in the hallway and infirmary should've clued me in though. Once a rapist, always a rapist."

"It hurts to know I made such a small impression on you. Clearly, I need to step up my game," Garrett laughed.

Shane looked like he was going to punch Garrett again, but the doors opened before he could. Dr. Reid entered the room wearing a white, button down lab coat, her blonde hair pulled into a tight bun.

"What's going on?" she asked.

The tension in the room was thick enough to be cut with a knife. Garrett and I stood still glowering at each other with Shane between us.

"Just rehashing some old memories, Doc," Garrett finally answered.

She glanced between the three of us and frowned. "Well, I hope my patient is still in one piece. I had just come to evaluate her. How are you, Lacey?"

"Just peachy," I seethed.

"Boys, go fetch this nice, young lady some food while I examine her. I'm sure she's starving."

Garrett and Shane silently stomped out of the room, but as soon as the doors slid shut, I could hear them yelling again.

"Those two are ridiculous." Dr. Reid rolled her eyes and turned to me. "Anyways, let's have a look at you. Have a seat."

I sat on the edge of the bed as she did her exam. All her

findings were completely normal. It was as if the last week had never happened.

"You've had an excellent response to the HyperStem administration. Considering how long you were out, I was starting to wonder if you were experiencing some kind of neurological side effect the EEG wasn't able to capture. You appear normal though. Any residual headache?"

"No. I actually feel fine."

"I see the puncture sites from your arterial line and IV are healing already. When did those come out?" she asked curiously.

I thought about lying but decided it wouldn't help anything. Plus, she could review the data from the monitor to see when the arterial line was no longer connected. "Maybe thirty, forty five minutes ago," I answered truthfully.

"Interesting." She didn't elaborate; however, I could see the wheels spinning in her mind. Clearly, she didn't expect the medication to still be active in my system either.

My two guards returned with a bowl of chicken soup and crackers. "Nothing too heavy to digest," Shane commented.

Dr. Reid turned on her heel and headed toward the door. "Bring her to the lab when she's finished," she called over her shoulder. "We have work to do."

The doors slid closed behind her, and the three of us were left alone.

# CHAPTER NINE

## *Tested*

I had absolutely no appetite after my quarrel with Garrett. As much as I hated him, I hated myself more for failing to recognize him sooner. *They could already be searching for Callen. But why would they keep asking me about him if they knew who my mate was?* I questioned internally.

The not knowing was somehow worse, but even if none of these people knew about Callen, it was only a matter of time. Callen would come for me. One way or another he will end up in this laboratory if I don't find a way to escape. If I die, he'll know it; he'll feel it. I just hope he isn't stubborn enough to try and avenge me. He knows I would never want him to put himself in danger, but that means nothing. Deep down, I know he will never stop until all these people are in the ground.

The thought of a bullet piercing Garrett between the eyes disappointed me. He didn't deserve to go out that easy. I wanted to pay him back for everything he inflicted upon me - strike for strike, kick for kick, pain for pain.

"What's on your mind, princess?" Garrett cooed from across the room. "You look ravishing when you're mad."

"Fuck off, Garrett," I snapped back at him, standing from the bed. I despised how much he put me on edge, his presence a constant trigger for my fight or flight response. Unfortunately, my only option was to fight, and so far, I had lost every time.

"You really need to clean that mouth of yours up before we take you to the lab. Although, I'm starting to think strangulation might be a kink of yours."

I grabbed the bottle of water and threw it at Garrett. He stepped to the side and dodged the projectile easily. A menacing smile lit up his face. "I do enjoy your feistiness though."

Shane looked like he was barely containing his temper. His arms were crossed over his chest and his jaw was tight. Staring daggers at Garrett, he said, "Stop messing with her. You might skew the results."

*Of course the test results were his only concern.* I scowled at him with the thought. Shane was blatantly a loyal soldier through and through.

"Eat your soup," Shane ordered.

"I'm not hungry."

"Eat it. You need your strength."

"No."

Shane closed his eyes and pinched the bridge of his nose. I wasn't sure what battle he fought inside, but he settled it quickly. "Eat it, or I'll make you eat it. Your choice."

We stared at each other for a long moment, a battle of wills flying between us. Deciding this wasn't the hill to die on, I sat down and started eating. It was lukewarm, but overall not bad. The silence grew thick as I tucked in the soup. When I was finished, I wiped my mouth and stood again.

"Time to get this over with," I announced, moving toward the door. Shane reached out his hand to grab my arm, but I snatched it away. "Don't touch me. I am perfectly capable of walking on my own. Garrett can lead and you follow. That's enough security."

Garrett laughed as he headed to the door, "I can't wait to take you down a peg in that attitude of yours."

Rolling my eyes, I followed him down the corridor, making several turns. Without a point of reference, I had no hope of finding my way through this maze alone. I cursed myself for not paying better attention when Shane took me to the infirmary.

When we stopped outside of the lab, Shane swiped his badge and beckoned me to enter first. The chair in the center of the room was gone. In its place stood a vertical table with leather bindings for the neck, waist, and extremities. My heart raced with fear. Whatever was going to happen, they wanted to make sure I wouldn't be able to get free.

I glanced around the room and noticed Dr. Reid at her computer. She was engrossed in her task and didn't seem to register our entrance. Shane cleared his throat as we waited. Her eyes snapped up and a dazzling smile spread across her face.

"Oh! You're here. Fabulous. Go ahead and get her set up if you two don't mind." Dr. Reid returned her attention to the computer, and Shane gestured for me to walk to the table before us.

"Absolutely not," I shook my head as I took a step back. Garrett, however, had moved behind me to block my retreat. My whole body stiffened with his touch. I took a small step forward to put some space between the two of us, but I refused to go any further.

"Why do you make everything so goddamn difficult?" Shane asked, looking up at the ceiling in exasperation. "It's going to happen whether you like it or not, so save all of us some effort and just do it."

I took a deep breath in an attempt to reel in my temper. "Look, I ate your soup. I put on your clothes. I've taken your medications. But, there is no way in hell I am going to walk over there and lay down like a pig for slaughter. I am a person not a science experiment!"

Garrett chuckled behind me. "Like I said, this one's as stubborn as a mule. You won't get anywhere with her through reasoning, Shane." He moved closer to me and pressed into my backside. His mouth felt hot by my ear as he breathed, "One day, I'm going to smoother that fire inside you, and I'm going to enjoy every minute of it."

I jerked my head away from him as he shoved me forward. I stumbled but corrected my footing, preventing a fall.

"I said no." Determination filled me, yet I knew deep down this was a waste of time. One way or another I would be strapped to that table, but I couldn't bring myself to comply. If I spilled secrets about Callen from whatever they were going to do to me, I wouldn't be able to live with myself if I didn't fight tooth and nail the entire time. I couldn't be complicit in their experiments.

"I see her brief purgatory in the infirmary did nothing for our guest's obedience," a voice rang out from the side.

I closed my eyes and took a deep breath. As much as I hated Garrett, I hated his boss more. If it weren't for him, none of this would even be happening. Opening my eyes, I shot imaginary daggers toward him. He wore a neat black suit minus a tie. As I watched him, he took his jacket off and draped it over a second chair by Dr. Reid. He slowly started rolling his cuffs as he waltzed toward me.

"I heard you and Garrett had a little one on one chat the other day."

"You could say that. There really wasn't much chatting the way I remember it though."

He laughed, "I'm surprised you remember much of anything to be honest; however, a good memory bodes well for me. Now, do be a good girl and walk to the table. We have much to do today." He was standing next to me and gestured for me to move forward.

"I am not go—" my sentence broke off as his palm collided with the side of my face. Heat instantly flooded to the skin's surface, and a ringing screamed in my ears. I staggered backward, running into Garrett. He wrapped his hands around each of my arms and pinned them to my sides to hold me in place.

The man stepped forward, grasped my chin, and angled my head to look up at him. "I will not ask again."

I peered over to Shane. His eyes were locked on mine, almost pleading for my compliance. With a stiff swallow, I shook my head in silent refusal. Shane closed his eyes and turned away from me as if he couldn't watch what was going to happen next.

"I had a feeling you were going to remain difficult. I did hope I was wrong though," the man said with a sigh. He dropped his hand from my chin and less than a second later, his fist slammed into my stomach. My knees buckled as I doubled over, but Garrett held me in place. A hand laced through my hair and yanked my head upright.

"Walk."

"Go. To. Hell." I managed to grunt out.

His fist connected with my jaw this time. Garrett threw me to the floor before slamming his foot into my right flank, pulling a scream from my lungs. Rough hands grabbed my ankle, dragging me across the room. Garrett hoisted me bodily and slung me against the table, holding me in place by my throat as I gathered my footing. Shane quickly began fastening the leather straps around me, splaying my wrists to the side and my feet a foot apart. Lastly, Garrett released his hold to allow Shane to tether my neck with the retracting elastic from last time. When they both stepped away, I pulled as hard as I could, but there was no give to the restraints. I wasn't going anywhere.

The man in charge strolled toward me with an air of amusement. "If you don't watch your language and start behaving, I may just give you to Garrett after all. He seems to think he can get you in line."

I bit my tongue to prevent a response from coming out. Somehow, the thought of him beating me while I'm spread helplessly across the table seems infinitely worse than any of the other times.

"Now, that's a good girl. Keep that mouth closed, and this will go much easier." He patted my cheek before turning and joining Dr. Reid at her desk. She was so absorbed in her computer, I couldn't tell if she even realized what just transpired in front of her.

*That or she doesn't care.* The thought did nothing to settle the knots forming in my stomach.

Garrett walked to the back of the room and returned with two chairs. He placed one on each side of me and plopped down with a smug smile. Shane spared me one last glance before taking his seat as well. My back and jaw throbbed from the strikes inflicted, but I did my best to regulate my breathing. I would need every facet I could muster to fight whatever they had planned next.

Dr. Reid stood from her computer and strolled over to me. She inspected my jaw where her boss had struck. "Hmm," she said with narrowed eyes.

"Is there a problem, Dr. Reid?" he called from the computer desk.

"Not a problem per se. It's just curious."

"What's curious?"

"Her face. It's not swelling."

"And?"

"Well, with a hit that hard, she should already have bright red bruising and swelling from the broken blood vessels, yet her skin looks completely normal." She went to pull the hem of my shirt up to inspect my abdomen.

"Stop," I said, almost as a plea.

She raised an eyebrow at me in question.

"You can't undress me in front of these men while I'm tied up."

She looked at me like she was going to refuse my reasoning. I knew I was just a science experiment to her, but I needed her to see me as a woman, a person, just like anybody else.

"Please." My palms started to sweat as I thought about how helpless I was tied to the table. They could do anything, and I couldn't even try to fight back.

Dr. Reid stared at me contemplating for what felt like ages, until she finally nodded in agreement. "I can do a physical exam later in private."

She strode off to a side room and disappeared from view. I sighed in relief, my eyes flickering over to Garrett to see him ogling my splayed form. Despite being completely dressed, his leering made me feel utterly naked.

"Too bad. Would've been a nice show," he mused.

I looked back forward to see Dr. Reid return with a cart in tow. Several pieces of machinery littered the two story tray. She placed two electrodes to my left wrist, entrapping my radial nerve. My crescent moon soulmark peeked out between the adhesives. She then placed an "L" bracket around my pointer finger and thumb.

Curiosity overwhelmed me, and despite myself, I asked, "Why are you setting up a train of four?"

"Ah, I forgot you are a nurse. Have you worked with this before?"

"Yeah, a few times. I had patients in the ICU we would use it on before I moved to the ER. You're not going to paralyze me are you?" Fear laced my words. The thought of being paralyzed was even worse than the bindings.

"Not exactly," she replied. She finished setting up the device and moved to her next task. She held two metal rings in her hand. Four small prongs that resembled hooks stood out on each of them. "These are my versions of lid speculums. They allow your eyes to stay open without worry of a traditional speculum shifting with movement. You'll feel like you're blinking, but your eyelids won't actually close.

"Now, it is very important that you allow me to place these correctly. If you don't, you could lose your eyes from injury, and none of us want that. Before I place them, I'll give you some numbing drops to prevent any discomfort."

I pursed my lips as I mulled over her instructions. As if he could read my thoughts about resisting, the man at the desk chimed in, "I will not delay any longer for injuries on your part. Either agree to the devices or I'll cut your eyelids off."

Dr. Reid shot him a disapproving glare before turning her attention back to me, mumbling something under her breath about interfering men. She had set the rings down and held a dropper of ocular solution in her hand. She pulled my lower lids down and instructed me to look up. Three cool drops spread across each of my eyes, followed by a slow numbing sensation. I blinked a few times trying to acclimate to the foreign feeling. Dr. Reid then placed the rings around my eyes, hooking each lid to prevent closing. I could feel the muscles contract to blink, but nothing closed over my vision.

"Next, I'm going to place a lens in each eye. It fits like a contact, but instead of improving your vision, it will track your eye movements."

"Why do you need to track my eye movements?" I questioned as she placed the contacts. I couldn't feel them thanks to the numbing medication, and they didn't appear to affect my ability to see.

"It will help me evaluate your nervous system, similar to the train of four. Only the lenses consist of nanotech. The sensors are too small for the naked eye to see to answer your next question."

Dr. Reid returned her attention to the cart. I glanced over at Shane. He was glaring at the floor. As if he could feel my eyes on him, he looked up at me. I swallowed as our eyes met. He clenched his jaw and looked away. I was a fool for letting my guard down around him. He may have provided medical care and food, but it never truly was for my benefit. I held the answers to the questions plaguing the world, and Shane did what he needed to do to get me to spill those secrets. I looked away from him as Dr. Reid refocused on me. She applied a sticky patch with a small box to my left carotid. The setting was odd due to the elastic band encompassing my neck, but she seemed satisfied with the placement.

"This is a heart monitor with smart capabilities. It will transmit your pulse rate, heart rhythm, and oxygen levels to the screen for monitoring."

It gave me very little comfort to know what all the devices she was hooking to me were, but it was better than nothing. It at least gave me something to focus on. Finally, Dr. Reid placed a heavy band across my forehead that was held in place by adhesive stickers on each temple.

"This is a memory projector. You are familiar with an EEG I assume?"

"An EEG shows brain waves and activity."

"Correct. This device, on the other hand, is much more advanced. It is able to follow the electrical impulses along the synapses of the brain; then, it extracts the information stored in the designated neuron and displays it on the screen over here for us to view just as you do. It's quite amazing really. Top of the line tech. Only a handful of people even know this technology exists. We will be able to watch the memory as you actively relive it."

"What if I don't want to relive a memory? Some things are private, you know."

"Sometimes we all have to do things we don't want to do," she replied with a subtle glance in Shane's direction.

Shane rolled his eyes but didn't respond. I don't think the other two men were even paying attention to our chatting at this point.

"Are we ready yet?" the man from the desk called.

"Just about," Dr. Reid answered before redirecting her attention to me. "Last, but not least, I'm going to put these blackout goggles on you."

"Blackout? I won't be able to see anything?"

"Right. It has proven easier for the subject to stay focused on the memory at hand if visual stimuli are not present to distract the brain. That's where the contacts come in hand. I'll be able to track your eye movements and pupil dilation or contraction. It helps predict emotional responses when compared to the other analytical data measurements."

She placed the goggles on me, and my vision went

instantly black. No shred or ray of light was detectable. Adrenaline pumped through my system as I waited helplessly in total darkness. I tried to move my head to dislodge the goggles, but the restraint tightened around my neck, halting my movements. Next, I tried pulling on my limb restraints again, but they were even less fruitful.

I took a deep breath to steady my nerves. This was completely unknown territory for me. Too many questions flooded my brain. *How was I supposed to block a memory? If they asked about my mate and I thought of Callen, would they immediately see his face? Or, did I have to actively engage in the memory?* My stomach churned with anxiety as my heart pounded against my chest wall.

"Alright, I think we are ready to begin," Dr. Reid's voice rang out from the direction of her computer. "Like I said before, this has only been tried on voluntary subjects, so I think we should ease into the line of questioning.

"Lacey, what color is the comforter on your bed?"

My bedroom popped into my head. A king sized bed covered with a light gray quilt sat in the middle of the back wall. The quilt stitching was done in navy blue which gave it almost a flowing, watery look.

"That is excellent. I see the gray quilt matches the curtains by the window," she called.

I shut off the image. *Stop thinking,* I instructed myself. My heart rate spiked even further knowing they all saw my home.

"Oh, and now the screen is blank."

A small sigh of relief escaped as I tried to think of how to keep the screen blank. I've never possessed the ability to shut my mind off. An internal monologue was a constant presence, narrating my life moment by moment. When I read a book, the scenes unfolded before me as if it were real. I even dreamed with nearly every sleep. My mind shot to an article I read about internal monologues differing from person to person in occurrence and intensity.

"I also read that article," Dr. Reid said. "I found it rather interesting that intrapersonal communication doesn't occur for some people."

"You can see the article I read?"

"Of course. It's a memory you have stored."

*Stop thinking! Stop thinking!* I scolded myself.

"And it's gone. Let's redirect. Where do you work, Lacey?"

The emergency room sprang forward, the trauma bays facing the nursing desk at the front. A long hallway branched off to three additional halls that connected in the rear of the department.

"Yes, the ER. I am told this is where you were found for your retrieval."

I flexed my fingers into a fist as the fear took over. *I was running from the building into the stairwell. A man grabbed me from behind, and I stabbed the scalpel into his leg.*

"That's Ben that had her there." Garrett's voice interrupted the memory. My breathing increased as the visual faded from the front of my mind.

*I'm not there. I'm not there*, I chanted, trying to ground myself to the present.

"I see you put up quite a fight, Lacey."

*Damn it, stop thinking!* my mind yelled.

"It's okay. Relax. Relax. You've got to bring that heart rate down," she scolded. "Did you ever meet a marked one while at work?"

*She'd been in a car crash. First responders had to extricate her from the crumpled vehicle. She tried to flee from the scene, but they caught her, put her in an ambulance, and brought her to the ER. She was so panicky they couldn't allow her to refuse transport in fear something was wrong.*

*She sat bolt upright in the trauma bay when I entered her room. She had refused to let the first responders and attending physician examine her. They were headed toward a psychiatric evaluation based on her emotional outbursts, but I already knew that was wrong. Only someone who had experienced this kind of panic would recognize it. I closed the door behind me and pulled the curtains when I walked into the room.*

*"Get up."*

*She sat there looking at me like a deer in headlights.*

*"Get up," I repeated, but she only continued to stare, her arms wrapped around her chest tightly.*

*"We are running out of time. You have got to get the fuck out of this ER before they send a crew of people in here to pin you down and examine you."*

*Her eyes bulged at my statement. I could see the fear growing in her eyes.. "Wh-why would they need to examine me? I'm fine."*

*"First off, you need to lie better, and secondly, you need better control. You're drawing too much attention to yourself by arguing with everyone. Now, get up."*

*She didn't budge from her spot on the bed. I huffed, marched over to her, grabbed her left wrist, and yanked it from her body. A white, circle soulmark shown on her inner wrist. She tried to pull her arm free as tears sprang to her eyes. I didn't let go and pulled her to her feet. My patience was wearing thin. Every minute she was here put her at risk.*

"Listen. I know you're scared. You're, what, eighteen? So your mark just showed up."

"Today's my birthday," she whispered.

"Well, happy birthday. Congratulations on the worst present of your life."

"I was trying to run. That's how I crashed. My family will report me. I know they will."

"I get it. I do, but you cannot be so rash. Under the radar. That's your life goal now," I pulled her toward the door as I spoke.

"Wait!" she yelled. "What are you going to do?"

"I'm not going to do anything. I left the stuff to start your IV at the desk. While I collect that, you are going to turn left when you walk out this door. If anyone asks, you are going to the bathroom to leave a urine sample. The bathroom is at the end of the hall by the ambulance bay. You are going to calmly - and I mean calmly - walk out those doors and get the fuck out of here. And, don't come back. They can't find you."

"You're not going to report me?"

"How can I report somebody I never even examined?"

"Why? Why are you doing this for me?" she asked with a trembling lip.

I wanted to comfort her, but we were racing the clock. There was no time for gentleness. "When I leave, count to three and go. Don't linger."

I dropped her arm and walked out the door toward the nursing desk. A doctor was headed for the room I just left with two security guards and a local officer in tow.

"I'm sorry, Dr. Simon. I just sent the patient to get us a urine sample while I get some supplies to start an IV," I said, doing my best to stall the men before me.

*"She can go later. This officer would like to talk with the patient urgently. I've told Katie to call the supervisor for a lockdown due to a suspicious person."*

*I did my best to school my features. "Suspicious person? She's just some kid shook up about a car accident. She's robably scared her parents will ream her for totaling the car." I waved a dismissive hand in the air with the statement.*

*"Maybe. Maybe not," the officer spoke. "Is that the patient there? Down the hall?"*

*I turned to see the girl halfway to the exit. She was walking quickly - too quickly - and looking around everywhere like she was expecting something. Before I could answer, the officer brushed past me, commanding her to stop.*

*Looking back, panic flooded her face. She went to run as the officer yelled for someone to stop her, tearing off in her direction. A male x-ray tech grabbed her arm and held her in place. My heart thrummed heavily as I watched. The untold horrors of what would happen to this girl filled my mind.*

*When the officer reached the pair, he grabbed her upper arm and went to pull her back to her room. "Let's go. I have some questions for you."*

*She ripped her arm free and started running toward the ambulance bay as the officer tackled her to the floor. The doctor and security guards joined me in racing down the hall as she desperately tried to fight him off. As soon as we made it to the scuffle, the patient broke free and stood. She held his service weapon in her hand. Unsure of the greatest threat, she constantly moved the gun barrel between the officer and security guards.*

*"Easy now, girl," the officer said as he stood. "No one needs to get hurt. We just want to talk to you."*

*I knew this wouldn't end well. If they didn't know for sure what she was before, they have no doubt now. I pursed my lips as*

*I stared daggers into her. I shook my head, trying to signal for her not to do this.*

*"Just let me go," she whispered.*

*"You and I both know that's not how this works," the officer answered.*

*She looked at me, but there was nothing I could do, not without risking myself.*

*"Put the gun down, then we can go and have a more private chat down at the station."*

*My breathing hitched as I looked at this poor girl. She was trapped. Done. They would take her, experiment on her, interrogate her. Her life was over before it even started.*

*She took a deep breath, glanced down at her left hand holding the gun, then back at the cop. A look of resolution masked her face. The air was heavy as she resigned herself to her fate. She dropped the gun to her side as a tear trickled down her cheek. Abruptly, she raised the gun to her temple and fired before anyone realized what was happening. Her limp body crumpled to the ground. The top of her head blew off from the bullet force, blood spattered the unit, and brain matter painted the wall behind her. My own blood drained from my face at the grotesque scene splayed out before me.*

"Fuck!" I yelled, snapping back to reality as the memory severed. I could feel the tears building in my eyes, my body shaking with emotion. The memory was so real. It felt like I was standing back in the ER with my now dead patient. I half expected to see her body laid out before me, but my vision was completely black. My breathing was rapid as I reacclimated to my situation. The girl had been right in her choice; death was better than being with these people.

"Who was that, Lacey?" Dr. Reid asked.

"I don't know who she was. Just some patient that

showed up in the ER."

"Do you regret telling her to leave? They could've brought her to me. She'd still be alive."

I sucked in a ragged breath. "The only thing I regret is stabbing that man in the leg. I should've slit my own throat instead."

"Why would you say that?" Shane spoke for the first time since we started this experiment.

My eyes flickered in his direction involuntarily, but I couldn't see anything. "I told you, some things are worse than death," I answered bluntly.

Silence swept the room. The boss cleared his throat and asked, "Did you ever meet another marked one at work."

"No." I had to come up with a plan. I didn't have the ability to cut my thoughts off completely, but maybe I could actively remember other things to block certain memory triggers.

"Where did you meet your mate then?" the man by Dr. Reid questioned.

*I like crazy daisies. You can buy bouquets of them at the store for cheap. The rainbow pedals shine bright and vibrant from the dyes. They do that by placing individual flowers in colored water. The flowers soak up the water, and the pedals change color.*

"What do flowers have to do with your mate?"

*My favorite bouquet I ever purchased consisted of various shades of purple and blue flowers: soft lilac, royal blue, and periwinkle purple.*

"Not flowers. Your mate. Show me your mate!"

*I put them in a clear vase with a black ribbon that I kept under my kitchen sink. The flowers came with a preservation packet of plant food to prolong the life of the flowers.*

"Focus!"

A shocking sensation zipped through my wrist. *The train of four. I can feel the shocks and twitching of my hand from the nerve stimulation. That means my neuro system isn't locked down. I need a deeper memory,* I thought before switching tactics.

*I stood in the middle of a softball field. My cleats dug into the dirt as I readied for the batter to swing.*

*"Strike!" the umpire called out.*

*The crowd erupted in applause. It was the bottom of the ninth, and we were leading by one run. The bases were loaded. We only had one out to go to win the game. I could see the player on third base edge a foot forward from the corner of my eye. I knew she wanted to steal home, but she wouldn't risk the game. The pitcher threw a second strike. The batter stepped away from the plate and rolled her shoulders. This was it - the pitch to determine the game. She stepped back to the plate. The pitcher wound up and threw the ball. With a loud crack, the bat connected. I held my glove up and tracked the falling ball, preparing for the catch...*

Pain shot across my left cheek, pulling me from the memory. Blood pooled in my mouth from the mucosa being ripped open by my teeth. The glasses flew off my face, and the light overwhelmed my eyes. I tried to clamp them shut, but the speculums prevented the movement.

Another blow struck me. Blood spewed from my mouth this time. I focused my eyes on the boss standing in front of me, heaving with rage, fists balled at his sides.

"I guess you'll never know if I caught the ball now."

He raised his fist to strike again, but Dr. Reid stopped him. "You're skewing the data!"

"What data? She was reliving a softball game instead of showing us her mate."

"She was actively remembering. It might not have been

the moment you wanted her to relive, but it was something. I told you this was only done with voluntary subjects in the past," Dr. Reid fussed as she started removing the head band, speculums, and monitors. "They were willing to focus on the memory requested. She was doing something never observed before by actively veering to unstimulated neurons."

"Dr. Reid, this is not about your brain mapping research. There's time for that later. I need answers that only she can provide."

Shane and Garrett were standing by my sides now. I blinked my eyes rapidly trying to dispute the dryness from being open for such an extended period of time.

My head began to throb as the two bickered back and forth. Despite the pain, I was pleased with the results. I don't know what data Dr. Reid abstracted, but information about Callen was safe. I can only hope they give up on the memory viewing after this. I might not be so lucky next time.

"Fine." His voice pulled me back to their argument. "Take her to her room." He turned and stormed out.

Garret and Shane began releasing my restraints as Dr. Reid returned to her computer. I flexed my arms and legs when I was free in order to return circulation to the stiffened limbs. Shane grabbed my arm and pulled me toward the door without a word. As much as I hated being manhandled, I was glad to leave the lab, if only for the time being.

# CHAPTER TEN

*Returned*

My guards took me back to my cement cell. When Shane opened the door, I tore my arm from his grip and walked into the room. I stopped halfway to the bed and turned when I heard their footsteps following behind me.

"Can I help you?"

Both men stopped about five paces from me. We stood staring at each other in tense silence.

"Why are you making this so difficult?" Shane questioned.

"Why are you?" I spat back.

Shane closed his eyes and took a deep breath while Garrett rolled his eyes at our bickering. "We all have a job to do. Yours is to answer our questions which you aren't doing."

"Just because you *want* it to happen, doesn't make it my *job*. I don't want to be here. I don't want to help you, and I have no intention of telling you a damn thing." I stamped my foot in frustration.

Garrett laughed, "You're cute when you're mad. You know that?"

I glared at him, wanting nothing more than to strangle him with my bare hands, to hit and hurt and rip him limb from limb.

"It is unfortunate that you feel that way, Lacey." A voice rang out from the hallway - his voice, the orchestrator of this hellish scheme. He strutted into the room with his hands in his pants pockets. He was calm and collected, as if ten minutes ago had never happened.

I ran my tongue across the cuts on the inside of my cheek expecting to find tender, mangled flesh; however, the cuts shockingly no longer hurt and felt like they were healing.

He stopped behind the two men in front of me, careful to never drop our eye contact. "Tomorrow, you will return to the lab, and you will answer my questions, or I will give you to Garrett. I am a very busy man, and you have wasted too much of my time already. If you won't volunteer the information and you won't comply even after being beaten into unconsciousness, perhaps a different approach can shred some of that stubbornness from your veins."

I clenched my jaw at his statement as a wicked grin spread across Garrett's face.

"I won't tell you anything."

"Oh, we will see my dear." He turned and walked out of the room. Garrett winked at me as he went to follow, a light airiness in his walk. He looked like a kid on Christmas getting his biggest wish.

Shane was furious. For a moment, he looked as if he was going to hit me himself, the tight grip on his self control wavering. I took a step back to put more distance between us. Just because he hadn't done anything yet, didn't mean he wouldn't. I wasn't going to fall for his nice guy routine anymore. It'd only be a matter of time before he dropped the facade.

Shane reined in what control he had left, marched out

the room, and slammed the door behind him. I took a deep breath and crumpled to the floor. So much had happened in the last week, I was about to reach my breaking point. I wasn't sure how much more of this I could take, how much more I could fight. I let go and allowed the tears to fall from my eyes. I channeled all the hurt, anger, and fear into those tears to purge my system. I missed Callen. I missed him so damn much it hurt.

When the tears no longer fell, I pulled myself from the floor. The time for weakness had passed. If I was going to keep any thought or memory of Callen locked away, I couldn't wallow with fragility. No, what I needed to do was sleep and rest and prepare for tomorrow.

Before I moved to climb onto the bed, a rapt sounded on the door. Dr. Reid opened it and walked into the room. "Oh good, you're awake. I wasn't sure if the session wore you out. Other subjects have expressed mental fatigue after their recollections."

"I would like to tell you I am fine, but truthfully, I am exhausted." Fatigue hit me like a brick wall as I spoke. All the adrenaline from before abandoning my system.

"I'll make this quick then," she said motioning for me to take a seat on the bed. I obliged and plopped down as she approached me. "I would like to check the injuries that you received in the lab. If you would be so kind as to pull your shirt up so I can check your abdomen and flank."

I bit my lower lip as I contemplated her request. If I refused, she would simply have the men restrain me, and I much preferred to do this without their supervision. I nodded my head as I pulled my shirt up to my chest to expose my midriff. She lightly palpated my stomach and tapped my flanks after she inspected the skin. Surprisingly, there were no bruises or swelling, nor any discomfort from her touch. She motioned for me to pull my shirt down when she was finished.

"There's not a mark on you," she observed. Dr. Reid reached into her lab coat pocket and withdrew a penlight. "Open your mouth please."

I opened for her to inspect the cuts to my cheek. The taste of old blood remained on my tongue, but nothing fresh came from the wounds.

"Interesting," she commented. "There is the faintest purple bruise to your jawbone, but the lacerations in your mouth are healing nicely. I anticipated more damage."

I shrugged at her not knowing exactly what to say. I was personally surprised how quickly the pain had dissipated as well.

"The HyperStem must still be scribed in your system."

"You sound surprised by that."

"I am. It's not meant to linger in the system and never has with any other participants." She spoke as if I was part of a voluntary drug trial, as if I wasn't here against my will and the drugs were a choice I opted for rather than an injection forced upon me. "I'm going to have Shane come collect some more blood samples. I want to see if we can isolate any chemical markers."

I nodded in recognition. My stomach churned at the thought of them taking more samples from me. Dr. Reid left and closed the door behind her, and I heard the soft click of the lock engaging. With a sigh, I pulled myself further onto the bed and allowed exhaustion to take over.

"Mmmmm," I moaned as a calloused hand caressed my face, pulling me from my slumber. The touch was so sensual and soft compared to anything I've felt in the last week. A thumb gently ran over my lips. I reached my hand up to hold Callen's, but I froze when my fingers found his. This wasn't Callen.

"What the fuck?" I yelled, jerking backward and flinging my eyes open.

Shane was sitting on the edge of the bed, his eyes shadowed in thought. "Sorry, I didn't mean to wake you."

"How long have you been here?" I asked, pulling myself to a sitting position on the bed.

"Not long."

I eyed him carefully, not believing his answer. *Why was he in here watching me sleep?*

He cleared his throat. "I brought you some food, and Dr. Reid asked me to come draw some new lab samples from you."

"What's with you and food?"

"Well, you have to eat to stay alive. I'm surprised a nurse doesn't know that," he said sarcastically.

"Did you ever stop and think that maybe I don't want to be alive?"

He pursed his lips at my statement. "Yes, you have made it perfectly clear how displeased you are with the current circumstances; however, death is currently not an option."

I rolled my eyes at him. "Get off my bed."

He laughed as he stood and took his seat at the table. A fresh peanut butter and jelly sandwich, chips, and bottle of water sat on a tray. I grabbed the water and drank greedily, my mouth parched and in desperate need of rinsing.

"Dr. Reid said your injuries from the lab were practically healed when she came by."

I nodded my head as I took a bite of the sandwich. I was hungry, and there was no reason to starve myself. It'd take too long to die from starvation. Plus, I needed the energy to fight and prepare. "I'm one special lady from what I hear."

He looked at me with a soft smile. Thoughts were churning behind his dark, brown eyes, but they were unreadable.

"How old are you, Lacey?"

"How old am I?" I laughed. "What's that matter?"

He shrugged, "It doesn't. I was just curious."

"I'm twenty-six."

He nodded. "How did you manage to keep it a secret?"

I swallowed as I considered his question. "Keep what a secret? My soulmark?"

He nodded, his eyes trailing down to the crescent moon on my wrist.

"It's not as hard as you would think. I mean you saw earlier that I had only met the one girl with a soulmark before."

"You said that's the only one you met at work," he corrected.

I elected to ignore his statement and continued, "There are so few marked ones out there, people don't really look for them anymore - at least not every day people - and we don't look any different than anyone else apart from the marking. So, I just keep my head down, my wrist covered, and blend in with the crowd. Besides, the last place anyone would look for a person being hunted is right in plain sight."

"That's fair. One would think you would try and hide a bit better than that though."

"Sometimes the best hiding places are the most obvious," I mused as I took another bite of sandwich. "Alright, my turn."

"For what?"

"To ask a question."

"I'm not promising to answer anything."

I rolled my eyes again. "Is Shane your real name?"

He laughed as he answered, "Yeah, it is. Shane Thompson."

"And your boss, what's his name?"

"That's two questions."

"So?"

"You said *a* question," he replied as he leaned forward in the chair and propped his elbows on the table.

"Well, answer that one and you can ask another."

"His name is Christopher McDaniels. He goes by C."

I grabbed the water and took another drink. "As in McDaniels Incorporated?"

"The one and only."

"McDaniels Incorporated is supposed to be compounding and researching intravenous nutrition, not hunting marked ones and meddling in everything else going on here," I said accusingly.

He shrugged, "Things aren't always what they say they are."

"Clearly." *No wonder Callen hasn't found me yet*, I thought.

A heady silence filled the room as I finished my sandwich, engrossed in my thoughts. *How long would it take Callen to see through their corporate ruse? He probably started searching within the known parties. It could take weeks for Callen to uncover this place. Plus, I have no idea how far they transported me. I could be anywhere.*

After a while, Shane asked, "Why won't you just tell us

who your mate is? We will find him eventually. Fighting it is simply delaying the inevitable, and you are getting hurt in the process."

"I've said a thousand times I don't have a mate." I set the water down and crossed my arms over my chest.

"Come off it, Lacey. We know you do."

"If you know so much, why do I need to tell you who he is?"

"Because the informant can't figure out who he is, so we brought you in alone to try and flush him out."

I pursed my lips in frustration. "I will never tell you a thing about him. It doesn't matter what any of you do to me."

"He's not joking. He's going to give you to Garrett, and Garrett won't stop until you break or we find him. *And, we will find him.* Save yourself."

"I will not sacrifice him to protect myself from Garrett! You don't feed the person you love to the lions in order to pull yourself from the den!"

"If he loves you as much as you love him, I have a hard time believing he would want you to be beaten and raped trying to shield him!" We were both standing and yelling at this point. Shane's fists were clenched at his sides.

"It doesn't matter what he would want me to do. I am the one that is here, and it is me who has to suffer the consequences. Besides, he might be my mate, but it's my body, my choice!"

"You don't think it's going to affect him? It won't tear him apart knowing you were violated and used because of him? Because he couldn't stop it? If that's what you seriously think, then you've lost your ever loving mind, Lacey!"

"Why do you even care, Shane? It doesn't have a

goddamn thing to do with you!" I was furious. The gumption of this man to presume to know what the two of us were going through was absurd and pissed me off to no end.

"The hell it doesn't!" he yelled.

"What's that supposed to mean?"

Shane stepped toward me and gripped my head between his palms, holding me in place. "You have no idea. You don't have a fucking clue."

"A clue about what?"

"Anything."

"Oh, and you do? You think you understand him? Or me for that matter?"

"I know more than you think." Emotion filled his eyes as he gripped me harder, twisting his fingers into my hair. "I know you are the most stubborn woman I have ever met. I know you care about yourself least in this world, and I know you won't do anything without a fight."

I swallowed as he spoke, his eyes pleading with me to listen.

"I also know you talk in your sleep, and you get a small furrow between your brows when you dream. You don't trust anyone and never have. I know you're scared whether you admit it or not, and there is no way in hell I am going to let you do this!"

I shoved against his chest, and he dropped his hands to his side. "You don't get to decide what I do and don't do. Your job is not to protect me. It's to follow orders and collect data and information. You've said it yourself this last week multiple times. Now, do your damn job and draw my blood, so we can get on with this!"

"This job has changed, and I don't want it!"

"Then what is it you want? Because you make zero sense!"

Shane stepped forward quickly, catching me by surprise. He grabbed my face again and crushed his mouth to mine. The kiss was angry and passionate and the last thing I expected. I shoved him backward again and slapped him across the face. His eyes widened as if he himself just realized what had happened.

"Lacey, I—"

"No," I whispered, tears pricking my eyes. "Just no."

The door swung open interrupting the moment. Dr. Reid entered the room in her pristine, white lab coat. She looked between us with a puzzled expression. Shane stood there staring at me with eyes full of regret. I wiped my hands over my face, willing composure to take over.

"Is everything okay?" she asked.

"Fine," I answered. "Shane was just getting ready to take some more blood samples like you requested. Right, Shane?"

"Yeah," he agreed, motioning for me to sit back down on the bed.

Once I was settled, Shane pulled a kit from his cargo pants pocket, wrapped the tourniquet around my arm, and drew four vials of blood from a needle he pierced into my inner elbow. When he finished, I held some gauze in place to staunch the bleeding as he rose and walked toward the door without another word.

"Want to tell me what just happened there?" Dr. Reid asked as he exited the room.

"There's nothing to tell," he called over his shoulder.

She turned back to me and strode toward the bed. "What about you?"

"What about me?" I asked curtly.

"Anything you want to share?"

"Nope."

She sighed, "I swear I am the only sane person left in this place. Anyway, I've come to talk to you about the recollection that will happen tomorrow."

I nodded, waiting for her to continue.

"I would really like for you to reconsider your memory lockdown."

I rolled my eyes at her and looked away.

"Just hear me out. If you cooperate, no one else has to get hurt. Yes, your mate will be brought in for questioning and examination, but you could both walk away from this. You are of no use to science if you are dead. These men will go to any extremes necessary, and they are capable of horrific things. Stop putting yourself at their mercy. If you comply with the studies, I can protect you."

I laughed dryly and shook my head, "What makes you think you are any better than the men you work with? You said it yourself, I'm a test subject for your project. Once you've gotten everything you want, do you honestly expect me to believe my mate and I will be able to walk out the door and go back to our normal lives? After everything I've seen? Everything I've endured? There's no way your boss is ever going to let me go. This isn't just business for him. It's personal, whether he admits it or not."

Nodding her head, she replied, "Perhaps, but it's personal for other people too. Not everyone is an enemy."

With that final statement, she exited the room, closing the door again behind her. The click of the lock engaged, and I threw myself backward onto the bed. I felt utterly drained, mentally and physically. The mind games from today were taking their toll. I didn't want to think about what Dr. Reid said, and I definitely didn't want to focus on what happened with Shane. My heart sank as thoughts about what tomorrow would bring flooded my mind. I buried my face in the pillow and waited for sleep to come.

*Callen came up and wrapped his arms around me while I was washing dishes. He gently kissed the sensitive skin beneath my ear, sending tingles down my body.*

*"So, I was thinking we could go away this weekend," he said in between kisses.*

*"Where would we go?" I asked, amused.*

*"It's a surprise. I thought a few days just the two of us, away from everything, would be nice. We could get to know each other a bit better."*

*"As much fun as that sounds, I have to work this weekend."*

*He nuzzled his nose into my hair and took a deep breath. "You smell so good."*

*I laughed, "What do I smell like?"*

*"Vanilla. It's soft and subtle, but it's there."*

*"If you say so," I answered as I dried my hands on a towel before turning around to wrap my arms around his neck.*

*"Come away with me."*

*"I really should go to work, but I suppose I can see if Claire can cover for me."*

*"Great. You call her, and I'll pack you a bag. We'll head right out."*

*"You mean leave now?" I balked.*

*"Yep. So you better get moving." He pecked me on the lips*

*and headed for my bedroom.*

*Shaking my head with a bemused smile, I pulled my phone from my pocket and dialed Claire.*

*"Hey! I was getting worried about you," she exclaimed from the other end of the line. "I've called a couple times since we went out, and you haven't picked up."*

*"I know, I'm sorry. I lost my phone and just found it," I lied. I hadn't even bothered with the phone since I woke up at Callen's apartment. Claire was probably worried sick.*

*"Michael said you weren't feeling well, so he put you in a cab. On his way back inside, he was mugged in the alley."*

*"Oh. Wow. Is he, ugh, is he okay?" I asked, trying to go with her story. I couldn't tell her what really happened.* How are you supposed to tell your best friend that her new boyfriend's friend tried to date rape you, and the only thing that stopped him was your soulmate - who isn't supposed to exist - beating the hell out of him?

*"I mean, he's pretty beat up and was unconscious for about an hour, we think, when Derek found him."*

*"That's good Derek found him then." It was hard to sound concerned for a man who had brazenly faked an apology just to do what he did. It takes a real bastard to be that methodical.*

*"Yeah, well, it was kinda weird. I mean, why would he put you in a cab from the back alley? And, why didn't he come tell us you were sick? I would've gone with you to make sure you got home okay or taken you back to my place."*

*"Ugh…it just came out of nowhere."*

*"Lacey, did something else happen?"*

*"Of course not," I answered a bit too quickly. "I was just really sick and puking everywhere. I think I have the stomach flu, actually."*

*"Do you need anything?"*

*Callen walked out of my room, carrying my flower duffle bag. He arched his eyebrow in question, catching the tail end of our conversation.*

*"I was hoping you could cover my Saturday and Sunday shifts at work. I was trying to avoid calling out so I won't get a short notice."*

*"Yeah, that's no problem. Derek is going out of town this weekend anyways. Are you sure nothing else is going on?" She sounded worried. I hated lying to her, but it was better for everyone the less she knew.*

*"I swear that's it. A few more days and I'll be good as new."*

*"Okay. Well, don't disappear like that again. You scared me to death."*

*"I promise. I won't. Thanks again."*

*"No problem. Feel better, girl."*

*I hung the phone up and looked at Callen. "You weren't joking about packing me a bag."*

*"Nope," he smiled. "Anything you need to do before we leave?"*

*"I don't think so. Claire is going to cover for me which was really the only hang up."*

*"Let's head out then."*

*We left the apartment and headed to Callen's truck. He tossed my bag in the backseat and cranked the engine.*

*"Are we going back to your place first?"*

*"Nah. I keep a go-bag in the backseat. I'll be fine with that stuff." He waved his hand like that was a perfectly normal response.*

*"Why do you have a go-bag?"*

"*Professional hazard. No big deal.*"

*I eyed him quizzically. Most professions that have a go-bag are, in fact, a big deal.*

"*So,*" *he said, transitioning the subject,* "*was your friend asking about the other night?*"

"*Yeah, she said Michael told them he was mugged in the alley after putting me in a cab when I started throwing up at the club. I just went with it and said I must have the stomach flu that's going around.*"

*He nodded,* "*That's as good a story as any.*"

"*Do you think Michael knew it was you?*" *I asked, chewing on my lip nervously. The last thing we needed was for Michael to come looking for revenge.*

*He shrugged,* "*Maybe. He was pretty put off with me when I ran back into him after I walked you home from the bar that first night. I doubt he forgot me any more than I forgot him.*"

"*What do you mean you ran back into him?*"

"*That's why I left. I had a feeling taking you from the bar wouldn't put an end to things so easily with the way he was looking at you that night.*"

"*How was he looking at me?*"

"*Like you were prey. Like you were going to be his one way or another. Even if you didn't belong to me, I still would've intervened. He's an animal. But, I already knew you were mine, and like hell I was going to leave you vulnerable.*"

*He looked over at me possessively. If anybody else would've dared stake claim to me in such a bold fashion, I would've been furious, but I wanted Callen to own me. And, I wanted to own him just as much. The feeling was completely foreign, yet it felt right all the same.*

"*So,*" *he continued,* "*I decided to walk back the way we came before retrieving my truck from the studio. I was about halfway to the bar when I saw him coming down the road. He was looking around. I figured he was trying to see if you were anywhere nearby still. I told him to back off and you weren't interested. We had a few words before drawing the attention of some onlookers. He seemed pretty pissed when he stormed off. I waited for a bit to make sure he didn't come back, but he never did. Why were you even out with him again anyways?"*

"His friend is dating Claire. She begged me to go out with them, and I finally caved and went. I thought the distraction would help."

"Distraction from what?"

"Well, honestly, from you. The night we went dancing and you touched my mark was when I realized who you were. I mean, don't get me wrong, I was drawn to you the moment I saw you, but I didn't realize why. I've spent so much energy locking that piece of myself away that I'd convinced myself I'd never find my mate purely because I would never look for you. With all the billions of people in the world, I didn't think there was a chance of running into you by happenstance."

"That's why you ran that night?"

"Mhm, and you know how I feel about how dangerous it is for us to be together. So, I left and tried to forget it ever happened."

"Did you?"

"No. I thought about you constantly. It didn't help that you kept calling either, because that meant you were thinking about me too. I thought you didn't feel the electricity when you touched my soulmark, so I figured you'd move on if I blew you off."

He reached over and grabbed my hand, lightly stroking the top of it with his thumb. "I felt it, Lacey. I felt it all the way to my bones. It was like nothing I could have ever imagined even though I already knew I had found you. I'm never letting you walk away *from me again. If I'd have just followed you and explained, you never would've been in that club. I should've protected you. I'm so sorry."*

"You have nothing to be sorry about. I'm the one that went to the club, I'm the one that believed his apology, and I'm the one who took a drink from a practical stranger. Everything that happened was my fault. I don't even want to think about what would've happened if you hadn't been there. You saved me when I pushed you away." I smiled at him and squeezed his hand in mine.

Callen kept his eyes forward, a serious expression on his face. "If I ever see him again, Lacey, I'll kill him."

"Callen," I looked at him with wide eyes, "you can't."

"If he ever comes near you again," he looked over at me, his tone completely serious, "I will kill him. Like I should've already."

I swallowed hard. I didn't know how I felt about that. On one hand, I didn't want anyone to die, much less for them to die because of me, but on the other, I never wanted to see Michael ever again. "I'm sure he's learned his lesson."

I looked out the window as we drove in silence, Callen holding my hand the entire drive. We turned onto a backroad that transitioned to gravel. Thick trees and undergrowth lined the narrow path. He pulled the truck up to a small cabin and parked.

"Where are we?" I asked as I hopped out of the truck.

"This is Paradise. I come here when I need a break from the world."

The roar of water echoed in the air, birds chirped in the trees, and nature completely surrounded us.

"The cabin's not much, but it does have plumbing and electricity from the waterfall," he said, guiding me up the four steps of the porch.

"Where did you find this place?" I asked, looking around at

*the beauty encircling us.*

*"I found the waterfall when I was out hiking one day. It was so peaceful here, so I bought the land and built the cabin shortly after."*

*"You built it? By yourself?"*

*"I had a few buddies lend a hand here and there, but mostly, yeah, I did it myself. Took about a year."*

*We walked into the cabin, and Callen flipped on the lights. The living room opened to a small kitchen in the right corner. Large windows lined the back wall providing a breathtaking view of the waterfall behind the house. A hallway down the left led to what I presumed was a bedroom and bathroom. It was small but cozy. The perfect image of peace.*

*"It's beautiful," I said, smiling at Callen.*

*"I'm glad you like it. Why don't you go take a bath and relax after being cramped in the truck. I'll make us some dinner. I'm sure you're hungry."*

*"Okay. That sounds good." I stood on my tip toes to peck him on the cheek and left down the hall with my bag.*

*The bedroom was at the end, and the only pieces of furniture it held were a king sized bed and trunk. After glancing around, I set my bag down and headed for the adjoining bathroom. A tiled, walk-in shower with a rainfall head stood next to a large garden tub. I turned the tap and started filling it with hot water as I undressed. The double vanity sink had a bag of epsom salts underneath, so I threw a few handfuls in as well.*

*I climbed into the tub and cut the water off. Laying back, the water came up over my chest, totally submerging me. I hadn't realized how sore I still was until the salts started relaxing my muscles. Bruises adorned my arms and wrists. My throat was tender to the touch, but it didn't hurt to swallow anymore. I closed my eyes and rested until the water turned cool. Then, I drained the tub and stepped in the shower to wash the salts from my skin.*

*Wrapping myself in a towel I found hanging from a wall hook, I returned to the bedroom to open my bag. I rifled through the contents and settled on a pair of pink bikini cut panties, but there weren't any pajamas. There was another bag laying on the bed that Callen must have brought in while I bathed, so I opened it to check for something to wear. It held a few of his t-shirts, a pair of jeans, sweats, shorts, socks, and boxers. I grabbed a navy t-shirt and pulled it over my head. The hem hit just above mid-thigh, the length showing off my legs. I ran my fingers through my hair and headed out to the kitchen.*

*A pot of water was boiling on the stove with some pasta, but Callen wasn't there. I went to look out the back windows when I heard his voice coming from the porch. I crept up to the door wondering who he was talking to.*

*"Yeah, we made it to the cabin. She says she's fine, but she's got some bad bruising from that bastard."*

He must be on the phone, but who the hell is he talking to? And why is he telling them about me? *I thought.*

*"I don't know his last name, but she called him Michael. Maybe it's real, maybe it's not. Add him to the list. I want to make sure he chose her at random and not because he knows she's a marked one."*

What list? Callen had talked about killing Michael so casually, and he was obviously a trained fighter. What kind of man was my mate? *The questions made my heart pound.*

*"I'll see you on Monday. Text me if anything important comes up before then."*

*Callen sounded like he was ending the call. Not wanting to be caught eavesdropping, I scurried back into the bedroom and shut the door. His conversation left me on edge. No one was supposed to know we existed, but he flat out admitted to whoever* was on the other end of that call that I was a marked one. Somebody I don't even know. I knew us being together would be dangerous, but I didn't expect him to cause the danger. I took a deep breath to steady my nerves. We would be here all weekend. I had time to figure this out before we went home.

You can always run. *The thought sent a pain to my heart. I didn't want to leave. It'd tear me apart. His words from the truck echoed in my head,* "I'm never letting you walk away from me again." *I'd have to be smart about it if I was to ever leave. I knew he meant what he said. He was possessive. Pushing my thoughts down, I reopened the door and walked back to the kitchen.*

*Callen was draining the pasta water and turned as he heard my feet padding on the floor. A smile broke out over his face as a gleam flickered in his eyes.*

*"I like your choice of outfit," he said with a coy expression adorning his face.*

*"Well, I didn't have many options since somebody forgot to pack me any pajamas. Your wardrobe had to donate to the cause."*

*"Oh, I didn't forget," he winked.*

*A blush rose over my cheeks at his meaning.*

*"Have a seat," he said gesturing to the bar height, two seater table. "I'll pour you a glass of wine."*

*"Dinner and wine? What else you got up your sleeve for me tonight?" I asked as I sat at the table.*

*"You'll just have to wait and see," he answered as he set two glasses of red on the table. He stood between my legs, and I felt my core clench at his proximity, my thin panties the only thing covering me. He kissed me lightly before returning to the kitchen, sending butterflies through my stomach. I crossed my legs to minimize my exposure and took a sip of wine. The tannins were light on the palette with a hint of lingering blackberry in the background. I twirled the glass in my hand and watched the legs*

*run down.*

*"This is lovely," I said as I saw him watching me, a smile tugging at the corner of his mouth.*

*"It's an Alexander Valley cab. It's one of my favorites," Callen replied as he returned to the table with our dinner. Spaghetti with marinara sauce filled the plates. It's aromatic smell wafting through the air. "It's nothing fancy. I tend to just stock the cabin with non-perishables. Next time we come back, I'll make sure to stop at a grocery store on the way," he said smiling as he popped a fork full of noodles into his mouth.*

*"I'm not a fancy type of girl. This is perfect," I said reassuringly before taking a bite. The sauce was heavenly. "What kind of marinera is this? It's delicious."*

*"It's mine. I made it."*

*"You made it?"*

*"Yeah. Does that surprise you?"*

*"Well, first I found out you built this cabin by hand, and now, you tell me you can make your own homemade sauces. Is there anything you can't do?" I teased, taking a sip of wine.*

*"Hmm," he tapped a finger against his chin, pretending to think, "I really suck at bowling. Does that count?"*

*"The contractor/chef can't bowl. Got it. We can do that on our next date, so you don't show me up so much."*

*"Oh, Lace, no one could show you up."*

*I blushed and looked down at my plate. Callen suddenly stood up and threw me over his shoulder.*

*"Hey! What do you think you're doing?" I yelled at him, slightly panicked.*

*He smacked me on the ass as he headed down the hall. "I warned you what would happen if you kept sucking and chewing* on that damn lip of yours." Reaching up, he spanked me again to punctuate his point.

"I didn't realize I was even doing it. It's a habit!" I squealed as I kicked my feet in a vain attempt to free myself from his hold.

"Well, it's a habit that's going to keep you on your back. Now, quit wiggling," he said as he spanked me harder, eliciting a surprised yelp.

When we reached the bedroom, he roughly tossed me on the bed. I bounced with the landing, and my unsupported bust jiggled with the motion. His shirt pooled around my waist, allowing my pink panties to peak out from the bottom. Callen stood over me, his chest rising as lust took over his breathing. His erection was pushing against his jeans, causing the fabric to strain. A wickedness twinkled in his eyes when our gazes met. My nerves twisted as he bore over me, but my core dampened with wanting.

"You're going to do exactly what I say or your punishment will be worse."

"You're going to punish me?" My heart raced with his words.

"I am, and I'm going to enjoy it too," he said as he pulled his shirt off and tossed it to the floor.

I lay there admiring his form, imagining running my tongue along his firm abs.

"Lacey, pay attention," he called.

My eyes snapped back up to his when he spoke.

"Now, it's time for that shirt to come off." He reached down, pulled me to a sitting position, and stripped me. "Stay," he ordered as he moved to the trunk at the end of the bed.

I shifted and crossed my arms over my chest as I waited for him, trying to cover myself. He rummaged in the trunk for a moment before he returned with a black tie.

"What did I tell you about being shy and hiding yourself?"

*"Ummm..." I froze.*

*"I believe I told you that wasn't something you were to ever do with me." He grabbed one of my wrists and wrapped the silky material around it. "Since you can't seem to control those hands, I'll have to provide you with some assistance," he mused.*

*Once the fabric was secure, Callen bent down and kissed me hard, his tongue plunging forward to ravish my mouth. He abruptly pulled away, picked me up, and moved me to the top of the bed. Throwing a leg over my waist, he straddled me and roughly pulled my other wrist up to tether me to the headboard. I tried to pull my arms free, but the knots only tightened.*

*"Those are arbor knots, baby. The more you struggle, the tighter they'll get." He winked before leaning down and kissing me again.*

*My heart was pounding with the thought of being tied down. "Callen," my voice shook as I said his name. Endorphins flooded my system. As nervous as I was about what was happening, the wetness between my legs increased, begging to be touched.*

*"Shh, shh," he hushed me as he slowly slid off the bed. He stood and looked me up and down, taking in every inch of my nakedness. The only thing covering me were my panties.*

*"You brought this on yourself, Lacey. Now, it's time to take your punishment like a good girl."*

*Callen unbuttoned his jeans and pushed them to the floor. My core clenched as his massiveness strained against his boxers. He climbed back on the bed and kneeled between my knees. Pushing my panties to the side, he slid his fingers between my folds, eliciting a moan of pleasure at his touch.*

*"God, you're so wet. You want me to punish you dont you?" he asked, pushing a finger inside me. "Is that why you've misbehaved tonight?"*

*I was panting with every stroke. Words refused to come as my mind scrambled with longing. He pulled his finger out and slid my panties back in place, making me whimper from the loss of his touch.*

*"Answer me when I speak to you, or I'll stop, Lacey."*

*I tried to pull my thighs together and rub for the much needed friction, but Callen held them in place. "I'll decide when you're pleasured. This is my punishment to give. Do you understand?"*

*"Yes," I breathed heavily, desperate to be touched.*

*Callen began rubbing me through my underwear as he bent down and pulled my nipple into his mouth. I moaned as he twirled it with his tongue. Then, suddenly, he bit down and pulled my nipple taut between his teeth. I gasped with the sharp pain in my breast, but a pulling between my legs caused a moan to follow. Lost in the moment, I tugged on my restraints again without thinking, tightening them further.*

*Callen released my nipple and peppered kisses down my stomach. "Stop fighting, Lacey." He reached my groin and rubbed his nose between my folds over my panties. "You're drenched," he said as he sat up and pulled them off. He brought his fingers back to my entrance and slid two in agonizingly slow.*

*"Oh, god, Callen, please."*

*"I don't believe I asked you to speak, my little mate. I think that mouth of yours may need to be occupied."*

*My stomach clenched as he leaned back over me. He moved as if to kiss me, but at the last minute, he shoved my wet panties in my mouth as a gag. My eyes widened in shock, and he snickered.*

*"That's better. Now, where was I?" he mused aloud to himself as he settled back between my legs, "Ah, yes, right about here."*

*He pushed his two fingers back inside me and curled them*

*forward, massaging the perfect spot. My breathing increased as pleasure filled my body. His mouth latched onto my clit and began sucking. I moaned into the gag and arched my hips. Callen used his free hand to press me back down into the bed. Alternating between sucking and licking with an occasional soft nip of his teeth, his fingers simultaneously pumped into me. The warm ball was forming in my stomach as he drove me toward an orgasm, but right before I reached the precipice, he stopped. The feeling dissipated, and I writhed in frustration, tightening my wrist bindings even more.*

*"Do not come, Lacey. Not until I say you can."*

*I took a deep breath and groaned. My body craved the release he snatched away. Callen planted gentle kisses on my inner thighs, ever so slightly grazing against my cleft. He was driving me wild, and the ache to be filled by him was almost unbearable. He slowly parted me open with his tongue and slid it into my entrance. My hips rocked forward demanding more, his thumb strumming my clit as he fucked me with his tongue. The ball of warmth filled my stomach as my climax began climbing again. Callen replaced his tongue with two fingers and pumped them in and out of me.*

*As I neared the edge again, my breathing became ragged, but just like last time, he pulled away. I whined needing a release. My body was so frustrated, tears threatened my vision. I needed to come more than ever. Callen straightened up on his knees, grabbed my legs and flipped me over onto my stomach. He pushed my knees underneath me and pulled my ass into the air. A hard slap connected with my right cheek, and I rocked forward, moaning as the pain changed to pleasure when he massaged the flesh he struck.*

*"Do you think you've learned your lesson, baby?"*

*I nodded my head the best I could in response.*

*"Are you going to chew on that beautiful lip anymore?"*

*I shook my head as Callen reached around me and pulled the gag from my mouth.*

"I'm going to take you now, Lacey. Hard. You are not to come though. Do you understand?"

"Yes, I understand."

My body shook with need as I knelt before him. In this moment, I'd do anything to end the torture and have him inside me. Callen lined his length up with my entrance and speared inside. I cried out with the delicious intrusion.

"Fuck, you're so tight." Callen forcefully thrust in and out of me as another smack landed on my ass cheek. He grabbed my hips and pulled me into him with a bruising force, yet I grinded down, begging for him to go harder. The ball formed in my lower stomach again as he plowed into me, setting a punishing rhythm. The urge to come was overwhelming.

"Please, I need to. I - I can't stop it." I pulled my elbows down trying to shift, but the knots further tightened around my wrists, holding me in place.

"Control it, Lacey. Or I'll stop," he said as he thrust into me harder. I pulsed around him as I tried to contain myself. Another slap jarred me forward with its delivery.

"Callen, oh my god, please, I can't take it," I begged him.

He bent over me and brought his mouth to my ear. "Let go. Come for me," he ordered.

My orgasm erupted at his words, and I screamed out in pleasure. Wave after wave rippled through me. My body locked so tightly, I couldn't breathe. I clenched firmly around him. His pace was unrelenting, determined to pull every ounce of pleasure from my system.

"Fuck," he yelled as he flooded into me, slamming into me one last time.

As our high dissipated, he pulled one end of the tie and released me from the headboard. Callen rolled to the side and brought me with him, never disengaging from inside me. Slowly, *my muscles relaxed as I breathed heavily in his arms, my hands still bound together and a lone tear running down my cheek. Callen wiped it away with his thumb and tightened his grip around me.*

*"Hey, what's wrong? Are you okay?" He pulled out as he adjusted to see me better.*

*"I'm fine. It's just...that was...I don't even have the words for it. It was intense and frustratingly wonderful."*

*He nuzzled into my neck as he inhaled deeply. "It's only wonderful because of you. You are perfect in every way, baby."*

*He reached around me and released the tie from my wrists. Soft redness highlighted my skin from my tugging. To my surprise, the sight of it made me ache for him all over again. I laced my fingers with his as he held me firmly against his chest. My eyes fluttered shut, sleep calling for me.*

*The last thing I heard was Callen whisper, "Rest, Lacey. I've got you," as he stroked my hair.*

# CHAPTER ELEVEN

## *Sampled*

I woke up alone in the cement walled room, my eyes heavy from sleep. Running my tongue over my cheek, I felt soft, whole skin. The cuts from yesterday were completely healed. *So far that injection was the only good thing to come out of this fucked up situation,* I mused.

My mind wandered back to Shane kissing me. It had been so unexpected - for both of us. At first I thought it was just a tactic, but the look of disbelief and shock on his face made me think otherwise. I rubbed my hands over my face, trying to clear my head. Taking a deep breath, I pushed the memory away. I needed to focus. I had no doubt today was going to be the worst day of my life. I knew Callen was looking for me - and he would come eventually - but what would be left of me for him to find? I'd never give him up which meant Garrett (or Michael) would finally get his way.

*You heal faster now. You can fight harder,* I tried to convince myself, but my body began to tremble despite my efforts. The memories of him kissing me in the club, strangling me in the alley, and groping me when he caught me in the hall rushed back. I could feel his hands on my body, his breath on my neck as he whispered in my ear.

Bile rose up my throat, and I sprinted to the toilet, vomiting until nothing else came out. Sitting down, I put my head between my knees. Fear enveloped me as my imagination ran wild with what was to come. I'd done my best to act tough and pretend the threats of Garrett having his way with me were nothing, but sitting alone, I had no one to be brave for.

Shane was right. Callen wouldn't want me to do this. In fact, Callen would've wanted me to spill my guts the first day in that vile man's office. He wouldn't care what happened to him as long as I was safe.

*Well, the feeling's mutual,* I thought. I took a deep breath as I stood from the floor. I paced the room, trying to calm the nervousness flooding through me. The waiting and unknown knowledge of when the hammer would drop were driving me mad. As I walked, I thought of Callen, the only thing to bring me comfort.

*I awoke the next morning to an empty bed. The smell of pancakes wafting in the air. I grabbed some new panties and my discarded sleep shirt and went to the bathroom to freshen up before padding quietly down the hallway toward the main part of the cabin. Callen stood shirtless at the stove. He wore gray sweats low on his hips with the band of his boxers peeking out the top. His chiseled back flexed as he reached over his head to pull a plate from the cabinet. I stood watching for a moment as I thought about running my hand over his broad shoulders, pressing myself fully against his back.*

*Just as my thoughts wandered to slipping my hand into his waistband, he called out, "Are you just going to stand there, or are you going to join me?"*

*I blushed as I walked toward him not realizing he knew I was there. He set the dishes down and wrapped me in his arms, placing a gentle kiss on the crown of my head before letting me go.*

*"Have a seat. I just finished cooking," he said, gesturing*

to the table and following me with our food. "I hope you like pancakes."

"I think everyone likes pancakes," I laughed. Picking my fork up to get started, my stomach growling in anticipation. "So, what's on the agenda for today?" I asked as I popped a forkful into my mouth.

"Well, if you're up for it, I thought we could go for a hike and a swim at the waterfall," Callen answered as he shoved a large bite of pancake in his own mouth.

"That sounds good to me."

"Did you sleep well?" he asked between bites.

"Like a rock."

"I thought so," he said with a smirk.

I arched an eyebrow at him in question.

"Has anyone ever told you that you snore?"

"I do not snore!"

"The hell you don't. You talk too," he teased, shooting me a wink.

I did my best to look irritated with him, but he made it hard. "Well, what is it I said then?"

"Oh, no. I'm not telling you that. That's for me to know and you not to remember."

"That is not very nice."

"I never said I was nice." A shadow flickered across his expression with his admission; however, it disappeared as fast as it came. I swallowed my last bite of pancake as I watched him.

"Why don't you go get dressed while I clean up?" he suggested as he took the plates to the kitchen.

I retreated to the bedroom, grabbed some clothes from my

bag, and entered the bathroom. I donned some black leggings, a sports bra, and a tank top, opting for comfort over fashion. When I exited the room, Callen was pulling a gray shirt over his head. The sleeves were snug on his biceps and his calf muscles bulged beneath his khaki, cargo shorts. I licked my lips as I checked him out. He had to be the sexiest man I had ever laid eyes on.

"Ready?" he asked, turning to me.

I nodded at him with a smile.

We headed out the door and started down a trail close by. I couldn't help thinking about his comment at breakfast and the phone call I overheard the day before. I wanted to trust him, but he clearly had a dangerous side. He didn't seem to mind fighting, and he spoke about killing like it was nothing.

"What's on your mind, Lacey?"

"Just enjoying the walk," I lied.

"You're thinking about something. It's written all over your face."

"You're nosey. You know that?" I shot back at him.

He laughed at my response. "Don't worry, you'll tell me tonight when you're asleep."

I reached over and punched his arm in irritation. He laughed harder at my outburst and rubbed his arm, feigning injury.

"It's not funny!"

"Oh yes it is." He reached over and laced his fingers in mine, sending tingles up my arm with his touch. "Wanna play a game?"

"What kind of game?" I asked, eyeing him carefully.

"Twenty questions?"

I snorted, "Why would we do that?"

"Well, the whole point of this getaway is to have some quiet *time to get to know one another. What better way?"*

*I rolled my eyes, "Yeah, okay. I guess since it's your idea you can go first."*

*He smiled as we walked on. The forest was beautiful. The trees were a lush green and formed a canopy overhead. Small sunbeams shown through the branches and leaves, leaving golden puddles of light on the path. Animals scurried in the undergrowth growth, and a light breeze tossed my wavy hair.*

*"What's your favorite color?"*

*"That's what you want to know?" I chuckled.*

*"For starters," he answered.*

*"Red."*

*"Like a stop sign?"*

*I shook my head, "No, darker than that. Like blood red. Crimson."*

*"Are you trying to tell me you're a vampire?"*

*I stuck my tongue out at his teasing. "What's your favorite color then, huh?"*

*"I would have to go with black. So, how long have you been a nurse?"*

*"Three years."*

*"Have you always worked in the emergency room?"*

*I shook my head, "No, I started in the intensive care unit. I worked up there for a year before transferring to the ER. I had done some cross training and liked the environment better. You said you are in research and logistics?"*

*"I did," his jaw tensed as he answered.*

*"What is it that you research?"*

*He thought for a moment before he responded, almost as if*

*he was mulling it over before he finally spoke, "Mostly different companies and corporations."*

*"What sort of companies?"*

*"Those that specialize in specific assets," he replied, clearing his throat. "Do you have any family?"*

*"That was too vague. Answer yours again."*

*"Nope. That's all you get."*

*"Then, maybe I won't answer any more of your questions," I quipped as I turned my nose in the air to snub him. It was childish on my part, but I wanted to know the secrets he was hiding.*

*"Why the sudden interest in my work? You could ask me anything, and that's what you want to focus on?"*

*"Yes."*

*"Why?"*

*I sighed, How was I going to explain this? I absentmindedly started chewing on my lip, trying to come up with an answer.*

*"Did you not learn your lesson last night about that lip?" He stopped walking and stared at me. His expression was serious and sent chills up my spine. Darkness flooded into his eyes as his pupils dilated for the hunt.*

*"We are in the woods, Callen!" I scolded him, promptly letting go of my lip.*

*"That changes nothing. Besides, you started it."*

*A ball tightened in my stomach, and my heart started racing as he took a menacing step toward me. Desire shot through me at the thought of last night - the spankings, the tie, the gag. However, I wasn't about to make it easy for him. I took a step back and eyed him.*

*"You wouldn't dare," I challenged.*

*"Bite that lip again and find out."*

*I took a deep breath as I watched him. He edged toward me ever so slightly, a wicked grin spreading across his face. He put me on edge, but part of me liked the chase. My defiant side won out over the rational, and I sucked my lower lip between my teeth in slow exaggeration.*

If he wanted to play, then we would play, *I thought.*

*A low growl ripped from his chest as he lunged for me, but I was ready, sprinting down the hiking trail as fast as I could.*

*"Oh, just wait and see what happens when I catch you, little mate," he called from behind me.*

*A smile spread across my face as I ran. I heard his feet slamming to the ground behind me. He was much faster than I was, but that wasn't going to stop me. The trail came to a fork, and I veered right. I had no idea where I was going, but Callen wasn't far behind. The roar of the waterfall grew louder as I ran. We had gone full circle to the cabin. I slid to a stop as a cliff loomed ahead. Looking down from the edge of the rock, it was only about a fifteen foot drop to the water, perfect for swimming.*

*In a blink of an eye, Callen grabbed me and rolled us to the ground. He straddled my waist and pinned my hands next to my head. I hooked my right foot up and around his ankle as I bucked my hips forward and pulled my other leg up, kicking my left foot firmly into his abdomen. I caught him off guard, and he plummeted off of the ledge, water splashing into the air when he landed.*

*I pulled myself over just in time to see him resurface, a wide smile spread across my face. "Enjoy your swim, babe! Thought you could use cooling off."*

*"You are in so much trouble when I get back up there," he threatened, but his voice was full of laughter. "I don't believe I taught that move in class."*

*"You didn't," I replied smugly.*

*"Why didn't you tell me you already had training?"*

*"You never asked. Maybe that should've been one of your questions."*

*"I guess so. Any more secrets you're hiding from me?"*

*"Only time will tell." I winked at him as I stood and cannonballed into the water, landing perfectly to send a wave over Callen's head. When I resurfaced, he grabbed my wrist and pulled me to him. Wrapping a hand in my hair, he kissed me, twirling his tongue in my mouth. I placed my hands around his neck as he pulled away and rested his forehead against mine.*

The door swung open to the cement room. I stopped pacing to face Garrett standing in the doorway.

"You're up early," he said, tilting his head. "Excited to get the day started? I know I am."

I scowled at him. Ironically, he looked pleased with that reaction as he stepped farther into the room. Peering around him, I waited for another visitor, but no one came. A nervous tremble shot down my spine from being alone with him.

"Where's Shane?" I questioned, trying to keep the fear from lacing my voice.

"He found himself otherwise preoccupied this morning, so I thought you and I could have a little chat." He stepped toward me, and I involuntarily moved away, backing myself into a wall.

"There's nothing for us to talk about." My heart was hammering in my chest as I appraised him.

He stood a foot in front of me, his eyes raking me up and down. "I think there might be." Grabbing a strand of my hair, he pushed it behind my ear. I twitched my head to the side not wanting him to touch me. "What do you remember from the night we were at the club?"

"What does that matter?"

"Answer the question, and you'll find out."

I swallowed hard, unsure of where he was going with this. "You gave a fake apology for being a pig, and I stupidly forgave you. Then, we drank and danced."

"Mmmm, you are a good dancer," he said, moving even closer. Our chests were almost touching as he looked down at me. "What else?"

"I, ugh, went to the bathroom, and when I came back you gave me another shot before taking me back to the dance floor. I decided to leave when I felt off. That's when I knew you drugged me," I trailed off. Anger was starting to refuel me as the glint in his eye showed how much he was enjoying my discomfort. "Then you took me to the alley and started to choke me since I was still awake."

"And?" he prompted.

"And that's it," I lied. "The rest is blank."

He watched me closely as I stood there taking rapid, shallow breaths. "I don't believe you."

"What was your plan?" I asked, trying to veer the conversation away from what actually happened.

"Were you going to fuck me once I was passed out and leave me god knows where to wake up on my own?"

"Don't be silly," he laughed. "It wouldn't have been any fun that way." He placed a hand on either side of my head and leaned down. I flinched as his breath landed on my neck and turned my head. "The drugs were just to get you out quietly. I knew you wouldn't leave with me on your own, and there was no way I was letting you get away twice."

I tried to move away from him, but he wrapped a hand around my throat and shoved me back into the wall, the impact eliciting a groan. I pushed against his chest in an attempt to extricate myself, but he merely pressed his whole body against mine. I closed my eyes, willing myself to relax. Garrett was the kind to thrive on fear from his victim.

"No, I was going to wait for you to wake up, before I had my way with you. Over and over again," he ran his nose up the side of my neck and into my hair as he spoke. "God, you smell just as good as you did three years ago."

He dropped his hand and took a step back. "However, all the fun I had planned for us never happened. Do you know why?" he asked, cocking his head to the side.

*Callen. That's why,* I thought. "No, I told you already, the last thing I remember was you choking me in the alley."

"What about before the alley?"

"We were inside the club. I could barely walk thanks to you."

"You are a terrible liar."

"I'm not lying."

"You're saying you don't remember the fight that broke out in the club before you ran into the alley on your own?"

"I don't know what you're talking about." My heart hammered faster as he observed my reactions. We were dangerously close to Callen which was the topic I was painstakingly trying to avoid from that night.

"Or that same man who started the fight following us into the alley? Or when he had you up against the wall by the bathroom before that? You're telling me you don't remember the same man being there who whisked you away from the bar the first night I should've had you?"

"No, I don't remember that," I said sternly. "Sounds like you have an active imagination. Are you sure you didn't drug yourself that night?"

"You know," he mused as he stepped toward me again, "all this time I just thought he was a jealous wanna-be-boyfriend, but you know what I think now?" He bent his head back to my ear with the rhetorical question. "I think that nosey asshole is your mate."

"You really are delusional, Garrett."

He laughed, straightening back up, "We both know I'm right."

"If you think you know so much, why don't you go on and tell your boss your theory? I'm sure he'd love for you to waste his time like you are mine. Or, do you actually know how stupid you sound?"

"Oh, I'll tell him," a mischievous smile spread across his face, "but not until you and I have our little playtime first. Once I've had my fill and that temper of yours is utterly shattered, I'll tell him you admitted it."

My chest clenched with his words. He was enjoying himself too much. He brought his hands to rest on my waist, watching me closely. Suddenly, he yanked me forward into him and planted his mouth on mine. I pushed off his chest and slapped my hand across his face with all my strength, making my palm sting. He caught my wrist, twisted it behind my back, and slammed me face first into the wall. I yelped as he twisted tighter, straining the connective tissues in my arm.

"You know what I find so intoxicating about you?" he asked as I poorly tried to extricate myself. "Even when you know you're beat, you fight even harder, and damn does it turn me on." He grabbed my other hand and pressed it to the front on his pants, forcing me to cup his erection.

"Get the fuck off me!" I yelled as I started thrashing against him.

He flipped me back around and held me to the wall by my throat, compressing my airway. His other hand dipped between my thighs and squeezed. My fingers shot to his hand holding my neck, and I dug my nails into his skin. He grunted as he threw me to the ground, small cuts weeping from his hand.

"Yeah, just like that, princess."

I jumped to my feet and ran out the open door, gasping for breath as I did so. I heard him cursing as I sprinted down the hall. I had no idea where I was headed, but anywhere else would be an improvement. I rounded the corner at the end of the hall and ran flat into Shane, both of us toppling to the ground.

"Lacey?" he asked in surprise, sitting up.

Garrett came around the corner looking furious. My eyes bulged as I scampered to my feet. I turned to run, but a hand wrapped around my ankle, tripping me. Someone climbed on top of my back and shoved a knee between my shoulder blades to hold me in place.

"Get the fuck off me!" I screamed as I tried to wiggle out from beneath the man pinning me to the floor.

"Calm down!" Shane barked above me.

I kicked and bucked trying to knock him off. He slid his knee to my side and straddled my waist as he flipped me over to face him. He grappled for control of my hands as I tried to strike him, panic wholly consuming me.

"Lacey, fucking stop!" He pinned my hands down by my head. I pulled my foot up to hook his ankle, but he tucked his knees up tight. "Lacey!"

Defeated, I finally stopped trying to throw him off me and laid there breathing heavily beneath him. "Let me go. Please, just let me go."

"What happened to your neck?" he asked as he scanned my features.

"Nothing," I answered with a shake of my head.

"Garrett what the hell did you do?" he demanded harshly, turning his head toward him.

Garrett shrugged, "We just had a small chat."

Shane looked furious, but as he started to retort, I interrupted, "Shane, please get off of me."

He gave me a long look before standing with a nod, resigning the conversation. He offered a hand to help me up, but I ignored it and stood on my own. I wrapped my arms around myself as if I could hold the fear inside that way. Swallowing painfully, I looked between the two men, unable to tell who was angrier at that moment.

"Can you just take me back to my room? Alone." I added. Garrett reached a hand out to grab my arm, and I jumped backward. "Not you!"

He smirked at my reaction. I knew letting him see how distraught he made me was a mistake, but I needed time to settle before I could muster any more strength to fight him. The small taste of what he had planned rocked me to my core, and he had barely scratched the surface.

"We, unfortunately, are due in the lab at any moment," Shane replied. "Garrett, after you." He gestured down the hall as he gently grabbed my upper arm. I let him lead me, since I didn't think I could will my legs to walk in that direction on their own accord.

The closer we got, the more I felt like I needed to retch again. This was the beginning of the end. Either I gave Callen up, or I gave myself up. These people were trying to break me, but I had to be the stronger one. *You can survive this,* I thought as the door to the lab clicked open.

# CHAPTER TWELVE

### *Dosed*

D r. Reid was at her desk when we arrived. Shane led me over to the vertical table from yesterday before releasing my arm and striding over to Dr. Reid. She shook her head as he whispered something in her ear. Garrett stood a few feet away, watching me coldly, almost daring me to run again. The fear had finally ebbed as a fresh wave of indignation washed over me. Hatred for him seeped from my every pore, and I did nothing to hide the glare of disdain in my eyes.

Dr. Reid strode toward us with a stoney expression. "Garrett, go grab our guest a bottle of water," she ordered. "She looks dehydrated, and I don't want anything to skew our results this time."

Garrett merely rolled his eyes as he left the lab, not bothering to argue. When the door clicked closed, Dr. Reid turned her attention toward me, "Let me see your neck."

Pressing a hand to my chin, she delicately moved my head back and forth in examination before placing her hands gently on each side to palpate the tissues of my throat. I stiffened with the pain and bit my cheek to hold in a grunt of discomfort.

"You have some severe bruising and swelling. When did the injury occur?" she questioned with a furrowed brow.

"Just a few minutes ago," I answered.

"Walk me through what transpired," she instructed as she continued my examination.

I shook my head in refusal. I had no desire to rehash the latest events of Garrett's never ending attacks. It wouldn't change my situation if I told her, and I desperately wanted to focus on anything besides his hands around my throat and his erection pressed into my hand.

"She came flying down the hallway in a panic. Garrett was chasing after her. She won't say what happened," Shane informed her.

I shot him a dirty look that he paid no mind to.

"Are you injured anywhere else?" Dr. Reid asked with a knowing look.

"No." It wasn't a lie. Physically I was fine, and there is nothing she could do to repair the mental and emotional damages endured. "Can we just get on with it?"

"Does that mean you have reconsidered the memory lock down?" She sounded hopeful with her question, but her expectant look immediately faded as she took in my disheartened expression.

"I'm not going to tell or show you anything, Dr. Reid. Hooking me up to that device is just going to waste everyone's time.

"Dammit, Lacey, enough is enough," Shane cussed.

"I agree. Enough is enough. I am done with all of these fucking games!"

"This isn't a game! You need to cooperate and save yourself."

I was shaking with frustration. Dr. Reid looked between us as we argued. Both of our faces were red with flaring tempers.

"I'm going to say this one last fucking time. I would rather die than be in this godforsaken place any longer or help you do this to any other marked one, whether it's my mate you insist exists or some random bitch your informant picks up off the street. I am a person just as much as any of you. I am not some guinea pig to be used for experiments, a punching bag you can beat into submission, or some whore to be fucked into spilling her secrets! Now, you can either hook me up to all those machines to look at a blank screen, lock me up with that bastard, or put a bullet in my head, because I'm not telling any of you another goddamn thing about my life!"

A slow clap started from behind. I turned to see C walking toward me, a smile on his face. "That was quite a performance. If only that powerful volition could save you now, but unfortunately for you, I *am* in a mood to play games."

Garrett stepped into the room with the bottle of water he was told to fetch. "I could hear her rant halfway down the hallway."

"I do think this young woman needs a reminder on how a lady behaves. Words such as whore, fuck, and bastard are for men to use, sweetheart," C cocked his head to the side as he gauged my reaction.

"You have some real backward ideas on men and women. I don't know if you are aware of it or not but it's the twenty-first century, the whole 'women are to be seen and not heard' standard doesn't exist anymore." I punctuated my statement with an eye roll, his belittling nickname grinding my already thin patience into non-existence.

C reached his hand up and backhanded me unexpectedly, sending my body crashing sideways to the floor. With a twist, I caught myself on my hands and knees, looking up just in time to see Shane stomp out the lab door.

"That's enough!" Dr. Reid barked. "You two men sit down while I hook her up to everything. I don't want her anymore damaged than she already is before the experiment." She continued mumbling under her breath about "altered results" and "testosterone filled jackasses" as she motioned to the table.

I backed up and allowed her to apply the restraints. When she was satisfied that I was unable to extricate myself, she started placing all the equipment. I remained silent throughout the ordeal and stared straight ahead. I wanted this done as soon as possible. Garrett and his boss were conversing at the computer desk deep in discussion while she worked. Finally, everything was in place - minus the blackout eyewear.

"We will put the goggles on when we are ready to begin. I just need to sync your monitors to the computer and obtain a baseline of the readouts," she said as she walked over to her desk.

The room was silent except for the clicking of her keyboard and mouse. The men stood beside her appraising me from the corners of their eyes as they discussed with one another in hushed voices. To my surprise, Shane came back into the room, barrelling toward me with a determined expression, his colleagues oblivious to the item clutched discreetly in his hand. Stopping inches in front of me, he displayed his smuggled object: a loaded syringe.

My eyes went wide, flickering between his stoney glare and the yellow-filled syringe. "What the hell is th—" my question broke off into a grunt as he roughly stabbed a needle through my pants and into the side of my thigh.

"If you won't save yourself, then I'll do it for you," he hissed into my ear as he withdrew the needle. Burning shot through my leg as the substance dispersed.

"Shane! What did you do?" Dr. Reid demanded.

"I gave her the truth serum your team has been working

on."

"You what?" Dr. Reid and I screamed in unison.

"That is experimental and has never been given to a marked one," she scolded.

If looks could kill, Shane would have dropped dead from the daggers I was shooting his way. "You had no right to do that," I said as a sluggish calm settled over my body.

"You refused to cooperate. You didn't leave me a choice," he growled so low I doubt the others could hear.

"Well, what's done is done," she said. "The chemicals shouldn't interfere with anything, and we honestly may get more information from her this way."

"How long does it last?" C questioned.

Dr. Reid shrugged, "I don't know. In normal hosts, it lasts about twenty four hours, but I'm not certain if the timeframe would be altered with a marked one. Afterall, the HyperStem was still active in her system as of yesterday. I couldn't say if this will have a prolonged effect as well."

My entire body felt heavy and a fog clouded my thoughts. Time seemed to move in slow motion as they conversed. The speculums held my eyes open, preventing the lids from drooping in my dazed state, but my vision blurred with the slightest movement of my head. Despite the overbearing feeling of weakness, I felt a calmness wash over, diluting the previous panic.

"What's...what's, uhm...what's in it?" I finally managed to articulate.

"It's a compound medication. It contains sodium pentothal, donepezil, and amphetamines. Previous studies showed that test subjects that were given sodium pentathol were more inclined to answer questions, while donepezil is a cholinesterase inhibitor that promotes and preserves memory functioning. The amphetamine is similar to adderall in its role by assisting the subject to focus while under the effects of the Pentothal," Dr. Reid answered.

"Oh," I muttered at her explanation. My head felt heavy, my thoughts groggy as I sifted through the mental fog.

"I think we should get started," she spoke. Shane grabbed the glasses and placed them over my eyes. The total blackness pushed me toward the edge of sleep, yet my body kept jerking itself awake.

"We will start slow like last time. Lacey, what's your favorite hobby?"

"Reading," I spoke aloud as the thought of being curled on the couch with a soft blanket, book, and glass of wine poked forward. "I like to read."

"Yes, I see. That is quite a large novel you have there. Can you tell me what that book is about?"

I could practically feel the thick, rough pages between my fingers as I turned the page. The smell of paper and ink flooded my senses.

"It was about a woman living in France during the revolution. She was fighting on the side of the resistance. She died," I sighed.

"It looks like she was beheaded?" Dr. Reid prompted.

"Yeah, she was. That was the last scene of the book." *Why am I telling her that? Stop talking!* I scolded myself.

"I see. Besides the marked one at the hospital, have you ever witnessed anyone dying?"

"I've lost count."

"Anyone you knew personally?"

"No, not that I saw die; but my parents died when I was

seventeen," I rambled.

"Tell me what happened."

"Car crash." That was all I was able to say before the memory took me.

*My pharmacology teacher stood at the front of the room dismissing the class after our latest three hour lecture. "Ms. Reynolds, I need a word before you leave," she called as I packed my things.*

*"Yes, ma'am?" I joined her after the last student exited the room.*

*"If you don't mind, I need you to come with me to the Dean's office,"*

*"I'm sorry. Did I do something wrong?"*

*"Of course not. We have some news to discuss with you."*

*My stomach knotted as I followed her to the office. The Dean of the School of Nursing only requested an audience for serious matters. I was an excellent student, top of my class in fact. I graduated highschool at sixteen and was accepted directly into the program.* Maybe it's where I turn eighteen next month? They probably just have some paperwork for me or something. *I tried to calm myself with encouraging thoughts, yet my heart raced on.*

*We entered the office to find Dean Garner waiting for us. "Ms. Reynolds, please have a seat," she greeted, her face grim and mouth pressed into a thin line.*

*I sat on the edge of my seat and waited patiently for her to continue, too nervous to break the silence myself.*

*"I am not exactly sure how to say this, so I am not going to beat around the bush...there has been an accident involving your parents."*

*"Excuse me?" I was confused. This was the last thing I*

*expected.*

*"There was a multi-car collision on I85 a few hours ago. Your parents car was knocked off the bridge - along with three others - when a semi failed to stop. There were no survivors."*

*I sat there staring at her in disbelief. "No. I talked to them this morning. They were going to pick me up for dinner this evening."*

*"I'm very sorry, Lacey. It took a while to extricate the vehicles. Your parents were some of the first to be identified. Since you are a minor and the only next of kin, the school was notified by police."*

*My heart felt as if it had been ripped from my chest. Tears wept from my eyes as a sob escaped.*

I tore myself from the memory and recentered to the present. "That's fucking private!" I did my best to yell, my breathing heavy and pulse booming with the recollection.

"I'm very sorry for your loss, Lacey," Dr. Reid spoke. "Take a deep breath to steady yourself. It's just a memory. I know it feels very real right now."

"Stop pitying me," I snapped. I tugged on my arms to reposition myself, but the restraints held fast, inhibiting any movement.

"Let's focus on something else. Do you like being a nurse?"

"I like certain aspects of it. Others not so much," I replied, automatically, the compulsion to speak overriding my irritation.

"Tell me about your favorite day at work."

"It'd been a busy day in the ER. All the beds were full, patients were lined up in the hallway, and even more were stacked in the lobby."

"What happened to make it so special?"

*The EMS radio sounded at the desk. Sirens blared in the background as the medic called in, "Chad County Medic eight to Ridgeview ER."*

*Katie pressed the com to reply as she wrote down the report, and I moved closer to the radio to hear better. "This is Ridgeview, go ahead Medic eight."*

*"Medic eight inbound emergency traffic with highly suspect CVA. Patient is a forty-seven year old male with complete left side limb immobility, left sided facial droop, and expressive aphasia. Daughter on scene reported last known well was forty-five minutes ago. Symptoms appeared spontaneously while the patient was eating lunch. Bilateral eighteen gauge AC IVs established. Heart rate eighty, BP 146 over eighty four, respers normal with a sat of ninety nine percent on room air. ETA one minute. Anything further?"*

*I shook my head, and Katie answered, "Negative. WPIS four-oh-six out. Room upon arrival."*

*"Brent, get trauma room three set up for an acute CVA. Katie, call triage to bring the scale down. I want an accurate weight on him first thing, not one from the bed. Then call CT to clear the table. I'll start mixing the tPA."*

*We all scattered to start on our tasks immediately. I admitted a temporary patient into the AcuDose under today's generated name: Blue, Blue, removed the kit of tPA, and began reconstituting the powder. The vial held one hundred milligrams at a one to one concentration. The max dose a patient with a pulse could receive was ninety milligrams, so I pulled off ten milliliters as waste.*

*I arrived in the room with the ambulance. The patient was alert and looking around, the left side of his body slumped on the stretcher. The medic began giving report to the primary nurse and doctor while I spoke with the patient. "Sir, can you tell me your name?"*

*"Mmmm....Maaa," he tried to respond. Frustration filled his eyes with his inability to speak. He knew what he wanted to say, but the words wouldn't compute.*

*"That's okay," I said as I peered at the EMS paperwork. "Is your name Mark?"*

*He nodded his head weakly in confirmation. "Okay, Mark, we need to get a very accurate weight on you. Brent and I are going to help you stand on this scale before we get in the bed. We will support you until your right leg bears all your weight. Okay?"*

*When he nodded his head in agreement, Brent and I helped him sit up on the side of the stretcher, placed his arms around our shoulders, and hoisted him onto the scale. The read out was 235. I called the weight to the scribe and estimated his height to be six feet and two inches to which the patient grunted in approval. Brent and I pivoted the patient onto the ER bed where we began hooking him to the cardiac equipment and performing an NIH Stroke Assessment - ranking him a nineteen - while another nurse drew his blood.*

*"Let's get him to CT to rule out a bleed," I barked when we had all finished. Brent rolled the patient out in accompaniment with the primary nurse. Turning to me, Dr. Branley asked if the tPA was ready.*

*"Yes, sir," I affirmed. "His weight qualifies for the max dose of ninety milligrams. I'll set the pump up now, so it's ready to go when you give the order."*

*"Excellent," he replied as he left the room to review the scans and consult neurology.*

*I programmed the pump to deliver a nine milligram bolus followed by an eighty one milligram infusion over one hour. Shortly, the patient returned, followed by Dr. Branley. With a bleed officially ruled out, he gave the order to administer the tPA. I connected the IV tubing to the access in his left arm after checking its patency and started the medication.*

*Fifteen minutes into the infusion, the patient was able to tell us his full name and birthday with only mild stammering. When his daughter walked into the room, he was able to greet her with a full smile. By the time the infusion was halfway completed, the patient had regained his full ability to speak and was able to move the left side of his body. Tears of relief streamed down his daughter's cheeks. Brent and I high-fived with the reversal of his symptoms. Ten minutes later, the patient had returned to baseline with no residual effects from the stroke. He had to be admitted for further testing and monitoring, but his outcome was expected to be excellent. Not only did we save a life, we performed a miracle.*

"That's quite impressive, Lacey. Clot busters are a miraculous drug," Dr. Reid commented, waking me to the present.

"Yes. It was fascinating to see it happen." *Stop showing them your memories!* I yelled internally. "But, I doubt the patient would be happy to know some strangers are prying into his medical history."

"It's okay. We are all professionals here," she assured.

The fog was heavy in my mind. *You have got to control it before it's too late,* I told myself. As if on command, the fog thinned to a hazy hue.

"Back to our original purpose...Where did you meet your mate?"

The studio from the self-defense class solidified in my mind. *"My name is..." the tall brunette began her spiel to open the class...*

"No!" I screamed as the image cut to blackness. "I won't show you that."

"Lacey, think of the studio," she instructed.

My brain registered the prompt and let the building pull forward again.

"Stop it!" I thrashed against the restraints as I screamed. Miraculously, I somehow managed to dislodge my right arm from its prison. I grabbed the goggles and ripped them off my face, gasping with panic as the elastic band compressed my bruised neck from the movements.

Shane grabbed my arm and held it tightly. "Lacey, stop. You're going to hurt yourself."

"I don't care. I don't care." I repeated as he tried to repair the strap. The haze around me started to dissipate some more, and I felt like I was able to regain control of my mind.

"I thought you said twenty-four hours?" C questioned.

"I did," Dr. Reid responded. "It's been less than an hour, and she's already able to resist the cocktail. That's fascinating; it had the opposite effect of the HyperStem injection."

"Well, give her some more," he interjected.

"I can't. That was the last dose. The compound takes about two weeks to prepare. We had halted the synthesis to focus on other compounds that were more in demand."

"So where does that leave us?" he asked.

She shrugged in return, "She's already proven the ability to memory select while sober, and now, she is able to dispel a chemical induced compulsion. Unfortunately, I don't believe she is going to allow further access to any other memories."

"What about while she's dreaming?" Shane interjected.

"Shane, it's like I told you before, the machine is designed for memories not dreams. Even if an image is displayed, there's no telling if it's real or not. Memories and dreams occur in different places in the brain." Dr. Reid had moved over to Shane and I as she spoke. "If she won't cooperate, there's nothing else I can do at the moment. I'll need a few weeks in order to adjust things before I'm willing to try neuronal mapping with the subconscious."

Dr. Reid started unhooking her devices as I let out a small sigh of relief. Stage one of today was over. *Now for the hard part,* I thought.

"That is not acceptable!" C yelled. "I want her mate. We've had her for a week, yet we are no closer to finding him than we were before she was brought in."

"I don't know what to tell you," Dr. Reid snapped. "I'm doing everything I can with what I have to work with. Get her off of there, Shane," she instructed as she strode back to the desk.

Shane removed the remaining equipment and restraints. I stretched my muscles as I stepped away from the table. My mind felt slow as if I hadn't slept in a few days, but I was in control now the haziness retreating further with each passing minute.

"Take her to her room," C ordered. Shane grabbed my arm and headed toward the door with Garrett trailing close behind us. "Garrett, a word."

We continued just the two of us. I didn't resist his urging as I was eager to put as much distance between the lab, its inhabitants, and myself as possible. When we arrived, Shane scanned his badge to my room and shoved me inside.

"You don't have to be so rough. I know you're mad, but still," I scolded him.

"How'd you do it?" he demanded.

"How did I do what?"

"How did you stop the serum? It's like you just cut it off, flipped a switch, and poof - it's gone."

"I don't know." I shrugged my shoulders. "I told myself to stop, then I did. I don't know how to explain it."

"You told yourself to stop? And, your brain just did?" he asked with a mix of mockery and indignation.

I nodded, "I guess. It's like I could recognize it wasn't actually happening, so I just cut it off."

"You could tell the difference between a live memory and reality?"

"Can't everybody?" I was confused as to why he didn't understand.

"No. No one has ever stopped memories like you do. They all live it out until the natural conclusion, and absolutely no one has been able to resist the serum. Subjects normally babble on for hours about anything and everything if they aren't asked specific questions to utilize the compulsion to speak."

"Great. Just one other thing for your boss to want from me. Thanks," I snapped as my temper rose to the surface again. "You had no right to do that. I told you it was my decision on what would happen, not yours."

"I had to do something. You are too stubborn for your own good! If I was your mate, I would never—"

I interrupted, "Well, you're not!"

"Don't you think I know that?"

I closed my eyes and took a deep breath, "I don't know what you think, Shane. I'm lost when it comes to you."

"Well, that makes two of us."

He walked out of the room and slammed the door behind him. The lock engaged, and I threw myself on the bed, exhausted and craving sleep.

# CHAPTER THIRTEEN

## Devoured

*A*fter our swim, Callen and I returned to the cabin hand in hand. "Do you want to shower before I make us some lunch?" he asked.

"A shower sounds great," I answered as I headed toward the bedroom. I stopped halfway down the hall when I realized he wasn't following me. "What about you? Don't you want to shower?"

"I will after you get done," he replied with a smile.

I knew he was trying to be respectful by giving me space, but I was hoping to continue what had started in the water. Just the thought of his hands running over my body and his mouth on mine were enough to turn me on. The simple idea of this man was an aphrodisiac.

Did I not have the same effect on him? Of course not. *The doubt cut deep.* Maybe he doesn't want me as much as I want him?

"Hey, what's going on inside your head?" He came down the hall and gently cupped my cheek into his palm.

"Nothing. It's silly. I'm just going to go get cleaned up," I answered as I tried to continue to the bedroom, but he held me in place.

*"I highly doubt it is silly," he pressed.*

*"Well, it's just...when we were in the water...I just thought..." I trailed off, embarrassment keeping me from finishing my sentence. I felt like an idiot unable to articulate a clear thought.*

*"You thought what?" he asked, confused.*

*I closed my eyes and took a deep breath to steady my nerves. "You don't want to come with me."*

*He laughed, "That's what's wrong? You think I don't want to shower with you?"*

*"Well, yeah," I answered, irritated by his reaction. "Don't laugh at me!"*

*"Why would I not want to shower with you?"*

*"Because you don't want me like I want you. I mean, I know I don't have a lot of experience, but I thought you enjoyed it..."*

*"You can't honestly think that, Lacey," he said, sounding surprised.*

*"Why wouldn't I? Any little thought of you drives me insane, and don't even get me started about how it feels when you touch me. You don't even want to be with me after I practically had my tongue down your throat five minutes ago!" I was angry from feeling vulnerable. Vulnerability was not something I was used to experiencing, and I hated that this man had such control over my body.*

*A serious expression shadowed his face. If I was angry, then he was furious. "You think I don't want you? Christ, I want you in every way possible." He towered over me, eyes boring into mine. "If I had my way, you'd spend the rest of your life naked in my bed."*

*My heart fluttered with his admission. My breathing increased as lust filled me and dampness spread between my legs.*

*"You bring out desires in me that I don't know how you'll react to. I'm doing my best to keep them contained," he continued.*

Glancing down, I noticed the bulge forming in his pants. I looked back up to see him staring at me, gauging my reaction.

"Maybe I don't want you to contain them."

"Lacey, I—" he began, but his sentence turned to a groan as I wrapped my hand around his hard length through his pants. I rubbed him as I pulled his head down to mine and plunged my tongue into his mouth, twirling it with each stroke of my hand. He wrapped his arms around my waist and pulled me to his body as he took us the remainder of the way to the bathroom.

Callen pushed into the shower and turned the hot water on as we kicked off our sopping wet shoes. Setting me back on my feet, he stripped me of my shirt and bra. My breasts bounced free of the fabric, permitting him to take a nipple into his mouth. He sucked and nibbled, massaging the other in his hand. I moaned as I slid my hands down his neck and chest, clawing at his soaked shirt until I was able to free it from his body.

He dropped to his knees and removed my leggings and panties in one swoop, followed by him planting kisses along my thighs and sliding his fingers between my folds. I moaned with his touch, my peaked desire spreading as he rubbed.

"You are so unbelievably wet. Is this what I do to you?"

"Y-yes," I stuttered out as he massaged my clit. He slid a finger inside and gently started thrusting it in and out.

"When do I do this to you?"

I moaned his name as he slid in a second finger. I pushed my hips forward, craving the fullness of him inside me.

"Answer me or I'll stop," he mused as he pulled his hand from me.

I whimpered, feeling empty with the loss of his fingers. "All the time."

"What's all the time?" he asked, pressing his thumb against

*my clit and slowly circling it.*

*"You make me wet all the time, when you look at me, when you touch me, when I—"* I broke off as he slid two fingers back inside.

*"When you what?"*

*"When I think about you."* The hot water flowed over my naked body, but my nipples were firm from arousal. I brought my hands up and tweaked them as he curled his fingers inside me.

*"Stop touching yourself. Those are mine."*

*"Excuse me?"* Did he really think he could tell me not to pleasure my own body? *I internally scoffed.*

*"I didn't stutter. Stop touching what's mine."* He pulled his fingers out and plunged them deep back into me, exciting his point.

I cried out and wrapped my fingers in his hair, desperate for something to hold. As long as he didn't stop, I'd do anything he demanded, his unwavering control only heightening the pleasure.

*"Good girl,"* he purred. Callen brought his mouth down to my core and licked, sending a shudder up my spine. Nothing in my life had ever felt this good. He pulled his fingers from me while he devoured me with his tongue, placing his hand on my backside and parting my cheeks.

A finger pressed into my rear entrance, and I gasped, *"What are you doing?"* I tried to wiggle away, but he held me firmly in place.

*"Just relax,"* he instructed between licks.

*"Callen, I don't—ahh."* He nipped my clit with his teeth, causing my sentence to break with the initial shock of pain; however, my eyes rolled backward with the following lick of his tongue. Spasms rocked through my core with the onslaught of heightened pleasure brought about by the snippet of pain.

*"Trust me, just relax. I'll make it feel good,"* he coaxed,

*adding a slighter pressure to my entrance.*

*I took a breath and willed my muscles to unclench. My body wanted the pleasure that his words promised, and, deep down, I knew my subconscious wanted to please him. I never saw myself as a submissive person, yet here I was, offering myself to his every demand.*

*"That's my girl," he praised as the tip of his finger slid through the tight ring of muscle. He moved deliberately slow, allowing my body to adjust as he teased me. He pulled out and placed his hand back between my legs. Two fingers plunged into me causing me to cry out once again. Rocking my hips, I rode his fingers, demanding more. He placed my right leg over his shoulder, displaying my center fully to him. "God, you are so fucking beautiful."*

*I bounced on his fingers as Callen watched me unravel, his eyes burning with lust. Suddenly, he twisted his hand and plunged his small finger into my ass.*

*"Oh, fuck," I screamed.*

*Shock morphed into intense pleasure as he fingered both my holes, his tongue lapping at my clit. My body was wracked with an overstimulation that I never wanted to end. The warm ball that had been forming in the pit of my stomach erupted, my left knee giving out as my climax tore through me. I fisted his hair and screamed his name, losing control. Callen held me up against the wall as he drew out my orgasm, my walls quivering around his fingers as he stroked them. Until finally, he withdrew and stood in front of me.*

*Crushing his mouth to mine, I reveled in the taste of myself on his tongue. He broke the kiss, spun me around and pushed my chest into the wall. Kicking my feet apart, Callen positioned himself between my legs while his shorts dropped to the floor. I could feel his tip pressing into me, and all I wanted was more. With one hard thrust, he speared himself inside.*

Callen buried his nose in my hair, grunting in pleasure. "Fuck, I don't think I'll ever get used to how tight you are," he muttered as he slipped his hands around to fondle my breasts, arching me backward. He pinched and pulled my nipples in time with his thrusts. The way he held me, my clit rubbed back and forth on the wall. Another orgasm grew, and I felt myself clenching around his massive length with the first waves.

"Are you going to come again for me, baby?"

"Oh god, oh god," I moaned, my second orgasm tearing through me at the sound of his voice. My entire body shook as I came. When I didn't think I could take much more, Callen wrapped an arm around my chest, holding me firmly to his front. His other hand fisted my hair, the control allowing him to take me harder. I whimpered as I dug my nails into his forearm. My core gripped him devastatingly tighter as I felt his warmth jet into me, a growl emitting from his throat.

Callen pressed me flat against the shower wall, pinning me in place while we both recovered. When our breathing was almost back to normal, he turned me around and gently kissed my lips. "You drive me crazy in every possible way. You know that?"

I laughed into his chest with the same feeling. "We probably should get cleaned up before the hot water runs out."

"Probably," he agreed after kissing me one last time.

The next evening we lounged on the couch in our pajamas and watched a movie with popcorn and a warm blanket. He stroked my hair affectionately as I snuggled into his chest. Nothing had ever felt so right in my life. I wanted to stay like this forever, but the weekend had come to an end.

"Will we be going home in the morning?" I asked to broach the subject.

*He sighed, moving his hand down to rest on the curve of my waist. "Unfortunately, I have a meeting to attend right after we get back. We will have to leave after breakfast. What's your schedule this week?"*

*"Well, Claire covered me today, so I only have Tuesday and Wednesday left."*

*"I'll pick you up Wednesday after work then."*

*"Are you asking or telling?"*

*"Telling," he said matter of factly.*

*"Maybe I have plans. Did you ever consider that?" I raised my eyebrow in question.*

*"Cancel them," he shrugged.*

*"I think the correct etiquette here is, 'Lacey, would you like to go on a date with me after work Wednesday?'," I teased.*

*He rolled his eyes. "Would you?"*

*"Would I what?"*

*"Would you like to go on a date with me Wednesday after work?"*

*I feigned surprise, "Oh, how sweet for you to ask. I would love to go out with you."*

*"Why are you so difficult?" He tried to sound irritated, but it wasn't working.*

*"I have no idea what you are talking about."*

*Callen grabbed me and flipped us over. His body pinned my back to the couch as he pulled my wrists together in one hand. The movement caught me by surprise, and I gasped.*

*"I do have a question for you though," he purred into my ear.*

*"What's that?" I asked breathlessly. Having him control me like this sent sparks of desire straight to my core. My arousal spread*

between my legs as he shifted his hips into mine.

"Are you ticklish?" he asked coyly.

"No!" I shrieked as his free hand tickled under my arms and over my stomach. I arched my hips trying to kick him off, but he countered his weight back into me. I wiggled below him, howling from laughter. He finally stopped and pressed his forehead to mine, both of us panting. Our lips met gently, sensuality filling the moment. I could feel his growing excitement press against me as our kisses deepened.

He released my wrists, and I pulled his sweats and boxers to his knees to free his erection. A fresh flood of wetness soaked my panties as I grasped him, my body responding to every inch of this man. His hand slid between my legs, and I moaned as he rubbed me through my panties, his touch driving me crazy.

I arched my hips and begged, "Callen, please." I needed him inside me, to fill me, to love me.

As if he needed me just as bad, he pushed my panties to the side and shoved inside me. I gasped at the wonderful intrusion and dug my nails into his back. It took several thrusts to work his way fully in, my core stretching in an attempt to suddenly accommodate his size. The hard lines between pain and pleasure blurred, but it only made me want him more. Callen groaned as we rocked, losing ourselves in one another. I wrapped my legs around his hips and dug my heels into his backside, urging him deeper and harder.

"Fuck, you feel so good," he exclaimed as he sat up on his knees, still thrusting in and out. He pushed his shirt up over my chest to free my breasts, their flesh bouncing as we gyrated together. The familiar ball of impending climax was building deep inside my lower stomach. He pushed my knees to my shoulders and impaled me deeper than ever before. I could feel him smacking against my womb with every movement as I took him.

"Oh my god," I moaned as my hands shot to my face, my

*body overwhelmed from the intensity.*

*Callen grabbed a wrist in each hand and pinned them to the couch by my head. "Don't you dare. I want to watch you come all over me."*

*"Callen, it's...god...it's too much...I can't...you're too big," I whimpered beneath him. Despite my claims I rocked with him. Each smack of him sent a pleasuring pain through me. It felt like he was deep into my abdomen, the feeling of utter fullness driving me crazy.*

*"Fucking take me, Lacey. Fucking. Take. All. Of. Me," he demanded, enunciating every word as he thrust into me over and over again.*

*I shattered around him, my back arching with the intensity of my orgasm. He held my wrists tight as he relentlessly drove into me while I clenched around him. I cried out his name through gritted teeth. My entire body convulsed underneath him as he drew out my climax. He pushed my knees apart to loom over me with a piercing look, penetrating me harder as his own release came. He spurted into me while my residual ripples pulsed around him. When he collapsed on top of me, he relinquished my wrists. I wrapped my arms around him and held his head to my breast as we panted against each other.*

*"So, I take that as a yes."*

*"Yes what?" I asked in confusion.*

*"That you're ticklish."*

*I laughed and playfully smacked him on the arm. This moment was perfect. Just the two of us holding one another. I wanted to freeze time and stay here forever. I knew once we left the sanctuary of Paradise that reality would set back in, so I held him close and decided to enjoy the time we had while it lasted.*

# CHAPTER FOURTEEN

## *Disciplined*

*I* respected the fact that we both had lives and history before one another, but I couldn't shake the feeling that Callen was hiding a huge part of his life from me. Between the elusive answers about work and the odd phone call I overheard, my imagination was running wild. If I was ever going to trust him, I needed him to be honest with me. But, will he be honest with me? I didn't have the answer to that question. I sighed as we drove down the road back to my apartment. Callen had a meeting scheduled for right after he dropped me off.

I could follow him and see what he's up to, *I thought*. I hated when he did that to me though. *I discarded that idea just like I did the idea of going through his phone last night while he slept.* How could I expect him to trust me, if my actions weren't trustworthy?

*"What are you thinking about so diligently over there?" he asked, breaking my internal debate.*

*I sighed again, it was now or never. "I need to talk to you about something, but it's going to make you mad."*

*"I won't get mad. If something's wrong, I need to know. Trust me."*

*"That's the problem. I don't trust anyone," I shook my head as I spoke. "Plus, it's not the asking that you are going to be mad about. It's what I did that's probably going to piss you off."*

*I peeked up at him not knowing what to expect. Callen didn't say a word as he stared out the windshield. He pulled off the road and parked the truck behind an abandoned convenience store in the middle of nowhere. My heart rate increased as he cut the engine and turned to look at me.*

*"Let's not put the cart before the horse. What's going on?"*

*I took a deep breath, "When we got to the cabin that first day, I originally came out of the bedroom and you were gone. I heard you out on the porch and realized you were on the phone. I didn't plan on eavesdropping, but I heard you talking about me. So, I did." I shifted uncomfortably in my seat before continuing. "Then, I went back in the room and acted like nothing happened. The next day you were really evasive about your work. So, that, combined with everything else, has me worried. What kind of person has lists for investigations? Or talks about murdering someone so nonchalantly? Why would you tell anyone about what happened at the club? And, why would you tell someone about my mark? You know nobody can know about us!"*

*Callen sat stoically silent, listening to my ramblings.*

*"I don't expect you to tell me everything about your life, but I know you are hiding some pretty big aspects. I don't want to be one of those crazy women that stalks their boyfriend or goes through their phone and messages. I'm so desperate I considered it, but I don't want to be that person, so—'*

*"Lacey," he interrupted me, "slow down. There's a few things to address."*

*I waited for him to continue, but he only stared at me with a look I couldn't quite identify.*

*"First, I am not your boyfriend, and you are not my girlfriend. Let's get that straightened out real quick."*

*My cheeks flushed as I chewed on my lip. "You're right. I'm sorry. Just because of this weekend doesn't mean that... " I trailed off not knowing how to finish the sentence. I felt like a fool jumping the gun about a relationship.* He said he wanted me, but that doesn't mean he meant long term. This is so embarrassing. You should've stayed quiet, *I reprimanded myself. I averted my eyes to my lap where my fingers fiddled with the hem of my sundress. "I think you should just take me home, Callen."*

*"Lacey, get out of the truck."*

*"What? You can't—"*

*"I won't say it again. Get out of the truck." Callen was furious. I expected him to be mad about my snooping, but this was beyond what I imagined. I opened the door and hopped out as Callen did the same; however, the previous apprehension I felt was gone. Instead, I was angry.* How dare he leave me in the middle of nowhere! *I opened the back door, yanked my bag out, and turned to stomp off.*

*"What the hell do you think you're doing?" Callen yelled as he came around the truck.*

*"Well, I am not going to let you leave me here without at least taking my stuff with me!" I shoved past him to march off, but he grabbed the strap of my bag and pulled me backward.*

*"You're not going anywhere," he said as he pushed me up against the passenger side door.*

*"What do you care? You just made it clear I'm not your girlfriend. I wouldn't have let you fuck me all weekend if I knew—"*

*"That's right. You're not my girlfriend," he yelled over me, "You're more than that. You're my soulmate, and I will not have you belittle yourself to the temporary, weak title of 'girlfriend.' You were made for me, and I will never let you go. I don't care how hard you try to push me away. I told you, you are mine, and I fucking mean it, Lacey."*

*I swallowed hard at his admission, the anger simmering inside me as we stood glaring at one another.*

"Now," he demanded, "get in the backseat."

"Callen, I—"

"Woman, you are desperately testing my patience. Get in the backseat, or, I swear to god, I will pick you up and throw you back there myself."

He pinched the bridge of his nose as he spoke in an attempt to rein in his temper. I chewed on my lip as I contemplated his seriousness. When he looked back at me, his expression darkened. He moved to grab me, but I held my hands up.

"Fine!"

I climbed into the back and slid over as he joined me. He slammed the door behind him and turned sideways in the seat. "Take off your underwear."

I gaped at him in shock, "What did you just say?"

"I said take off your underwear." He stared at me until I complied. The simmered anger completely disappeared with blooming nervousness. I kicked off my sneakers, lifted my hips, hooked the band of my panties with my fingers under my dress, and pulled them down. Callen held his hand out expectantly. I handed them over as I repositioned in the seat, feeling self conscious.

"Is this because of the phone call?"

"This has nothing to do with the phone call. We will come back to that. This has a bit to do with you thinking I would throw you away after a weekend and everything to do with you chewing on that damn lip of yours."

My eyes popped as the memory of him throwing me over his shoulder and tying me up flashed in my mind yet again. "You can't be serious. Callen, we are in public," I fussed at him.

"Oh, I'm completely serious. Now, get on your knees and face the window."

I sat perfectly still as I looked at him in disbelief that he *thought we were going to have sex in his truck in broad daylight.*

*He shook his head. "I've got all day, but the longer you disobey the worse it'll be for you."*

*I wanted to be furious with his crassness, but part of me wanted this. I wanted him to have all the control to dominate and punish and pleasure. With one last look at him, I turned toward the window and moved onto my hands and knees.*

*"Good girl," he said as he pulled my dress over my hips to expose my backside. Goosebumps covered my skin as he gently caressed my soft, delicate cheek. Suddenly, his hand smacked my ass so hard I yelped, but he soothed the skin instantly with his continued rubbing. "Do you remember your punishment last time?" he asked almost casually.*

*I nodded as he spanked me harder.*

*"Words, Lacey."*

*"Yes, I remember."*

*"Good," he said with another swat. My back arched with the impact, the stinging sensation fading quickly with his gentle kneading. "This time, you aren't to come at all. I don't care how bad you want to. This is for me, not you." He swatted me again, and I groaned.*

*"Your cute little ass is bright red," he said as I heard the zipper of his jeans. "Do you understand your punishment?"*

*"Yes," I answered breathlessly with anticipation. My every fiber wanted him inside me. I wanted him to fuck me like I belonged to him.*

*He reached his hand between my legs and stroked. "I should've known you'd be ready to take me like the perfect little mate you are," he said as he pulled his hand back. He pushed me forward so my head was down and positioned himself at my entrance. My core clenched in anticipation.*

"Remember, this is for me, not you," he stated as he spanked me again. My skin was on fire beneath his palm. I sucked in a breath as he plunged into me and propped my hands against the door to steady myself. The pleasuring pain ripped through my body as he roughly thrust in and out. Callen wrapped his hand in my hair at the nape of my neck and yanked my head up, the movement causing my back to arch so he could push in farther.

After a few more thrusts, he was finally sheath completely. Another smack landed on my ass making me moan. I rocked into him, his roughness only serving to spur me on and make me want more. I closed my eyes as he rutted into me. The familiar sensation started forming in the pit of my stomach, my body demanding a release.

"Do not come, Lacey. This isn't for you," he ordered.

I whimpered as he thrust harder, smacking the top of my womb. Suddenly, he pulled my hair, causing me to gasp. He then shoved my panties into my mouth and pushed my head down into the seat. He relinquished my hair and placed the palm of his hand between my shoulder blades. I tried to sit up, but he shifted his weight to hold me down. The way he had me pinned, I couldn't move. All I could do was lay there as he had his way with me, and damn did it turn me on. He landed another smack to my backside, and I whined around the gag. Everything he did to me felt so good. I was rapidly building to my climax. I needed to come, but I willed my body to obey his denial.

Just as I was about to lose the battle of control, Callen groaned and released himself into me. His pulsating orgasm sent a shiver through my core. He pulled out and tugged me onto his lap when he finished, my dress fluttering around us as a cover. The loss of him was utterly devastating, leaving me with the feeling of emptiness. My core clenched, aware of how close his partially remaining erection was to my entrance in this position.

He kissed my shoulder and said, "There's definitely going to be a handprint on your ass," as he pulled my panties from my *mouth.*

*I laughed as I looked at him, the frustration was gone and his eyes were clear as he stared at me. He trailed his hand up my spine, and I squirmed with the tickling sensation.*

*"Do you have any idea how sexy it is when you submit to me like that?"*

*I blushed as he looked at me. The way he roamed my body with his eyes adding fire to the lust pulsing between my legs. I shifted again, uncomfortably aware of the wetness dripping from me.*

*"Now, back to the phone call," he said, changing the subject.*

*"Are you mad?" I didn't think I could take another punishment like that. I was too close to the edge already.*

*"Mad that you listened? No. I don't like that you worried yourself about it all weekend and didn't tell me. We should've talked about it. I took the call outside so you wouldn't worry; and, it appears to have had the opposite effect."*

*I swallowed as he spoke, not wanting to interrupt.*

*"You said you didn't want to be the person that snooped through my things behind my back. If you were so concerned, what stopped you?"*

*"Honestly?" He nodded in reply to my question, so I continued, "I want to be able to trust you, but I also want you to be able to trust me. Going through your things is not a good way to earn your trust and not telling you about hearing the phone call was basically a lie of omission. I can't expect you to be truthful with me if I'm not truthful with you."*

*"I do trust you, Lacey. There's things - like my work - I didn't want to tell you about, because I'm trying to protect you. I don't want you to freak out and try to leave again, but if it bothers you so much, I'll tell you. I can't know what you need if you don't tell me."*

"So, you're not mad?" I half smiled at him.

"No, I'm not mad," Callen laughed. He kissed me, and I melted into him with relief. His tongue slipped into my mouth, causing my core to clench with need. I shifted again in his lap to squeeze my thighs together for some friction. His kisses became more demanding as I felt him growing hard again. The feeling of him being so close to where I wanted him made me even wetter. I whimpered into his mouth as my arousal escalated to agonizing levels.

"What do you need, Lacey?" he asked seductively.

I blushed again as I continued to squirm.

"I can't help you if you don't tell me," he teased.

"I need to come, Callen. Please."

His excitement grew even more with my begging. His hand slid under my dress and up my thigh. He slowly parted my legs and ran his fingers between my folds. I was drenched from my wetness and his release. I moaned as he pressed his thumb into my clit and rubbed circles while leaning forward and popping the handle to push the front seat up with his other hand. Without interruption, he spun me around to face forward, lifted my hips, and guided me back down onto his erection in a wide straddle position.

"This one is about you, Lacey," he whispered into my ear as he pulled me backward to lean against his chest. He rubbed my clit agonizingly slow, driving my already frazzled nerves farther over the edge. I began gyrating against him, and he picked up the pace to match mine. I moved up and down, plunging him deep inside me. His other hand moved to my breast and pulled it from my dress. He tweaked my nipple as I rode him faster. I wanted every inch of him inside me.

It took only moments for the familiar sensation to return. My release ripped through my whole body. I bolted upright and froze on top of him, so he wrapped his hands around my hips and moved me against himself. I panted as my climax completely consumed me, the intensity skyrocketing as Callen continued to move.

He grabbed my hair and pulled my back to his chest again, nuzzling my neck as I resumed grinding against him with my feet on the back of the front seat for leverage. I wanted to make him come again. I wanted him to feel as good as he made me feel, and he apparently felt the same way. He ran his hand back between my legs to continue his massaging. He sucked and nibbled my neck as I rode him harder. Each stroke pulled me closer to another release. I bounced on him faster as the sensation built again. This time, we toppled over the edge together. Wrapping his arms around me tightly, he held me in place. I screamed his name as his warmth coated me inside once again. When the final climactic spasms ceased, I dropped my feet to the floorboard as we caught our breath.

"I think you're going to be late for your meeting," I finally panted out, beyond sated.

"I'll be late everyday for this," he laughed into my hair.

I shifted onto the seat, causing us to disengage. The emptiness he left behind was abrupt, but not agonizing like before. Callen grabbed his bag and pulled out a t-shirt. He handed it to me as he pulled on his boxers and pants.

"What's this for?"

"I thought you might want to clean up before redressing. You'll be more comfortable during the meeting since you won't be able to shower."

"You want me to go to the meeting with you?" I asked, surprised.

"I thought you might like to have some answers to your other questions. Does that sound okay?"

"Yeah. That sounds wonderful. Thanks," I replied with a full *faced smile.*

# CHAPTER FIFTEEN

## *Altered*

We pulled up outside what appeared to be an old warehouse. The parking lot was empty, and the building looked vacant.

"Where are we?" I asked clambering out of his truck. I swung the door shut behind me as I straightened my dress.

"This is home base," he answered as if it would clear up everything.

I arched my brows at him in response.

"I promise, it's more impressive on the inside," he laughed, wrapping his arm around my waist and guiding me to the building.

The entry door looked to weigh at least a ton in metal and required a palm scan to unlock. It seemed like excessive security for an old warehouse. When Callen scanned his palm, several bolts clicked as the locks disengaged. He nudged it open and gestured for me to enter first. I took a hesitant step inside of a long, dark hallway. The only other exit was at the end, where faint rays of light escaped the cracks of another door.

"It's alright, Lace," Callen said as he stepped in behind me and shut the door. Goosebumps covered my skin in uncertainty. I was putting a lot of trust in Callen right now, and my hammering heart didn't let me forget it. He placed his hand gently at the base of my spine and landed a delicate kiss atop of my head.

You made it this far; you might as well keep going, *I told myself.*

*Callen trailed his hand around my hip and grabbed my hand. He began walking forward with his fingers laced between mine, toting me along. I hesitantly put one foot in front of the other as I obliged. When we got to the door, Callen typed a six digit passcode into a keypad.*

*"Ready?" he asked over his shoulder.*

*"Yes," I answered with a swallow.*

*He squeezed my hand in reassurance as he turned the knob. The room was large with several rows of industrial lights lining the multistory ceiling, the walls encircled with balconies from the offices and rooms above. Three men were sitting around a table in the center of the room. I tucked tightly behind Callen when they looked up at our entrance.*

*"About time," a voice called from the group, "I was starting to think you got lost. That or you couldn't tear yourself away from your weekend romp after all."*

*A snicker came from the table, followed by an audible punch.*

*"Hey!" the voice hollered, "What was that for?"*

*"I think Callen has some company with him, you idiot," another voice rang out.*

*"Oh, shit," he replied. "Sorry, man. I didn't see her behind you. I thought you were taking her home."*

*I peeked around Callen to see the men watching us curiously.*

*"Gentlemen, I would like you to officially meet Lacey, my mate," Callen tacked on as he pulled me around in front of him and placed his hands on my shoulders. I shot daggers at him with the introduction, making him chuckle at my reaction to the word "mate".*

"Lacey, this is Jake," he said, gesturing to the man yet to speak. He was about my height with wavy, blonde hair mopping his forehead. He smiled at me and tilted his head in hello. "Nick," he continued as the one in the middle waved, "And the asshole with the big mouth on the end is my annoying brother, Travis."

A huge smile adorned Travis's face as he watched me. He was about an inch shorter than Callen and had a dimple in his left cheek; however, his eyes were the same striking, emerald green. Travis appeared to be closer to my age than Callen's, and an air of eccentricity vibrated off of him.

"Well, isn't this a pleasant surprise," Travis said, standing and quickly striding toward us.

My eyes popped out in shock. A fleeting feeling of panic washed over me, and I kicked him in the shin when he reached his arms out for me. Travis hopped up and down and rubbed where my sneaker scraped the skin. Callen suppressed a laugh and pulled me to his side as the other two men cackled.

"You're right Callen, she is a little spit fire," Nick called from the table. They strode over to join us as Travis regained his footing.

"What did you tell them, Callen?" I asked, accusingly. He had never mentioned these men, but they all seemed to know about me.

"I certainly didn't tell them about you throwing me off the diving cliff, that's for sure," he joked in an attempt to ease my tension.

"She threw you off the cliff at Paradise?" Travis asked with a disbelieving howl.

"I didn't throw him, per se. It was more of a kick..." I trailed off as a blush creeped over my cheeks.

"Well, you do have one hell of a kick, that's for sure," Travis teased with a wink.

"Alright, leave her be," Callen said, rubbing his hand over

my hip. "Why don't you take a seat, Lacey? I'll go grab us some coffee." Callen gestured to the table as he put his hand in the small of my back. I let him lead me forward and pull me out a chair. He pecked my cheek as he scooted my chair in before leaving with Travis. They playfully shoved each other as they walked off, talking and laughing.

Nick and Jake sat down opposite me at the table and pulled their already filled coffee cups to their new seats. Nick sported a buzz cut and a jagged scar to his left eyebrow. His entire body was well muscled, and he stood as tall as Callen. His overall demeanor was daunting, causing me to regard him carefully. I noticed the two men's eyes skirted from my bruised neck down to my arms, examining the injuries from the club. The marks had faded from dark purple to various shades of yellow and green which made them look even worse in my opinion. Hard expressions came over their faces, and I looked down in embarrassment.

"Sorry about Travis," Jake said, clearing his throat. "He gets a bit overzealous sometimes. He means well though."

"He's been driving us crazy wanting to meet you," Nick chimed in.

"How long have you all known about me?" I asked hesitantly.

"Well, I told Travis that I found you the night you came to Janet's class, and he and his big mouth told these guys shortly after," Callen answered as he sat down at the table beside me with two mugs of black coffee. I wrapped both hands around mine and took a small sip. It was rich and smooth in flavor. The warmness curled in my belly, dissipating some of my discomfort.

"In my defense, you didn't say it was a secret, but I probably would've told them regardless," Travis mused, taking a seat on Callen's other side.

"You've been a pain in my ass since you were born."

*"So, they've known from the beginning?" I pursed my lips and shot an irritated look at Callen.*

*He noticed my temperament change and arched his eyebrow at me.*

*"Are you crazy?" I hissed.*

*"What?"*

*"You can't just go around blabbing about mates and soulmarks like it's nothing!"*

*Smiles spread across all the men's faces, and I could tell they were trying to suppress their laughter. The fact they found my disdain funny did nothing for my temper.*

*"Lacey, it's okay," Callen said, patting my thigh reassuringly.*

*"It most certainly is not," I countered, pushing his hand off of me. "There was not a single person on this planet that knew I had a soulmark until I met you. That's kind of imperative when it comes to staying hidden. Marked ones are hunted, and you've told three people I've never even met about me? How do you know they won't report us? How have you made it this long when you're so reckless?"*

*"Will you calm down for a second?"*

*"No, I won't calm down! I am so mad, I have half a mind to —"*

*"Dude, did you not tell her anything?" Nick interrupted.*

*"I thought she'd have a better time believing it with her own eyes," Callen answered as he watched me. "I trust these guys with my life, Lacey, and I promise I am not reckless. This group is a family in more ways than one. Besides, they would never expose either of us. They'd be damning themselves if they did."*

*"What is that supposed to mean?" My voice was softer than it was before, but I was still mad.*

*Callen put his hand back on my thigh, and this time I didn't push him off. He nodded at the men, and they each stuck out their left arm, palms up to display three unique soulmarks. Travis's wrist bore a tight three loop spiral while Jake's was a plain singular line - both of them white. Nick was the odd man out, his soulmark was shaped like a "V" and deep black in color.*

*"You're all…" I trailed off speechless. Never in my wildest dreams did I ever imagine I would be sitting at a table with four other marked ones. A table where we didn't have to hide who we were. "All of you?"*

*Callen smiled, "All of us."*

*The men pulled their arms back and returned to comfortable sitting positions, sipping on their coffees. Questions flooded my mind so rapidly that I didn't even know where to start. I opened my mouth to speak, but promptly shut it again.*

*Callen gently rubbed his hand up and down my thigh, pulling my attention to him before he spoke, "We protect each other here. I was serious when I said you didn't have to hide anymore."*

*"Why are you all together? It's a gamble. If one of you were caught or identified, the others would be put at risk."*

*"That's why we make sure to find them first," Nick said.*

*I looked at Callen questioningly. He sighed before answering, "This is the part you might not like…we track and eliminate the parties hunting marked ones."*

*"It's more of a kill them before they kill us mindset," Travis added.*

*"You've got to be fucking kidding me," I took a deep breath and ran my free hand through my hair. "I tell you that I've spent the last five years hiding from the world, and you tell me you've spent your time scouring the earth in search of the people trying to kill you." I spoke aloud, but the thought was actually meant for*

*myself.*

"We shouldn't have to hide who we are or live in fear of discovery. The people and corporations after us are evil, and they won't stop until someone makes them. So, we've formed a team with the goal of destroying the status quo," Callen explained.

"And how many, ugh, places, have you shut down?"

"Seven. There are two more we are currently investigating. Most corporations aren't upfront about their interest in marked ones, so they have to be vetted. That's my job. Jake is basically our in-house PI. He searches for marked ones and investigates persons of interest. He would be who I was on the phone with while we were at the cabin. Nick is in charge of training and supplies, and Travis is our money maker. He keeps the banks full to broker our expenditures."

"Are there more of you?"

"A few, like Janet, mine and Travis's sister that you met during class; the four of us, however, pretty much run things."

"How do all three of you have a soulmark? It's not supposed to be genetic."

"Why do any of us have a soulmark? Luck of the draw," Travis shrugged.

"Well, you were right about one thing," I said looking at Callen, "I wouldn't have believed you if you hadn't shown me."

Callen squeezed my leg as he looked at Jake, changing the subject, "Have you found anything yet?"

"No, it's either an alias or he scrubbed his public record like we did ours. I thought I'd try a different angle and check into his friend. I'll see if that proves fruitful with a lead."

"Are you talking about Michael?" I interjected.

"Yes," Callen answered, "Jake is going to track him down. It may take some time, but he will find him." His hand tightened on *my thigh as he spoke. I knew his thoughts flickered back to the alley when he pulled Michael off of me. I could feel the eyes of the other men settling on the bruises around my neck, and I covered them with my hand self consciously.*

*"Callen, I want you to let it go."*

*He turned in his seat to face me directly. "You can't be serious."*

*The guys shifted in their own seats and averted their eyes.*

*"I am. I want to put it behind me, and I can't do that if you look for him. I hate how stupid I was that night. I don't want what could've happened to haunt whatever is happening between us. It needs to be left in the past," I pleaded with him.*

*"He doesn't deserve to skate by with what he did," Callen argued.*

*"I know he doesn't, but this isn't about him. It's about me. Promise me you will drop it."*

*He looked at Jake who shrugged at him in response.*

*"Promise me, Callen," I pressed.*

*He sighed, "Fine, I promise; but, if I ever run into him again, he's dead."*

*"Same here," Travis added as the other two nodded in agreement.*

*"Fine," I resigned myself to the compromise. I knew I was lucky to get that much from Callen. I could tell he was still furious about what had happened every time he looked at my neck or when his fingers grazed the discoloration on my arms; however, it was over, and I needed it to stay that way. I lifted Callen's hand from my leg and wrapped my fingers between his. With a slight squeeze, I changed the subject, "So, what's next?"*

*Callen took me home after the meeting Monday, and I spent the day piddling around my apartment attempting to process everything I had learned. Callen and his team had intervened three years ago when Nick and his mate, Angela, were trying to escape an ambush in Vancouver. Heavy fire had been exchanged between both parties. Nick's face had been grazed by a bullet, and he went down. Angela saw one of the attackers aim at Nick again and threw herself in between him and the bullet. The round went straight through her heart, killing her instantly.*

*Callen's team was able to neutralize the attackers before any more lives were lost on their side, but when Angela died, Callen said Nick went insane. They had to drag him away from the scene and sedate him. He was out of his mind screaming and attacking anything that moved. That's when Nick's soulmark turned black, half his soul died that day. To make matters worse, they had to burn her body to ash in order to prevent any stragglers from obtaining it for research purposes. He lost his other half, and he wasn't even able to bury her properly.*

*My heart ached at the story. I couldn't imagine the pain he felt losing Angela so violently. I barely knew Callen, yet the mere thought of losing him in such a grotesque manner hurt. I understood their desires to right the wrongs inflicted upon our kind, but I didn't know if it was a life I could live. It was dangerous, and I wasn't a killer. Callen insisted there was no need for me to be part of their organization, and he would only tell me what I wanted to know.*

Could I let him go off on these missions not knowing if he would return? Could I complacently sit at home knowing they were on their way to eradicate the world of our persecutors? *I didn't have the answer to either of those questions plaguing my mind. The thoughts stayed with me throughout my entire shifts Tuesday and Wednesday, until the moment I finally had my answer.*

*I stood in the hallway staring at the crumpled body of the girl who shot herself rather than be taken. Her blood had splattered everywhere, covering my face and clothes in crimson spray. One of the security guards began retching at the site. This eighteen year old girl was essentially a child, yet she felt there was no life left for her to live. And, she was right. I turned my back to the scene and walked to the charge desk, collapsing in my chair. Claire was instantly at my side checking me for injuries.*

*"I'm fine," I whispered. "It's all her blood. I, um, I need to go, Claire."*

*She nodded, "Let me call the supervisor and get someone to take my patients. I'll take you home."*

*I shook my head, "No. You stay. They'll only be able to send one float nurse. You take over charge. I'm just going to walk." I stood and exited out the ambulance bay before she could argue with me. I didn't care about the paperwork and investigation that would follow such an event. My only concern was putting as much distance between that wretched scene and myself as possible. I pulled my phone from my pocket and dialed Callen's number.*

*"Hello?" he answered on the first ring.*

*"Um, hey, do you think you could pick me up at Greenwood Park down by the hospital?"*

*"Yeah, I'm actually just down the road. I'll be only a second. Are you okay? I thought you didn't get off work for another two hours."*

*"I left," I replied, my voice blank of emotion.*

*"Did something happen?"*

*I could hear the revving of his truck in the background as I plopped down on a bench by the road.*

*"Lacey?" His voice was more demanding when I didn't answer. His truck pulled onto the road, and Callen stopped right in front of me, practically jumping from the vehicle. "Oh my god, are you hurt? What happened?" He ran his hands over my body*

*looking for a wound.*

*"It's not my blood, Callen," I whispered to him.*

*He picked me up and cradled me to his chest as he carried me to the passenger side of his truck. He fastened my seatbelt as I sat there utterly numb. Before I knew it, Callen was pulling up at his apartment, yet I had no recollection of the drive. I had seen countless people die before, but I had never witnessed someone take their own life - much less someone do it so calmly.*

*He came around the truck and lifted me out to carry me inside his apartment and to the bathroom. We were silent as he gently removed my bloody clothes and turned the hot water on for the shower. Shock had taken over my system, and I couldn't will myself to move as I stood there watching the water rain down.*

*Callen stripped and guided me into the shower with him. Positioning me under the water, he ran his hands through my hair. I watched as the water faded from red to pink to clear as the blood washed away. Callen lathered his hands with shampoo and worked the suds into my hair. Next, he soaped up a washcloth and gently washed my body, paying extra attention to cleanse my skin of the heavy make up I had used to cover my healing bruises. His touch was so tender, so mild, my shocked system barely registered what was happening. He gently nudged me back under the water and tilted my chin up to direct the soapy water backward, away from my eyes.*

*As the water swept over me, my system finally began to recover enough for me to recount the events to Callen. He kept his features neutral as I spoke, but his eyes flashed with grim anger. He pulled me to his chest and rubbed circles on my back with the palm of his hand.*

*After a heavy silence, I whispered, "I want to help you."*

*"Help me what?" he asked with uncertainty.*

*"I want to help you kill every last one of those fuckers. No*

*more of us should have to die because of them."*

*"No, we shouldn't," he whispered as he held me close.*

*Later that night, Callen had ordered us pizza for dinner - my favorite, sausage and pineapple stuffed crust.*

*"That was the weirdest pizza combination," he teased.*

*"It was delicious, and you know it," I replied, nuzzling into his chest.*

*We were curled up in bed watching a comedy after we ate. The remainder of the night called for lightheartedness after the tumultuous events of the day. Callen's fingers twiddled with the hem of his t-shirt I had donned after the shower. He slowly pulled it up and skated his fingers across my hip, running his palm back and forth a few times before he groaned, "Lacey, are you not wearing any underwear underneath here?"*

*"No, I'm not," I coyly smiled up at him.*

*I shifted slightly, causing his hand to slide over my bare backside. I wiggled my hips and pressed my cheek into his palm seductively. His other hand reached to the crotch of his sweats as he adjusted the fabric straining against his growing erection.*

*"Is that a problem?"*

*I slid my hand down his abs, tauntingly slow. When I reached his waistband, I ran the tips of my fingers underneath and gently grazed the skin. A low growl rumbled in his chest as he watched me. I felt myself instantly go wet with the thought of grasping him in my hand and stroking his hard length.*

*Sliding my hand to the side, I tugged his pants and boxers down as I sat up and climbed on top of him, his t-shirt gathering around my hips. Arousal flooded out of me as I grinded against him. With a breathy moan, I gently rocked upward and reached a hand to position him at my entrance, our eyes locking onto one another as I slid him inside me.*

*"Lacey," Callen moaned as I took all of him in.*

*A sigh of pleasure escaped as I moved up and down. I clenched my walls around his large girth as I bounced, squeezing him tighter with each movement.*

*"God, what are you doing?" he breathed heavily as he softly rocked his hips into me. His eyes were closed and his head was thrown back in ecstasy.*

*I bent my head down to his ear and whispered, "I'm making love to my soulmate."*

*I pressed my lips to his neck for a kiss and gently nipped him with my teeth. His hands skirted up my hips as he grabbed the hem of his shirt and pulled it over my head. I sat up straight as I rode him, taking him deeply. We locked eyes again as he brought his right hand to my breast and cupped it. He massaged his hand into the delicate tissues, and I moaned in pleasure. Sitting upright, he pulled my naked nipple into his mouth, twirling it with his tongue. I panted as the sensation made my core twinge in delight.*

*Lying back, he placed his hands on my waist as he picked up momentum. My breasts jiggled with each thrust. I abandoned any self consciousness I may have had as he watched me move on top of him. His gaze roamed my body, a feeling of worship emitting from him. I felt like a goddess, a siren from the sea, beckoning my lover forward to eternal bliss. His eyes were full of lust and wanting when they met mine again, and it made me want to pleasure him even more.*

*"I could watch you all damn day. You're so beautiful," he groaned, digging his fingers into my hips. I bit my lip as I bounced faster. The warmth in my stomach rapidly building. Each stroke felt like he buried himself impossibly deeper. Small spasms rippled through my core, clenching around him. His left hand found mine and his fingertip grazed my mark.*

"Oh," I whimpered as electricity shot through me, "you feel amazing."

"Tell me again. Tell me again what you're doing," he commanded.

I placed my right hand over his heart and took a deep breath. I stilled on top of him as we drank each other in. "I'm making love to the man that owns me, to the man that I love."

In one swift movement, Callen flipped us over, his stiffness never leaving me. I gasped at the sudden position change, and he pressed harder into me. "Again. Say it again, Lacey." His eyes glistened down at me, his expression serious.

I pulled his left hand up by my head as I wrapped my legs around him. My thumb danced across his soulmark before I pressed down on it, saying "I love you, Callen."

He pulled in a deep breath, "God, I love you so much. I loved you the second I laid eyes on you, Lacey."

He pressed his lips to mine and kissed me softly. Slowly, we started moving against each other again and more spasms rippled through me. He wrapped his fingers in the hair at the back of my head, holding me against his pillow. Our eyes locked together as our bodies fed one another. Callen gripped me tighter when I felt his release pump into me, and it was all I needed to fall over the edge. We wrapped our arms around each other squeezing as hard as we coul. When our mutual highs receded, he stilled inside me, pressing his weight into me with our heavy embrace.

I was done running, hiding, and living in fear. It was time for my life to finally begin. I never could have imagined the completeness I found in this wonderful man. He was everything I never knew I needed.

"Don't ever leave me," I whispered as we lay linked together.

"I'm not going anywhere," he answered, bringing his lips back to mine.

# CHAPTER SIXTEEN

## *Mesmerized*

**W**e spent the following weekend moving my things to Callen's apartment. I had no attachment to mine, and I liked the idea of living in his home. Callen had stepped out to run a few errands while I settled in. I was perched on our bed folding the freshly washed laundry I just took out of the dryer when memories of the first time we were together swept over me. I could almost feel his hands pressing me to the wall and tugging on my hair.

I didn't think I would ever get enough of him. My body yearned for him constantly. I wanted to run my hands across his broad shoulders and feel his breath on my neck as he whispered in my ear. The ache between my legs grew with my lustful thoughts. I found myself sliding my hand up the leg of my shorts, craving a release. I closed my eyes as my fingers skirted the edge of my panties, imagining that it was Callen touching me. A slight moan escaped as I pictured his hands firmly stroking me through the thin fabric.

A throat cleared from the doorway, startling me. I jerked my hand away as I turned around. Callen stood there leaning against the frame, a mischievous glint in his eye. Blood flooded my cheeks from embarrassment. "How long have you been there?"

"Long enough to see you get yourself all hot and bothered," Callen answered. "Tell me, Lacey, what were you thinking about?"

"Well, right now I'm thinking I should've locked the door!"

He strode over to the bed and leaned down so we were face to face. "That's not what I asked. When you were touching yourself, what were you thinking about?"

My face was bright red at this point. It was embarrassing enough that he caught me touching myself. It'd push me over the edge to mortification to admit I was thinking about him.

"Lacey, answer me when I speak to you," he commanded. Dominance laced into his voice this time, pushing me to comply.

"I-I don't want to talk about it," I stammered.

"I didn't ask if you wanted to talk about it. Now, I'm not asking anymore. You're going to tell me what you were thinking about," he said, standing up to tower over me.

A fresh surge of wetness flooded between my legs as I looked up at him. I shook my head, and a wicked glint flickered into his eyes.

"Last chance to play nice, Lacey," he warned.

I cast my eyes to the side wondering what he was going to do. There was no way I'd last through a punishment like the one in his truck. I was too far gone already.

A growl came from Callen as he grabbed my chin and pulled my lower lip from my teeth. "Get on your knees."

"What? No! I didn't realize I did it. I'll tell you."

"Too late. Get on your knees. Now."

I slid off the bed onto my knees as he instructed. My heart rate accelerated at not knowing what was to come.

"Since you don't want to use your mouth to chat, I think I should occupy it another way," he smirked as he looked down at me. His erection was pressing into the fly of his pants as he loomed over me. "Unbutton my jeans," he ordered.

*I squeezed my thighs together as I knelt before him. The authoritative voice he used made my core ache with need. I slowly reached my hands to his waist, unfastened his jeans, and slid the zipper down. I hooked my fingers at his hips and pulled his jeans and boxers to the floor. His erection sprang free, and my mouth watered at the sight. I wanted to taste him. I licked my lips in preparation and grasped his length in my hand to guide him to my mouth.*

*"No, I make the rules now."*

*I looked at him in bewilderment, "But, you said—"*

*"I said I would occupy it. Now, put your hands on your lap."*

*I set my hands palms down on my legs like he commanded. Butterflies filled my stomach as he looked down at me.*

*"Open your mouth."*

*I opened for him as he wrapped his fingers in my hair and pushed himself inside. His saltiness danced on my tongue, riling all of my taste buds into a frenzy. He guided my head back and forth as I bobbed up and down his length, bringing my hand up to rest on his thigh instinctively. Callen pulled out of my mouth and said to me sternly, "Hands on your lap, Lacey."*

*I swallowed and dropped my hand back down. He pushed back into my mouth and thrust to the back of my throat. I gagged and my hand shot up again, but this time I moved it back without him telling me.*

*"That's a good girl," he crooned as he pulled back to a comfortable depth.*

*I stuck my tongue out to cover my teeth and began sucking him again. He tasted so good that I had to constantly battle with myself not to touch him. He moaned as he fisted my hair. I glanced up to see him watching me intently. The look of pleasure in his eyes sent another wave of arousal through me.*

*"You want to touch me so bad you can barely control it."*

*I whimpered around him in agreement as I tried to shift to ease my aching core.*

*"You can touch me, but if you do, I'm going to fuck your mouth as hard as I can."*

*My eyes bulged at his brazen statement, but all it did was make me want him more. Without a moment's hesitation, I wrapped my hands around his backside and pulled him to me.*

*"Oh, you are such a naughty, little mate," he hissed as he slammed into the back of my throat. "Is this what you want?" he asked rhetorically as he pushed my head down onto him. He wrapped both hands in my hair to hold me in place with each hard thrust. Moving my hands to his thighs, I braced myself from the motion. Another whimper came out of me as he pushed into me farther, and I loved every second of it. A sliver of precum slid onto my tongue, encouraging me to take him deeper.*

*Callen did as he said and thoroughly fucked my mouth. His long length slammed into my throat over and over again, the base of his shaft never reaching my lips. I gave up trying to suck as he thrust harder, saliva running down my chin as I gagged. The roughness in which Callen used me only fueled the desire in my veins for him. I could tell he was nearing his finish, but he suddenly wrenched me backward, wrapped his hands around my upper arms, and tossed me onto the bed.*

*"Ladies first," he said as he climbed between my legs. He lifted my hips and pulled off my shorts, leaving me spread before him in my black panties. "Tell me what you were thinking about when I came into the room," he said as he ran his nose between my folds.*

*My panties were drenched, and I knew he would feel it with that slight touch. "I was thinking about what it feels like when you touch me," I panted.*

*"Like this?" he asked as he cupped me in his hand. I moaned as his fingers teased me through the cotton fabric. I arched my hips*

*forward searching for more. "You are so fucking sexy when you do that."*

*"Do what?"*

*"When you beg for me." He pulled his hand away and climbed off the bed.*

*"Callen, please. You're driving me crazy," I groaned as he left me lying unfulfilled.*

*"That's the plan," he winked as he pulled off his shirt and dug in the bottom drawer of his nightstand. He circled behind as he demanded I sit up with my back to him. I did as he instructed, and he quickly removed my shirt and bra. Wrapping his hands around me, he held my breasts in his hands, rolling my nipples between his thumbs and fingers until they stood pointed from stimulation. He squeezed and tweaked them as he leaned into me. Abruptly, he withdrew his hands, and blackness covered my vision.*

*"What are you doing?" I gasped.*

*He tightened the fabric around my head and tied a sturdy knot. "You'll find out soon enough," he mused. "Now, put your head at the top of the bed."*

*I hesitated with uncertainty, losing the sense of sight rattling my nerves.*

*"Do as you're told, and obey me, Lacey."*

*I took a deep breath before shifting up and laying on my back.*

*"That's a good girl," Callen praised, running his fingertips along my thigh. Goosebumps riddled my flesh as my sense of touch spiked from the sensory deprivation. Callen dropped his hand and climbed on top of me in a straddle position. He bent down and kissed me forcefully while pulling my hands above my head. Silky fabric laced around my wrists and tethered me to the headboard.*

*"Do you trust me?" he whispered in my ear.*

"Yes," I answered with a nod, the response coming without a second thought.

He shifted off me and rummaged in his drawer again. His fingers gently stroked between my legs before pulling my panties off. Callen wrapped his hand around my left ankle and pulled my leg straight. He bound my ankle in more silk before securing the other end to the bed. He followed suit with my other leg, leaving me spread before him. My heart hammered in my chest as I twisted my limbs experimentally, but Callen left no slack for movement. I became hyper aware of my nakedness, anxiousness for what was to come gripping me tightly.

"I'll be back," he said as his voice faded toward the door.

"Don't you dare leave me like this!" I yelled after him, but he only answered with a laugh. I tugged harder and rubbed my head back and forth in effort to dislodge the blindfold, but the knots were firmly secured.

Callen came back into the room and positioned himself between my legs. He ran his nose between my folds causing me to moan, his breath oddly cool against my skin. He spread my folds apart with his hands and sucked my clit into his mouth.

"Oh, shit," I screamed at the sudden sensation.

His mouth was freezing, but the drastic temperature stirred something unexpected inside me. He twirled his tongue and pushed an ice cube against my delicate skin, eliciting a full body shudder. Quickly, he pulled it away and dropped it into his hand. His mouth warmed around me, and I sighed. He ran the piece of ice up my stomach to my breast, gently grazing my nipple with it. The sensation sent chills down my spine, and I arched into him. I heard a slight vibration noise click on as he climbed the bed to kiss me. His tongue plunged into my mouth as he held the toy to my cleft. The vibrations caused me to instantly escalate from wet to soaked between my legs. He positioned what felt like a small oval over my clit and let my folds come around it to secure it in place.

*"Have you ever used a bullet, Lacey?"*

*"N-no," I stuttered as the vibrating rhythm increased. It felt so good it was almost overwhelming. I squirmed against my bindings as Callen sucked my cold nipple into his mouth. The contrasting warmness shot tingles through my body.*

*He drew his mouth away and sat up. "Well, I have a remote that controls that little toy. I can turn it up, and I can turn it down with a click of a button," he explained as he demonstrated.*

*I gasped with the fluctuations. I had never used any kind of toy before, but the pleasures were more than anything I could have conjured.*

*"Squirm all you want, Lacey. You aren't going anywhere," he mused as he toyed with the speeds.*

*"Callen! Please, please, I need you to touch me. I need you to do something, anything!" I begged. My nerves were frazzled, and my limbs were shaking with need.*

*"That's right, beg for me," he answered with a growl.*

*"Please, I need you!"*

*He quickly plunged two fingers inside me. "Damn, you're wet. I love when you do this for me."*

*He moved his fingers in and out in a steady rhythm, the vibrations slowly escalating with each stroke of his fingers. It took less than a minute before I detonated around him. Callen pumped me faster, drawing out my excruciatingly intense orgasm.*

*When I finally came down from my high, my limbs felt like jello. My breathing was labored as I laid there on full display for him. He slowly pulled his hand from between my legs and dislodged the bullet before untying my ankles.*

*"That was...wow," I was barely able to whisper as he positioned himself between my legs, pulling my knees up to my hips.*

"I'm not done with you yet," he exclaimed as he thrust himself into me.

I screamed in unexpected pleasure. He buried himself to the hilt before stilling inside. My walls clenched around him, adjusting to his large size. Reaching up, he removed the blindfold from my eyes. Our gazes locked as he slowly started moving. I thrust back against him wanting him to take me harder. I loved when he was rough and claimed me as his. Outside of the bedroom we were equals, partners in each other's lives; however, behind closed doors, my body was a slave to his. Callen never pushed too far, and I knew, without a shadow of a doubt, everything would stop if I ever said the word. I never wanted him to stop though. He brought me to new heights every time we played, and I craved for him to be my master.

Callen took my movements as encouragement and slammed into me harder. He braced himself on my bent knees as we watched each other move. "God, I could fuck you for the rest of my life."

"Please, Callen, please," I begged, needing more of him. I tugged on the silk binding my wrists to the bed, but the knots wouldn't budge.

"Tell me what you need, Lacey."

I whimpered beneath him as he held me in place by my knees.

"Do you want me to fuck you harder?" he asked.

I whimpered again with a nod of my head. I needed more of him. I needed the pleasuring pain that tore through my body when he claimed me. He brought his movements to a standstill, pulling back so his tip barely broke my entrance.

"All you have to do is say the words, Lace. Tell me what it is you need. Beg me for it."

"Callen, please..."

"Please what?"

*"Please, harder, I need you to take me harder."*

*"That's my good girl," he whispered, before slamming inside me, sheathing himself completely.*

*I cried out as he rode me harder than ever before. The pain was so good I couldn't form coherent words. I tugged on my restraint again. Knowing my desire, Callen leaned forward and freed my hands. I instantly entwined my fingers in his hair and pulled his mouth to mine. He licked his tongue down my neck and bit down on my breast. I screamed, and fisted his hair harder. He groaned around my flesh as his release took over, his warmth flooding inside me. His deliberate thrusts became erratic while he lost himself before collapsing on top of me.*

*His teeth had left indents on my soft skin, and he gently kissed them when he saw. Rolling to the side, he pulled me to his chest. I snuggled into him completely sated and satisfied. "That was quite a homecoming. I'd have moved in sooner if I knew I'd get that kind of welcome."*

*My head bounced on his chest as he laughed, "I missed you today."*

*"I missed you too, but I think you already saw that when you snuck in."*

*"You're cute when you're horny, you know that?" he teased.*

*"Shut up," I said, lightly smacking his chest.*

*I stood at the sink washing dishes after dinner. I had made a meatloaf with roasted veggies and mashed potatoes. Callen had eaten two platefuls and stuck his stomach out like it was going to pop afterward.*

*There was a peacefulness that came with being at home with him, a happiness in having dinner with the one you love most in the world. A wonderful closeness bloomed from casual* conversations as we delved deeper into one another. Sensuality filled me as we built a bond past a soulmark. We discussed likes and dislikes, friends and family, music and movies. I wanted to know him as a person, not just as my mate. This was intimacy on a completely different level than I had ever experienced. A smile skated my lips as I thought about the light that twinkled in his emerald eyes when he laughed, the butterflies that filled my stomach when I caught him staring at me. He had wholly and completely consumed me, heart and soul.

Callen snuck up behind me and wrapped his arms around my waist, pulling me from my thoughts. He placed a gentle kiss behind my ear, and the familiar sparks of affection fluttered under his lips.

"Are you almost done?"

"This is my last dish. Did you need something?"

"I have a surprise for you. It's part of the errands I ran today."

"That was thoughtful. What is it?" I asked as I dried my hands and turned around in his embrace.

"Come see for yourself."

He relinquished my waist in exchange for my hand and led me into the living room where he took my breath away. The overhead lights were off, and soft, white string lights ran across the wide window to the balcony. Candles flickered on the television stand, wafting a subtle aroma of vanilla into the air. He had pushed the coffee table against the wall and sprinkled red and pink rose petals in the shape of a heart across the glass top. The center of the heart held two flutes of champagne with the remaining bottle on ice. He released my hand and pressed a button on his phone to play soft music from the television speakers before setting it down.

"What's all of this about?" I asked, unable to contain the happiness bubbling inside me.

"I wanted to do something special for you," he answered as he reached his hand out. "Dance with me?"

A blush creeped up my cheeks with a full fledged smile as I placed my hand in his. He pulled me close and planted a delicate kiss on my lips before leading us to the music. I laid my head on his chest with a content sigh.

"Thank you. This is wonderful."

"I don't know how I made it this long without you, Lace," he whispered into my hair, "and I promise to spend the rest of my life trying to make you as happy as you've made me."

"I'll always be happy as long as I have you, Callen."

He squeezed me tighter as we danced, letting the music take over. The lyrics felt like they were written just for us as they echoed in the air:

> All my life I have wandered,
> Living but not really dreaming.
> Then, into the room you sauntered,
> A radiant light brightly beaming.
> One look from you
> And my world stopped on a dime.
> I swear it's true,
> A moment forever stuck in time.
>
> I knew I loved you then.
> I couldn't fight what was happenin'
> I swore up and down that night,
> I'd always treat you right.
> Let me tell you again,
> I knew I loved you then.

I lost track of how long we danced that night. Hours felt like minutes when I was wrapped in Callen's arms. Nothing in this world compared to him. It was shocking how something so *unexpected could lead to such a happy adventure.*

# CHAPTER SEVENTEEN

*Depraved*

"**I** know you're over there," I announced as I lay on my back staring up at the ceiling. The entire room was pitch black. Someone had cut the overhead light out for the first time since I'd arrived.

"How long have you been awake?"

"Since you came in."

"Why didn't you say anything?"

"Why didn't you?" I challenged.

His answer of resounding silence was deafening. I lay there waiting for him to speak, to offer some kind of explanation for his presence in the dark, but nothing ever came. Instead, angst permeated the air, instilling terse foreboding with every breath.

With a sigh, I sat up and dangled my legs over the side of the bed, allowing my toes to skim the cool cement floor. "What do you want, Shane?"

"I'm supposed to let them know when you're awake."

"Well, I'm awake, so you better get on it, and while you're at it, turn the light back on."

"Dr. Reid said turning the light off would help you recover faster from the serum. Something about reducing stimuli during REM sleep; but, since you're awake, I guess it doesn't matter any more."

The light flicked on, and my pupils constricted as I squinted my eyes against the brightness. After a brief adjustment period, I shot him a dirty look. "You could've warned me first. I thought you'd have to leave to do that."

He shrugged as he walked over and sat down on the bed. His eyes were bloodshot, and he looked like he hadn't slept in days. We both faced forward as the silence grew between us again.

"Why are you still here, Shane? What do you want?" I whispered.

"I don't know," he replied as he leaned forward to prop his arms on his knees. "I honestly have no fucking idea anymore."

"You don't seem to fit in with these other guys. You know that?"

"How do you mean?" he asked, sitting up straight.

"You seem to have a conscience, whereas they obviously don't. They like the power and control this place affords them. Your boss can do pretty much anything he wants with no consequences. He doesn't care what he has to do to get his way or who he hurts in the process, and don't even get me started on Garrett. You seem to care though. I don't know if it's sympathy or what, but you're different."

"I'm not better than they are."

"I didn't say you were better," I laughed. "I said you were different."

A half smile ticked across his face. He reached over and grasped my left hand in his, turning it over and running his fingers over my soulmark. It was nothing like when Callen touched me. There was no spark, no current, no pleasure. The touch felt just like any other - plain and dull.

My heart ached for Callen. It felt like a literal piece of me was left behind when I was taken. I missed his smile, his voice, his possession. My skin itched for his touch. If I had known I wasn't going to see him again, I would've kissed him longer, held him tighter, and loved him harder. I allowed one lone tear to shed before I locked them back up inside. Shane dropped my wrist to wipe my cheek with his thumb, cupping my face in his hand as he stared at me.

"You should go," I said. "Tell them I'm awake, so we can get this over with. I'm tired of playing these games."

The door slammed open causing us both to jump to our feet. Garrett and their boss strode into the room. "I think we have a few more games left to play, don't you sweetheart?"

"Shane, if you wanted to fuck her so bad, you should've just asked. I'd give you a turn before I finished with her," Garrett interjected, winking at me.

I clenched my jaw as I took a deep breath and moved several steps away from the men around me. Shane's fists were balled at his side with ferocity dancing across his features as he glared at the other men. It was no secret he didn't approve of their methods, but like he had said multiple times, he had a job to do.

"Garrett, you're free to take Ms. Reynolds," C said with a nod in my direction. "Shane and I will be in my office if you need anything."

Shane turned his head to give me one, last, long look before he walked out the door. His boss followed, leaving Garrett and I alone. I backed into the wall as he strode toward me. My heart clambered farther into my throat with each palpitation. He stopped a foot in front of me and brought his hands up to crack his knuckles.

"I've been instructed to get you to talk or kill you trying," he mused with a tilt of his head.

"You should just kill me now and save everyone the time and energy." Despite the raging storm of turmoil flooding my veins, my reply held a flat, even tone of indifference.

He closed the distance between us and wrapped a fist around each of my upper arms, squeezing them with a bruising force. "Between me and you, I hope this takes a real fucking long time," Garrett hissed, dropping my right arm and yanking me forward by the other.

"Where are you taking me?"

"You'll see. I don't want to spoil the surprise."

He forced me down the hall, tightening his grip as I tried in vain to free myself from his grasp. We turned down several corridors before finally stopping at a plain metal door. Unlike the badge scanners securing the other entrances, this one was adorned with a digital keypad. Garrett typed in the passcode, and the door swung open with a quiet beep.

"Only my boss and I have access to this room. We don't want any unnecessary interruptions now, do we?" he asked rhetorically as he shoved me inside.

The room housed the same windowless, cement walls I had come accustomed to; however, the remainder of the scene was a shock to my system. Handcuffs dangled from chains attached to the ceiling, the cart of instruments from before sat in a corner, bats, rods, and whips were displayed on the wall, and a cabinet sat next to a metal framed bed on the far side of the room. I felt like I was going to hurl as my eyes danced across the exhibit. My heart fell to my stomach when the door shut and locked behind me. I ducked just in time to prevent Garrett from grabbing a handful of my hair and took several steps before turning to look at him.

A sinister smile spread across his face. "There you go resisting again even though you know there's no way out of this room. You're going to fight me anyway, and I fucking love it." He shot toward me, and I dodged him again. We danced in a circle watching each other.

"You don't have to do this," I tried appealing to him.

"I know I don't have to, princess; I want to. That's the difference."

He lunged forward, caught my wrist, and slung me to the ground. Pain reverberated through my hip and elbow from the fall. Before I had time to recover, he grabbed my hair and drug me to the center of the room. I screamed and clawed at his hands as my roots desperately clung to their home. He released my hair, dropping me onto my back. With a firm stomp, he bore his weight onto my chest, pinning me to the ground. I grunted as my ribs pressed inward under the crushing strain, preventing air from filling my lungs. Garrett brought the cuffed chains down as my hands desperately fought to lift his foot from my chest. Fire burned in my lungs from lack of oxygen as I teetered on the edge of suffocation.

When he bent down to grab my wrists, I reached my hand up and dug my thumbnail into the corner of his eye. He cussed, grabbed my arm, and slammed a fist into my jaw. My head whipped to the side as the taste of copper filled my mouth. Aggressively, he slapped the cuffs on my wrists before removing his foot. I gasped and gulped, greedily inhaling the much needed air.

Blood trickled down Garrett's cheek as he stood over me with a scowl etched across his face. "That's the last time you make me bleed, bitch."

Without another word, he walked to the wall and pressed a button. The chains quickly retracted, hauling me upward until I was dangling, the tips of my toes barely able to skim the ground. The metal bit into the base of my hands and wrists as I tried to support my weight.

"I fucking hate you, and I swear to god that I'll kill you when all of this is over!"

He merely laughed at my exclamation as he slowly sauntered back over. "You won't be able to walk by the time I'm finished with you, much less kill anybody."

I kicked my foot at him, but he side-stepped the weak attempt with another laugh. The metal dug deeper into my wrists as I tried to regain some traction on the ground. Circling behind my dangling body, he ran his hand up my spine. My muscles stiffened when I heard the swish of a pocket knife flinging open.

"Let's start by getting this shirt off, hmm?" he mused.

"Piss off, Garrett," I barked, letting the anger burn to keep the fear at bay. I wouldn't give him the satisfaction of letting the panic burst through.

Slowly, the tip of the knife trailed up my back, following the previous path of his fingers. He was careful to lightly pierce the skin, drawing a thin cut from the small of my back to the band of my bra. I winced as the skin split open, doing my best to hide the pain. The collar of my shirt pulled on my neck as he stabbed the knife through the back fabric and slit it down to my waist. He made quick work of the sleeves, letting the tattered garment fall to the floor. I hung suspended in my pants and sports bra, my hands throbbing from the digging metal. Thin rivers of blood trickled down my arms from opening wounds. The knife clattered to the floor, and the sound of his belt buckle echoed in the quiet.

I closed my eyes as I started to shake. *Get it together. You have to be tougher than this,* I thought.

Garrett walked around in front of me as he pulled his

belt from his pant loops. "I thought we could start with a game," he said as he folded the belt over onto itself. "Let's see how many lashings you can take before you scream, but once you do, those pants are coming off next."

A grin spread across his face as his eyes roamed my suspended form. When he took a step toward me, I quickly pulled my knee up and connected with his groin. He doubled over in pain, stumbling backward. The abrupt movement caused the cuffs to cut further into my wrists, eliciting a throaty grunt of discomfort, but the rebellion was worth the pain. I wouldn't go down without a fight, no matter the cost.

"You'll pay for that," Garrett finally gritted out. He straightened his spine and squared his shoulders once he recovered. Any trace of amusement was gone from his expression, and in its place stood outright fury.

Stepping forward, he whipped the leather belt into my abdomen. I bit my tongue to prevent a scream as a welt sprung instantly on my exposed skin. He swung again, the end of the belt connecting with my breast. Grinding my teeth, I shut my eyes, refusing to make a sound.

Trailing his fingers over my midsection, he circled around me. When his touch fell away, I tensed my muscles in preparation for the next blow. The leather lashed into the skin between my shoulder blades. My body involuntarily arched forward with the sharp pain, causing me to lose my footing. Blood ran down my arms from the cuffs, and tears pricked my eyes as I settled myself back onto the tips of my toes.

"You really are something else, you know that, princess?"

When I didn't answer, he whipped me again, the strike landing on my lower back.

"Answer me when I speak to you."

I gave him a derisive huff in response, not trusting my

voice to remain steady for a true answer. I knew pissing him off would only make things worse, but I would never be able to live with myself if I didn't do everything I could to derail his plans to use me.

The fifth and sixth lashings came as consecutive blows. My knees buckled with the pain, but I managed to keep the noise in my throat to a minimal grunt. My skin was burning hot from the resultant welts littering my back.

"One little scream, and it'll be over. Let it out. I know you want to," Garrett coaxed from behind me.

I shook my head in answer, willing the tears back behind the dams of my eyes.

"Have it your way then."

The belt swished through the air, connecting with my upper arm and clipping the top of my ear. A soft yelp hung in my throat, but I refused to let it out. I could hear him chuckle behind me as another hit landed to the backs of my thighs. I brought my legs up instinctively, only for the cuffs to bite into me even further. The blood trails began running down my torso as the rivulets thickened. The leather then connected with an already formed welt across my spine, causing bright patches of light to flit across my vision. I bit down on my lower lip to stifle the scream threatening to ring out.

"We are getting closer," he mocked, trailing back around to face me. He brought his arm back, aiming the strike toward my face. I squeezed my eyes shut and turned my head, but instead of the slap of leather I expected, the metal buckle caught my cheek, prompting the cry I had fought so hard to bury.

"There's that scream I was looking for."

"That wasn't fair. You cheated."

"All is fair in love and war, princess," he said as he tossed the belt to the ground. "However, I'm willing to make you a deal."

I observed him warily as he paced back and forth in front of me.

"I'll let you keep your pants - for now that is - if you tell me where I can find your dear, precious mate. Callen, I believe his name is?"

"That's not his name," I lied through panting breaths.

He laughed, "Come on, Lacey. We both know it is. I would just like a bit more information to hand over after we finish." He pulled his phone from his pocket and dialed a number. "Yeah, it's me. I thought you may want an update. Her mate's name is Callen, boss."

I growled as I tried to kick him again, but he stepped to the side with a grin.

"No, she hasn't given a last name or location yet. I'll call you back when I have more," he said before hanging up the phone.

"I should've let him kill you three years ago, you bastard."

"Aww, that's not very nice. We wouldn't get to have this magical time together if he had."

Stepping forward, Garrett pressed his chest flush against me, knotted his hand in the nape of my hair, and crushed his mouth to mine. I kept my lips clamped shut against his tongue seeking entry. He snarled as he yanked on my hair, causing me to gasp. His tongue darted into my mouth and lapped at mine before retreating. Unable to turn my face away, I bit down on his lip until I tasted blood. He jerked away and drove his fist into my stomach. My knees buckled as I retched forward, the chains groaning and squeaking as the cuffs dug mercilessly into my ripped flesh.

"Useless bitch," he snarled.

I gasped trying to recover my breath as he yanked my pants off, leaving me clad in my bra and panties. He grabbed his belt off the floor and struck me another dozen times from all directions. My body writhed and arched in the suspended chains with each lashing, but no matter how much I moved or how loud I screamed, the smarting sting of leather found my bare skin over and over again.

By the time he dropped the belt, his breathing was ragged from the force behind each blow. Tears streamed down my cheeks as long welts bloomed to decorate my skin. I gave up trying to support my weight with my toes and hung limply from the cuffs. My body felt like it was on fire from the whipping, and my wrists throbbed. I let my chin sag to my chest, unable to muster the strength to hold my head high any longer.

Garrett moved back in front of me and, once again, fisted my hair to bring us face to face. A charged silence filled the air as we stared at one another. Silently, the neverending tears continued trickling down my face. He leaned forward and ran his tongue over my cheek, lapping up the saltiness. I cringed from the contact, but his grip held me firmly in place. After what seemed like a small eternity, he released my hair and smirked. Just when I thought he was going to turn away, he shoved his hand down the front of my panties and cupped me in his hand.

"You're fucking dryer than a desert."

"Stop it!" I yelled at him through the tears. "I don't want you touching me."

"I can change your mind. If you'd just give in, you might even like it," he said as he slid a finger though my folds and over my clit. I thrashed in an attempt to dislodge his hand. The pain driven tears receded as panic started to take over my every sense. I'd only been with one other man before Callen, and the feel of Garrett touching me shattered my stoic resolve of bravery.

"Stop!" I screamed again.

"No." His mouth perked up into a wicked grin as he roughly shoved his thick fingers inside me. I felt myself tear at his violent intrusion and cried out. There was no lubrication to dampen my soft tissues, no dilation from wanting.

"Damn, you're even tighter than I could've hoped for," he groaned as he pumped his fingers in and out. Each movement sent sharp pains through me as my tissues continued ripping. A sob tore from my chest with the forced violation. The pain and humiliation were almost too much to bear.

He removed his hand and allowed the waistband of my panties to snap back in place as he walked to the wall and released the chains from the ceiling. I toppled to the ground in a heap without even attempting to break my fall. My arms landed in front of me, revealing blood-caked skin and deep lacerations around my wrists. The wounds throbbed as he unfastened the cuffs. I lay there, helplessly trying and failing to pull myself together as he worked.

He grabbed my ankle and drug me over to the bed. I dug my nails into the floor in an effort to resist, but I found no purchase with the cold concrete. Lifting me by my upper arms, he slung me on the bed before climbing on top to straddle my hips. I bucked and writhed trying to throw him off as I shoved my hands against his chest. Grabbing my wrists, he pinned them above my head in one of his hands. I screamed when he squeezed the wounds lefted from the cuffs with an evil smile dancing across his face. He was getting off from the pain he inflicted.

*Where's Callen? Where is he?* The desire to lose myself to memories of him pulled at me. The thought of abandoning the present and drowning myself in memories of him were hard to resist. *No. He's not part of this. I will not connect him to this moment,* I decided, shoving the thoughts of him from my head. I wouldn't let him be part of this memory.

"Last chance, princess. Tell me what I want to know."

"Your bartering information for you not to rape me? You're fucking sick," I cussed. I did my best to resurrect my anger. Continuing to panic would only make things worse, but anger, at least, would protect me from breaking.

*Fight and you'll survive,* I chanted to myself.

"Oh, I'm going to fuck your either way; however, if you give me his last name, I'll be nice enough to get you some lube first."

I jerked my knee, aiming for his groin again, but he blocked it.

"I had a feeling that would be your response," he laughed while digging his free hand into his pocket to pull out two zip ties. He shifted his weight onto my shoulders before binding my wrists. We grappled for control, but he was markedly stronger than I was, making my resistance futile. He then used the second zip tie to tether me to the metal bed frame.

"That's better," he huffed, sitting up straight. "So what's it going to be, a dry hump, or would you actually like to enjoy yourself?"

My breathing was heavy from fighting him. My breasts heaved up and down with exertion. "It doesn't matter what you do to me. I'll never tell you a goddamn thing about him." I clenched my jaw as I stared at him, the trails of salty tears drying on my face as I pulled at my final reserves of bravery.

"I was hoping you would say that," he smiled. "You never fail to disappoint, princess." He pinched my cheeks between his fingers, squishing my lips out. "I think I'll start by fucking this mouth of yours."

I jerked my head to dislodge his grip before replying, "Come near me with that prick of yours, and I swear I'll bite it off."

"You bite me, and I'll go grab that knife from over there and slit your throat."

"You better go get it then."

A throaty laugh rumbled out of him, "You are too much fun."

He patted my cheek, wiping my blood off his palm as he did so. He bounded off the bed, grabbed his knife, and climbed back on top of me. He pushed the blade against my throat, piercing the skin. I felt the warm blood pool on my neck before running down onto the bed. One swift movement and everything would be over.

"This is what you want? You'd rather I cut you from ear to ear than answer my questions?"

"Yes," I whispered, not taking my eyes off of him.

"You'd trade your body, your life for his? No second thought? Right here, right now?"

"Yes," I repeated louder. Callen was my life. I'd do anything, endure anything, if it kept him safe.

Garrett laughed again as he tossed the knife to the ground. "Maybe later. We have things to do first."

He leaned up to unfasten his pants. For the first time, I noticed his hard erection bulging against his zipper.

"Get the fuck off me," I yelled as I spat in his face. His palm slapped hard against my cheek in response. He jumped off the bed and grabbed my ruined shirt from the floor, ripping a chunk off before stomping back over to me.

"That's enough from you," he seethed as he crammed the fabric to the back of my throat and settled himself between my thrashing legs. Just as he went for his zipper the door slammed open.

"Who the he—" he broke off as he was thrown backward onto the floor.

I could hear fists hitting flesh as I twisted into a sitting position, my back to the brawl. Adrenaline flooded my system as I yanked my wrists. Somehow, I managed to snap the tie binding me to the bed. Arms grabbed me from behind, and I screamed through the gag as I swung my tethered fists. Electricity shot over my skin, and I stilled when I heard his voice calling my name.

"Lacey, it's me! It's me!" He spun me around on the bed and pulled the gag from my mouth.

"Callen?"

# CHAPTER EIGHTEEN

## *Liberated*

"It's okay. I'm right here," he wrapped his arms around me as a sob ripped through my entire body. I buried my face in his chest as he gently kissed the top of my head. Relief flooded my system at the sight of him. Garrett groaned from the floor, shattering the moment and reminding us that we weren't free yet.

"We need to go," Callen said as he released me.

Pulling his own knife, he sliced the tie binding my wrists together. Blood glistened on the blade as he shoved it back into the sheath at his waistband. I bent down and grabbed Garret's discarded knife from the floor. My vision was red with anger as the relief from seeing Callen faded. I headed toward Garrett's sprawled out body, ready for vengeance.

"What are you doing?" Callen demanded as he grabbed my arm. His eyes raked down my body taking in the numerous welts, cuts, and blood trails. "My god…" he trailed off.

"I'm going to fucking kill him!" I yelled as I tried to move forward, but Callen pulled me toward the door instead.

"Lacey, we don't have time. We need to leave. Now."

Callen snagged my pants off the floor as we exited the room. He shut the door behind us and handed them to me in exchange for the knife, which he promptly tossed to the ground. I pulled them on quickly and looked at him.

Callen was staring at me intently, a mix of emotions on his face. "I'm sorry it took me so long. Are you okay? Did he... did he..." he trailed off clenching his jaw.

"I'm okay. Let's go. We can talk about it later."

Callen nodded, his lips set in a hard line. There was too much to say to start now.

"Where are the others?" I asked as we set off down the hall in a soft jog, itching to leave.

"They are in the city. Travis served as look out while I breached the building, but I gave him orders to leave once I was inside. We couldn't risk them getting a hold of any more of us if we were spotted, and we weren't sure how many guards would be here. So, I thought it would be best if I entered alone," he answered as we passed through the maze of corridors. Callen seemed to know where we were going, so I followed his lead without question.

"I've only had direct contact with four people since being here, but there were two other soldiers at the hospital when they took me. One is dead, but there has to be more."

"How do you know he's dead?"

"Because I killed him." Callen stopped to look at me in surprise, so I continued, "When I was trying to get away at the ER, I stabbed him in the leg with a scalpel. He bled out."

He kissed my forehead and took a deep breath, "I'm sorry I wasn't there."

"Don't apologize. None of this is your fault."

He pulled away and nodded. "Let's go."

We made it to the foyer without an encounter, but before we could head for the last hallway and exit, the office door swung open. C, Shane, and Dr. Reid stepped into the foyer.

Shock flitted across their faces as they took in the sight of the two of us. Callen quickly shoved me behind his back, using himself as a shield.

"And, who do we have here? Lacey, has your mate come to join us after all?" C called to me.

"We were just leaving," Callen casually stated.

"Dr. Reid, please return to my office," C instructed.

She retreated back inside without any hesitation. We all knew this would not be a peaceful confrontation, and she wasn't a fighter.

"Shane, if you would be so kind as to escort Ms. Reynolds to her room. I'll handle - I believe your name is Callen - if I am not mistaken," he said, gesturing to us.

"Touch her, and I'll rip your arm off," Callen growled at Shane.

A hand snaked through my hair and yanked me backward, causing me to yelp with surprise. A man I didn't recognize held me. Callen spun around and the other two men took the opportunity to attack. Shane and his boss lunged toward Callen, but he turned just in time. Callen flipped Shane over his shoulder to the ground and landed a fist to C's jaw. My captor let go of my hair and grabbed my arm instead. I took the latitude to spin around and threw my fist into his throat. His hand released me as it shot to his airway protectively.

"Lacey, run!" Callen shouted as he traded punches with C, but there was no way I was leaving without him.

Shane got to his feet and went for the pair. I dove on top of him, the momentum sending us to the ground in a heap. The soldier I hit lifted me off Shane and threw me face first to the ground before he headed for Callen. Shane climbed on top of me and pinned my arms behind my back. I flailed my legs to knock him off, but he pressed a knee into my lower back to hold me in place.

"Stop fighting!"

"Get off of me, Shane!"

I looked up in time to see the unknown soldier pull a gun from his waistband. He aimed at Callen, and a blood curdling scream ripped from my chest. The three men snapped their heads to look at me.

"Don't! Don't hurt him!" I cried out.

"You are not in a position to make demands, sweetheart," C disparaged as he nodded at the soldier to continue.

"I'll tell you about the bond!"

"Lacey!" Callen fussed.

"I'm not going to let him shoot you!"

"What bond?" C questioned, walking toward me. I arched up against Shane, and this time he let me stand; however, he wrapped a hand around my upper arm to hold me in place.

C stopped a few feet in front of me, his eyes locked on mine. "What bond?" he repeated.

"The soulbond between mates. Have you asked yourself why my mark is brown when every other one you've seen is white?"

"Yours wasn't brown from the beginning?" he asked with a cock of his head.

I laughed and jerked my arm from Shane's grip. I closed the distance between C and I as I spoke, "You think you're so smart with all your gadgets and scientists. You think you know what it is to be a marked one, but you're nothing but a fool."

The other soldier moved closer, shifting his aim toward

me. Callen subtly moved behind him utilizing my rant as a distraction.

"You'll never find what you're looking for in DNA. I can answer questions you didn't even know you had. Do you want to know why your fancy truth serum didn't work - why it never worked? Why the only damn memories ever displayed on that screen were ones that I wanted you to see?"

"You're lying," he answered, but I could see the doubt in his eyes. He didn't know for sure. Everything he thought he knew about his medicinal compounds and machines, I had proven wrong so far. His attention was captivated, his surroundings lost to him. I dangled everything he wanted like a carrot on a string, luring him to me.

Callen nodded, and we moved together. I brought my knee up fiercely into C's groin. When he doubled over, I drove my elbow into the base of his neck. I looked up just in time to see the soldier crumple to the ground after Callen snapped his neck with one clean twist. C was struggling to stand when Callen pulled him into an arterial choke before tossing his limp body to the ground as unconsciousness claimed him. He then grabbed the dead soldier's gun and aimed it at Shane.

"Callen, no!" I screamed, placing my hand on his arm.

"I told him not to fucking touch you."

"Shane didn't hurt me! I'm fine, look at me. I'm fine."

Callen slowly lowered the gun, not taking his eyes off of his target. I turned toward Shane once I was positive Callen wouldn't shoot him.

"You two need to get out of here. Quickly," he said. He reached into his pocket and pulled out his security badge. "You'll need this to get through the exit. A silent alarm triggered earlier, alerting to a containment breach. Only C and I can unlock a door when that happens."

He moved toward me, holding the badge out. His eyes were filled with longing as he bore his gaze into mine. Callen stiffened at the intensity and reached his own hand out to take the badge. Shane shifted his attention to Callen, saying, "He can't know I helped you. You're going to need to rough me up a bit."

"Come with us," I interjected. "Don't stay here."

He shook his head in refusal. "This is the only way."

"Lacey, we have to go," Callen urged. I looked between them wanting to argue, but I knew Callen was right. Time was ticking. As if to prove the point, C groaned on the ground.

"Do it," Shane ordered.

Callen nodded and landed three punches to Shane's face without hesitation. My muscles jumped with each blow as I watched. Shane spit a mouthful of blood onto the floor, his left eye instantly swelling.

"Now, get her out of here."

Callen grabbed me by the elbow and steered me down the hallway. I glanced back over my shoulder to see Shane watching our retreat, pain in his eyes. Callen scanned the badge at the exit and shoved the door open. It was pitch black outside. I squinted into the darkness, making out what looked to be an empty parking lot. No other buildings were in sight. Callen grabbed my hand and pulled me around the building.

"Do you think you can make it a mile up the road?" he asked.

"Yeah, I can. What's up the road?"

We took off in a sprint, ready to put as much space between us and the facility as possible. I looked back over my shoulder to see if anyone followed, but the building was dark and the lot remained empty.

"There's a getaway car parked up there."

We let the conversation lapse as we picked up our pace. By the time we made it to the car, my breathing was ragged and a stitch had formed in my side. The car was plain and black, something easily camouflaged in the night. We climbed in, and Callen cranked the engine, speeding off down the road as he hammered the gas.

"Where are we going?"

"Travis and the guys are at a safe house. We've been using it as a headquarters while we searched for you," he reached his hand out and placed it on my thigh. The familiar electricity I had craved since being taken zipped through me despite the fabric pants barricading my skin.

"How long do you think it'll be before they come after us?" I asked, checking the side mirror for a tail.

"Depends on what that guy tells them," Callen answered as he gripped the steering wheel tighter.

"You didn't have to hit him so hard. He was helping us."

"Yes, I did," Callen said. "He's part of the reason you were there. Plus, I didn't like the way he looked at you."

"How was he looking at me?"

"Like he wanted to kiss you, touch you - like letting you go was tearing him apart. He's lucky I only hit him three times."

"I don't think he would do that again," I spoke before realizing I said the words out loud.

"Again?" Callen yelled as he slammed on the brakes. My seatbelt locked and held me in place as we came to an abrupt stop.

"Callen!" I chided. "We have to go."

"I should've shot him."

"No, you don't understand. He's the reason I'm alive. And, well, I think he got the point when I slapped the shit out of him."

Callen half smiled as he looked at me, "How hard did you hit him?"

"As hard as I could. Made my palm sting," I answered, smiling back.

With a small smirk of amusement, Callen started driving again. I looked down at my body to see the leather inflicted welts standing high on my skin. Two inch thick stripes littered my abdomen, chest and arms. I knew there'd be even more on my legs and back. I hated Callen seeing me like this. I looked down to see raw, open wounds ringing my wrists from the cuffs. Dried blood trails stained my arms and torso. My wrists ached all the way up to my shoulders from the strain of holding my dangling weight.

Pulling the visor down, I inspected my face. This was the first time I had seen myself since I was taken. The outline of the belt buckle was bright red on my cheek, and a small hole indented the skin where the prong had pierced under my eye. Even though the cut was small, a purple bruise had already formed around the edges. A smear of blood ran over my cheek from Garret's hand. My lips were swollen, and a shadowy bruise lined my jaw. Additional remnants of fading bruises littered my neck. Callen squeezed my thigh tighter as I took in my appearance.

"It's okay," I assured him. "It's not that bad compared to the other injuries I had. Besides, everything will be healed by tomorrow."

"Lacey, there's no way. I don't think you realize how bad those marks are. When your adrenaline fades, you're going to be in a lot of pain. And, what other injuries?"

"It's a list about a mile long. I would have to say the biggest were some broken ribs and severe concussion that knocked me out for a few days. Oh, and probably when the acid was injected into my arm. I almost forgot about that."

"What all did they do to you?" he gritted out.

"I don't want to talk about all the details right now. Let's just get somewhere safe. I promise to tell you later," I tacked on at the end before he could argue. "My point for bringing it up is that there is a neuroscientist - the woman that ran inside the office - that has a team working on all sorts of crazy medical stuff. She gave me an injection called HyperStem-247. It rapidly accelerates the body's ability to heal. It's only supposed to last forty eight hours, but it's several days past that benchmark and still working as of yesterday."

"How is that possible?"

"I honestly don't know. I wouldn't believe it if I hadn't experienced it myself. Apparently, I'm the first marked one to receive it. Even the scientist was shocked at the results. They have some real messed up things going on there - truth serums and memory projectors - and I'm sure that doesn't even scratch the surface," I babbled.

He moved his hand to hold mine as he drove. His eyes were locked on the road like he was afraid to look at me. Callen would always blame himself for my abduction, but there was no way it could have been prevented. These people were unknown to us before it happened.

Callen parked the car in a dark alley before cutting the engine. He leaned against the headrest and finally looked at me. His eyes were dark as he drank in my appearance. He was torturing himself with unbridled blame.

"I promise, it's not as bad as it looks," I said, trying to ease his internal strife.

Callen clenched his jaw, never taking his eyes off me. "We better get inside."

I nodded in response, released his hand from mine, and stepped out of the vehicle. Callen led the way down several alleys before stopping at an old door. It opened to a dimly lit flight of wooden stairs. Callen shut the door behind us and ascended first. When he reached the top, he pulled his keys from his pocket and unlocked a second door. The room was large and open. Jake was splayed out over the couch while Travis and Nick stood in the kitchen talking in hushed voices. All their heads whipped in our direction as the door clicked shut behind us.

"Lacey!" Travis exclaimed, practically running to us. He picked me up in a bear hug and swung me around. I couldn't help but giggle at his antics. Travis was essentially an adult sized teenager sometimes. He set me down and held me at arms length. The color in his face drained away with his relief of seeing me as he took in my appearance. "What the fuck happened to her?" he demanded to know, turning to Callen.

"She keeps saying she will tell me later, but if the scene I walked into—"

"Callen," I cut him off, "not now." I took a deep breath after I spoke. I didn't want the guys to know about what Callen saw. I didn't even want Callen knowing about it to be honest. I knew there was nothing for me to be embarrassed about, but I blamed myself for not fighting harder, for not being stronger than him.

"Lacey, why don't you go in the back bedroom and clean up? There is a connecting bathroom, and I brought some clean clothes for you," Callen suggested.

I nodded in response before turning to leave. I passed a second small bath and bedroom as I strode down the hall. A tear trickled down my cheek that I hadn't realized formed.

I wiped it away while I rummaged through a duffle bag. I grabbed some clothes without really looking at them and headed toward the bathroom. After cranking the hot water all the way up, I stripped off my remaining clothes. A light pool of blood shown in my panties from the forced entry of Garrett's fingers.

Closing my eyes, I stepped into the shower for the scalding hot water to pelt against my skin. Immediately, I grabbed the bar of soap and scrubbed every inch of my body with a lathered washcloth. I needed to rid my skin of all the blood and lingering touches of my tormentors. Standing alone in the shower it almost felt like I was still there. Flashbacks of my first shower hit hard as I watched the blood flow down the drain.

The bare flesh on my wrists and back stung from the soapy water, and the welts that covered my body smarted with every movement I made. I ignored all of it though as I desperately tried to clean myself; however, no matter how hard I scrubbed, I couldn't get clean. I felt dirty in so many different ways. Collapsing into the shower floor, I sobbed, the whole ordeal resonating in my mind. I could practically feel every hit, slap, kick, and touch all over again as the memories washed over me, my brain permitting itself to finally process everything that occurred.

The air shifted as the shower curtain pulled away. Callen stepped inside completely clothed and dropped down beside me. He pulled me into his lap and took the cloth from my hand. Wrapping his arms around me, he held me against his chest as the water ran over us. I wept until tears physically refused to continue falling. My eyes burned from the salt and snot ran from my nose.

"You're safe. I've got you. I've got you," he repeatedly whispered into my ear.

*You need to get yourself together. You survived, and you're only hurting Callen now. He's hurting enough on his own. It's time to be strong again,* I told myself.

We sat under the water until it ran cold. Begrudgingly, I stood and quickly washed my hair while Callen stepped out of the shower. I turned the water off and pulled the curtain open. Grabbing the towel hanging from the wall, I dried myself before looking at him. He stood as still as a statue with my bloody panties in his hand.

"It's not what you think," I whispered.

Callen dropped the ruined garment to the ground as he looked at my welt ridden body. Pain was written all over his features.

"He didn't...it was just...he just touched me," I tried to explain but words failed me. "I tried to get away, to fight. I'm so sorry I wasn't strong enough."

Callen strode toward me and wrapped me tightly in his arms, "You were strong enough, Lacey. You're the strongest person I know. I'm so sorry it took me so long to find you. We turned this city upside down searching. I didn't protect you. I'll never forgive myself." He squeezed me tighter as he spoke. Callen was torturing himself over something out of his control.

I gently pushed against his chest and cupped his cheek in my hand, "You've done nothing that needs forgiven. You found me. It's over. I just needed a moment." I dropped my hand and moved away from him, "Now, get dry and dressed. I have to tell you guys a ton of stuff before we can make a plan."

# CHAPTER NINETEEN

*Resurrected*

"So, you're saying they can project a person's memories onto a screen, but the person has to be thinking about the memory?" Travis asked with a furrowed brow. We were all in the living room. Callen and I were on the loveseat, Jake and Nick sat across from us on the couch, and Travis paced back and forth between us all.

"I know it sounds crazy, but yes. There's a bunch of equipment that has to be hooked up first. A lot of it is to evaluate the nervous system, but I don't know what all data is collected. I'm not really sure how the projection works either. She would ask me a question or mention a topic to trigger a memory, then it would start playing in my head and on the screen simultaneously. It took a few tries, but I was eventually able to block their triggers and display other memories that I focused on."

"That sounds like something out of a science fiction movie," Jake said.

"It should be. I never would have thought something like this was possible. Apparently, all the other subjects that they tested were unable to interrupt a memory once it started. Everyone was pretty shocked when I did it."

"What did they ask you?" Callen questioned. He had been careful not to touch me since we left the bathroom. All I wanted was to be wrapped in his arms, but I wasn't sure what was going through his head.

"Mostly about you," I answered looking over at him, "The boss, Christopher McDaniels - he goes by C - said he wanted both of us. He said his informant identified me and knew I had a mate but didn't know who. He never told me who the informant was or how he knew me though. The good news is that they have absolutely no idea about the rest of you guys," I said, gesturing to Travis, Nick, and Jake, "or the others. But, we may have a small problem..." I trailed off.

"Just one?" Travis asked sarcastically.

Nick kicked him in response when Travis paced in his direction. "Let her finish."

I took a deep breath, "The last time they hooked me up to the machine, they injected me with some kind of truth serum cocktail. It makes your thoughts all cloudy and things just spill out. Supposedly, it lasts a day, but I was able to push through it in less than an hour. But, before I broke out of the haze, they accidentally triggered the memory of us meeting at Janet's class. They briefly saw the studio and Janet before I was able to shut it off. They never saw you though, Callen. I don't know if they'll be able to connect the dots from there or not."

"Ah, damn," Travis sighed, running his hand over his head and through his hair.

"I'm sorry," I blurted out, guilt riddling me. "I did the best I could to fight it off. I never told them anything voluntarily. Not even when I was tied to a chair and tortured or when I was beaten into unconsciousness with broken bones or when he had me strung from the ceiling and he—" I broke off, unable to complete the sentence. Tears pricked my eyes as I droned on, "The mind games were just so much harder to navigate."

Callen jerked himself off the couch and strode to the

window, every muscle flexed with tension. The sun was starting to rise in the distance, casting a luminous glow on his skin, a stark contrast to the dark and twisted reality we were living.

"Hey, hey," Travis said as he crouched and wrapped me in a tight embrace. "You did amazing, Lacey. No one would even be upset if you couldn't have fought it off. I'm sure you were more resilient than any of us could have been."

"Yeah, you could have told them everything as soon as they grabbed you. We would've understood. You didn't have to sacrifice so much," Jake added from his seat.

"I never would've done that. I don't even remember how many times I told them to just kill me, but they wouldn't."

I shook my head to dislodge the memories threatening to take over my mind. Travis sat down on the floor in front of me, leaving one hand to rest on my knee. Nick stood and walked over to the window. Callen and him spoke in hushed yet harsh voices. I glanced over just in time to see Callen slam a fist into the wall. Thankfully, he missed the studs and only smashed the drywall. I looked back at Travis and closed my eyes.

"Callen said they gave you an experimental drug to treat your injuries," Jake prodded.

I told them about receiving the HyperStem injection, and its lingering effects days later. "I don't know how much longer it'll last," I concluded.

Travis and Jake held grim expressions as I named the injuries treated by the injection and those that happened after; however, I didn't go into details about how they were inflicted. They didn't need to know, and I wasn't ready to relive all the nitty gritty details yet. I also left my most recent injuries off the list. They could infer from one look at me what had happened.

My eyes were heavy from exhaustion. The night had been long and eventful. Recounting pieces of the last week drained me mentally and emotionally. We sat in silence in the room while Callen and Nick finished their heated discussion.

"She needs to get some rest," Nick finally announced to the group. "Callen, take her to bed. The three of us will alternate guard duty while the others grab some shut eye. We will make an extraction plan this evening and head out tonight."

Callen nodded in agreement and walked back over, offering his hand to me. I grasped it and let him lead me back to the bedroom. I permitted one, last look over my shoulder at the guys; they all looked furious as they spoke in low voices to one another. As soon as the door shut, Callen pulled me to the bed. I climbed in and patted the mattress beside me, inviting him to join. He hesitated for a moment before settling himself beside me. I turned on my side to face him, his eyes lingering on my injured arms.

"Stop looking at me like that," I said in exasperation.

"What are you talking about?" Callen asked.

"I'm not some wounded, lame duck. I don't regret fighting. I'd do it all again, so stop beating yourself up about it."

Anger flashed in his eyes with my statement. "You should have told them who I was or where to find me. You shouldn't have sacrificed yourself to shield me."

"You're mad that I didn't give you up? Are you freaking kidding me?" I yelled in question as we both sat up.

"You're damn right I'm mad. It should've been me in that building. It should've been me protecting you! You shouldn't have been beaten and raped—"

"He did not rape me!" I screamed at him. "Yes, he was going to, and yes, he made me bleed from his fingers, but he didn't get to rape me because you showed up! You found me, and you stopped him!" I knew the guys could hear us fighting, but I didn't care. "So, stop looking at me like I'm some poor, little, broken thing, you stubborn jackass!"

His face contorted with anger as he jumped off the bed, "Lacey, what they did to you—"

I cut him off as I clambered off of the bed after him, "I know what they did! I lived through every godforsaken moment to save you!"

"It shouldn't have been you!" He rounded and grabbed me, his fingers further bruising my arms as he squeezed. "You should have told them whatever they wanted to know, so I could've been there with you! You never should've ended up in that room!"

"If it had been the other way around, would you have told them about me? Would you have given in?" My voice dropped to a whisper as our eyes locked onto one another's.

"That's not the point," he softly answered, the anger deflating from him.

"Yes, it is," I said as he dropped his hands from my arms. "You would've done the same thing I did, and I don't regret a second of it, Callen. You have to let it go and stop blaming yourself," I whispered as I stepped toward him. Lacing my fingers in his hair, I pulled his lips to mine. I channeled all the love I had for him into that kiss. I needed to show him that we were still us. Nothing could ever change that.

Callen wrapped his arms around me and kissed me back. The kisses were slow and sensual as we savored the taste of one another. Fireworks danced across my skin, lighting that familiar burning inside me. I walked backward toward the bed and fell, pulling Callen with me. Wrapping my legs around his waist, I pushed my hips to his. I could already feel his bulge growing and pressing into me. I ran my hands under his shirt and up his back.

"Lacey, you're hurt. We don't need to do this right now," Callen protested as he pulled his mouth from mine; however, desire danced in his eyes despite his resistance.

"I want to though. I need to feel you, Callen. I need your touch. I need you to make it all go away," I said as I pulled his shirt over his head.

He lifted up and tossed the shirt to the floor. I sat up and put my arms in the air, encouraging him to do the same to mine. Slowly, he disposed of my shirt and bra. His hands delicately tracing the welts on my chest. Pain flickered in his eyes before he met my gaze again.

"You're sure?"

"I've never been more sure of anything in my life," I sighed, bringing my lips to his again.

I collapsed backward as I fiddled with the button and zipper of his jeans. He pushed them off with his boxers in one swoop. I lifted my hips allowing him access to remove my leggings and panties. Gently, he peeled them off me, careful to mind my injuries. He started at my ankles and kissed every welt and bruise that littered my skin all the way up to my neck. The wetness grew between my legs with every touch, my body demanding his.

Callen possessed a sense of healing I could only get from him. He pressed his body to mine and grinded our hips together. My breathing rapidly increased as I felt him pressing into my entrance. He steadily slid into me, my walls swollen and tender. I winced in pain, and he abruptly halted his advance halfway in.

"Don't stop," I breathed into his ear.

"Lacey, we should wait. I don't want to hurt you even more."

"No, Callen. Please, don't stop. I need you," I begged as I squeezed my legs around his hips urging him forward. Callen slowly slid the rest of the way into me. My breathing hitched as I adjusted. He groaned into my ear when I started rocking into him. The pain rapidly transformed into pleasure as we made love wrapped tightly in each other's embrace, moving as one.

"God, I missed you," I moaned as he pushed into me. "I missed you so much."

"You're all I thought about, Lace. I love you so much it hurts. I thought I lost you," he whispered back, his face buried in my neck.

I squeezed him impossibly tighter with his admission. "I love you too."

I was so caught up in the moment I didn't register the orgasm creeping up until it was too late. I cried out, my entire body stiffening beneath him. He grunted as he found his own release and flooded into me. We stayed wrapped together as our breathing evened out.

Callen gave me a long kiss before standing up and lifting me to the head of the bed. He climbed in behind me and covered us with the blanket before wrapping his arms around my waist. I laced my fingers between his and pressed my back into him. I wanted every inch of his body touching mine. Callen hummed the song we danced to in our apartment all those years ago into my ear as I gave into the exhaustion and drifted off to sleep.

I woke up still wrapped in Callen's arms. The room was well lit from the afternoon light peeking around the window curtains, Callen softly snoring in my ear. I moved to get out of bed, but his arms tightened around me. I smiled to myself as I snuggled back against him, deciding to enjoy the moment. I traced circles around his bruised knuckles as I examined the small cuts lining his hands from yesterday.

Doing my best not to wake him, I twisted in his arms. A shadowy bruise adorned his left cheekbone, and dark circles lined his eyes from exhaustion. When they took me, I knew he wouldn't rest until he found me, but the evidence of him not sleeping for a week pulled on my heartstrings. As bad as my time away was, I can't even fathom what it was like for him. Callen thrived on control, and it had been wrenched from his hands. The not knowing alone would be enough to drive anyone to the brink. His imagination must have tormented him the entire time.

We would need to get a plan together today. Staying in the safe house long term wasn't an option. C and his soldiers would never stop searching for both of us now. I ran my fingers through Callen's hair and kissed the tip of his nose. His eyes fluttered open and locked onto mine. A smile spread across his face as we watched each other. His hand skirted over my hip and to my backside as he pulled me closer to him. He took my mouth to his and slid his tongue across my bottom lip. I opened to give him access which he eagerly accepted.

After a moment, he pulled away and brought my wrist to his lips. He kissed where the cuffs had cut me, but abruptly pulled away when he felt the skin. Instead of scabbing wounds, my wrist was lined with thin pink scars, and all the pain from yesterday had disappeared. Callen pulled my other wrist out and examined it to find the same results. He flung the covers off and searched my body. One small welt remained on my breast, but all the others had dissipated while we slept. Callen grasped my chin in his hand and tilted my head up to examine the puncture wound and bruises to my neck. Finally, he flipped me over, causing me to squeak in surprise. He ran his hand over my spine where the cut had been.

I rolled myself back over, giggling from the ticklish

sensation his touch left behind, "Will you stop it?"

"Everything's healed," he exclaimed.

"I told you I'd be fine by today. Give it another day or so and the scars will be white and silvery as if they happened years ago."

"I know you said it, but it's hard to believe until you actually see it."

I laughed again, "Tell me about it."

After placing a quick peck on his bruised cheek, I climbed out of bed. "I need to freshen up before we head out to the living room."

I walked to the bathroom, took a fast shower, and dressed in my briefly worn clothes from earlier. Callen came into the bathroom just as I was finishing.

"I'll go see if there's any coffee hidden around here somewhere while you clean up," I said as I hung my towel back up to dry.

"I won't be long," he promised, planting a kiss on the crown of my head before stepping into the shower.

I ran my fingers through my hair and found a spare toothbrush under the sink while he bathed. A smile spread across my face as I headed for the living room. I could hear voices rumbling as I walked. Entering the room, I found Nick and Jake in the kitchen, sipping on coffee. Travis was sprawled out on the couch, fiddling on his phone.

"You are ridiculous," he called without looking up. "We haven't even had her back for twelve hours, and you've already buried yourself balls deep inside her."

"You're such a damn idiot, Travis," Nick said, shaking his head from the counter.

"What?"

"Did you ever consider it was *me* who buried *him* balls deep and not the other way around?" I quipped as I strode over for the cup of coffee Jake was pouring me.

Travis sat bolt upright, his face bright red. "Oh, shit! I thought you were Callen!"

"Obviously," I teased.

"Dumbass," Nick muttered under his breath despite a small smile pulling at his lips.

"I swear he's only like that because Janet dropped him on his head too many times as a baby," Callen said as he joined us in the kitchen.

"That's not funny, Callen," Travis pouted as he swung his legs around to stand.

"You're right. Brain damage is a very serious condition, but luckily you don't appear to have a brain. So, you should be fine," Jake added with a grin.

"Man, you guys suck," Travis rebutted but even he couldn't hide the amusement in his voice.

When the laughter faded away, I realized everyone's eyes were glued to me. "Why are y'all staring at me? Is there something on my face?" I asked, wiping my hand over my mouth expecting to find a coffee mustache or something similar.

"No, there's nothing on your face," Nick answered, "Or your neck or your arms for that matter."

I rolled my eyes, "You are as bad as Callen. Now, stop it. All of you are making me self conscious."

"If you're going to be self conscious, it should be about that sex scream you let out earlier, not about your healed skin," Travis taunted.

My eyes popped, and I gaped at him as Callen yelled,

"Dude!" Turning, he punched Travis as hard as he could in the arm.

"Oof!" Travis grunted, grabbing his injured arm, the skin turning instantly red. "That's going to bruise!"

"Good!" I said sternly, shooting Travis a dirty look. "Mention it again, and I'll shove my foot so far up your ass you'll taste shit for a month!"

"So, Lacey's back..." Jake trailed off as he fought another laugh.

"I missed you, sis," Travis said, wrapping me in a backward hug.

"Yeah, yeah. I missed you, too, Travis," I admitted, patting his hand.

"Alright, that's enough. Remind me to kick your ass for real later," Callen said to Travis as he pulled me to him. I leaned my head onto his chest as we stood in the kitchen talking.

"So," Nick started after a few minutes, "let's review what you know about the people that took you. We need all the information we can get to make a solid plan."

I nodded, "Four men took me from the hospital. They wore masks, but two of them ended up being my guards while I was there - Shane and Garrett or I guess y'all know him as Michael."

"Michael?" Jake asked, raising his eyebrows.

"That bastard from three years ago?" Travis interjected.

"Yeah, that's him. Callen, ugh, found me locked in a room with him." A blush creeped up my cheeks with their knowing looks. I'm not sure if Callen told them what he saw or if they pieced enough together from our yelling match in the bedroom.

"I knew we should've fucking killed him back then,"

Travis muttered.

"He'd be dead now if Callen wouldn't have stopped me," I said, shooting a disapproving glance at Callen.

"We had to get out of there, Lacey, and you know it. Besides, I stabbed him once, he could be dead, depending on how fast someone found him," Callen replied with a shrug.

"Plus, you aren't a killer," Travis added.

"Tell that to the soldier I stabbed. His dead body would disagree." Any remorse I had for killing that man had long since left me. There was no place for guilt. This was kill or be killed.

"Lacey—" Travis started, sympathy in his eyes, but Callen held his hand up to stop him. He knew I didn't want sympathy or pity from anyone.

"It's okay, Travis. Anyway, Shane was the guy that gave us his badge to escape. I'm not really sure how he got mixed up in all this, but he's not a bad guy."

"Lacey, he helped kidnap you," Nick said in a cold voice.

"Yeah, he did. I don't know how to explain it..."

"He has feelings for her," Callen scoffed.

"Callen, I think he was just confused with the situation," I replied, trying to ease the tension.

"How do you know he has feelings for her?" Travis asked.

"Oh, trust me. You should have seen the way he looked at her. I would've shot him then if I knew he fucking kissed her—"

"Okay, that's enough!" I scolded. "No more commentary until I'm finished." I looked at each of the men expectantly until they agreed. "So, Shane helped us leave and had Callen beat the crap out of him to dislodge suspicion. He didn't agree with the techniques the other men used to gain information," I added when I saw Travis open his mouth to speak.

"Anyway, I'm not sure if the soldier Callen killed was the fourth from the hospital or not. I'd be surprised to find out there were only four soldiers. There has to be more. I just didn't see them," I continued. Next, I filled them in about C, Dr. Reid, and McDaniels Incorporated. "Unfortunately, that's pretty much all the information I have. I know it doesn't help much."

"On the contrary, it helps a lot knowing who the key players are," Jake spoke up. "When we get somewhere better, I can do some digging. I might be able to uncover a few more of the minor people involved."

"Where are we going to go?" I asked.

"Well, we have a few options," Nick began, "We can run together, go into hiding for a while, let things cool off. If we get caught, we all go down. Or, we can load up on supplies and take the fight to them, but without a head count that's highly likely to fail. The third option is we split up, go to our individual safe houses, communicate through scattered IP addresses, do some research and hire some mercenaries to help when we do attack. If one of us is found, that'll prevent everyone else's locations from being compromised."

I shook my head, "Those are crap options."

"Agreed," Nick sighed, "but I don't know what else to do."

"We can let them find me again. Take out the ones that show up. Do a bait and switch," I suggested.

"Hell, no. That's not an option," Callen said. "Whatever we do, you aren't going to be involved. I'm not risking losing you again."

"I'm not just going to sit in a hidey-hole while you are out there. I thought we put that to bed years ago."

"Things are different now."

"No, they aren't. I go where you go. I'm not going to let these people take my life from me, from us." My eyes pleaded for Callen to understand as I spoke.

"Fine, but you aren't going to be bait."

"Yeah, none of us would ever agree to that, Lacey," Jake added.

"Well, what are we going to do then? Storming the place is a death sentence. That leaves options one and three, and I don't like those either."

"I'd rather all of us get caught, or all of us go free," Travis said. "We are in this together."

"They are after Lacey and I," Callen argued. "They have no idea about you three. I think the best idea to get out of the city is for us to split into two groups. You three go first, then we will follow."

"No, we stay together," Jake countered, siding with Travis.

"Callen is right. It's best if we disperse until we get out of the city. We can meet up at a prearranged time and place to regroup. Then, we can go underground together until we have a better plan and some back up," I agreed.

Callen turned to Nick, "You're the tie breaker. Plus, this is your area of expertise."

Nick sighed, "I don't like the idea of splitting up, but in reality, it gives us the best chance of success. Anybody we run into on the street could be working for this McDaniels guy, and he will definitely be looking for you two together."

"Dammit to hell, Nick!" Travis yelled as he started pacing, "I'm not leaving without them."

"Yes, you are, Travis. Think about Janet. She doesn't

deserve to lose both of her brothers at once if we don't make it out. Besides, I told you yesterday they saw her studio. You guys need to grab her on your way out," I reasoned.

"She's going to be really pissed off when we show up," Jake replied, rubbing his hand over his face. Janet had refused to speak to any of us for the last six months, after her world combusted. She blamed Callen even though there was nothing he could have done, and when the rest of us told her so, she cut contact with us all.

"I know, but hopefully, it'll go better since I won't be with you," Callen sighed.

"She's going to come around, Callen," I replied, rubbing his upper back in a soothing gesture. "You're her brother. She was angry and needed someone to blame, and unfortunately, it's sometimes easier to take it out on who you're closest to."

"Yeah," Nick agreed, "it's just going to take her some time."

I nodded at his statement, the room growing quiet. All of our hearts ached for Janet. The pain of losing a mate is unfathomable. Nick, being the only other one to lose his mate, knows that destruction all too well. He fights every day to survive the emptiness left behind, and we can only hope Janet will keep doing the same.

"All this fucking sucks," Travis finally said, breaking the silence; however, he reluctantly agreed to the plan.

# CHAPTER TWENTY

*Hunted*

I stood at the window watching the three guys disappear down the street. It was dinner time, and Janet's studio would be closing soon. The plan was for them to grab her and get out of town. Nick offered his personal safe house as a temporary residence for them all since they were unknown to our pursuers. The house was stocked with nonperishables and weapons, and only Nick knew its location. They would wait there with a burner phone to hear from us. The number was preprogrammed into the other burner waiting for us at Callen's tertiary safe house in Montana. It was a good plan, methodically designed. The safe houses were a contingency we hoped to never need, yet here we were.

We went over countless versions of how this could fail, but Nick had back ups for his back ups. Despite all the planning, I couldn't shake the feeling this wouldn't work. Callen came up behind me and encircled my waist with his arms. He bent down, allowing his chin to rest on my shoulder as he spoke, "I know that look. You're worried."

I sighed, "I know this is what we all agreed to do, but I can't shake the feeling that something's going to happen. I can feel it in my bones."

"I know what you mean. It's like the air is heavy with something."

"I'd feel better about it if we could figure out who the

informant was, but there really isn't much to go on," I said as I turned in his arms to face him. "Do you think they'll make it?"

"They'll make it. They know how to blend in."

I nodded before leaning into his chest. He smelled like honey and warm spices. His scent was intoxicating, like a drug designed especially for me. After a long moment, I pulled away from Callen and headed to the kitchen for a bottle of water. When I turned around, I practically ran flat into his chest.

"You know," he said as he tucked a strand of hair behind my ear, "we have a good two hours before it's dark." His voice was laced with carnality as he slid his hand over my neck and down my curves. Goosebumps riddled my skin with his touch.

"A whole two hours, huh?"

"Mmmhmm," he purred into my ear as he placed delicate kisses up and down my neck. His warm breath sent chills down my spine, and an ache shot through my core with his suggestion. I took his mouth to mine, kissing him deeply. Lifting me onto the counter, he pressed himself between my legs.

"What is it you had in mind?" I teased, running my palm down his bulging length.

His hand wrapped around my wrist as my fingers moved to his zipper. "I had a different idea."

Callen whisked me off the counter and laid me firmly across the kitchen island. In a flash, he had me stripped to my bra and panties. He roamed around the table drinking me in. I dampened with need as I lay there, practically feeling his gaze caressing every curve, every inch of my body laid out before him. His breath was heavy as he circled me. Lust filled in around us displacing all of the unease from earlier. Callen reached his hand out to lightly trail up and down my inner thigh. I moaned as the electric current his touch always brought washed through me.

"What do you think I should do to you, Lacey?" he asked in a deep voice. "What do you deserve?"

I swallowed as my breathing quickened. My heart was hammering in my chest with the hint of anger that seeped into his words. I moved my head to look at him. His eyes were a glistening emerald, his jaw clenched with a stern look.

"Answer me when I speak to you," he said as he pinched one of my nipples through my bra and twisted.

I yelped with the pain, but my other nipple pebbled instantly. "I think you should punish me," I whispered.

"Tell me why that is," he demanded, releasing my nipple and sliding his hand to my throat.

"Callen, what are you doing?" My voice faltered with the question.

"Are you afraid?" he asked, slightly increasing the pressure on my windpipe.

"No," I lied, fighting back the memories of the other men's hands around my neck, squeezing the life from me.

"You're lying," he hissed as he let go. Trembles raked my body as he paced down to my waist. He wrapped his hand around my thigh and squeezed until my leg jerked before he continued, "You realize you've only cried once since we've been here? You keep saying that you're fine, that I shouldn't blame myself, that I saved you. You only seem to care about how I feel and what I went through. You're trying to act like you weren't affected at all. Well, I'm not buying it!"

I sat upright on the island and glared at him, "There's nothing to buy. I *am* fine. Look at me. I barely have a scratch on me!" I was so past angry I didn't even have a word for it, so I merely shoved his hand off of my leg as I jumped from the counter and took a few steps away. "You've got some fucking nerve to try and tell me how I should be feeling."

"Someone has to do it, because you sure aren't telling yourself," he retorted. "You might be physically okay, but I know you better than anyone, Lacey. You smile, but you don't really mean it. The light in your eyes is gone, and telling everybody your fine is the biggest fucking lie to leave your mouth."

"What do you want me to say, Callen? What do you want from me?" I grabbed my shirt and pulled it back over my head.

"I want you to be honest! You've never been scared of me before, and just then you were lying there shaking but still willing to let me do whatever I wanted to you!"

We stood there glaring at each other. I didn't want to have this conversation. I wanted to be a million miles from here. I moved to walk away, but Callen launched himself at me and pinned me to the wall a few feet behind us. He aggressively groped me between my legs, and my hand swung at his face. He managed to keep his head straight, yet a red handprint already bloomed on his cheek. My palm stung from the slap, but I smacked him again anyway.

"Don't you dare touch me like that!"

Callen moved his hand up and grabbed my jaw in his hand as he yelled, "That's right! Be angry, be mean, be anything besides this timid creature trying to make me feel better about what happened to you! Don't lay there and tell me I should punish you, because you think it'll make me feel better!"

"I didn't say it because I thought you wanted me too," I gritted out between my teeth and shoved him. Callen released me and took a step backward. I was so furious that fire felt like it flooded through my veins. "I said it because I fucking deserve it! I hate myself! I hate what they did to me. I hate that I let them lay a finger on me. Don't you fucking get it? It was my fault I was there. They didn't take you or Travis or anybody else. They took me, and I fucking *let* them. They kidnapped me and beat me and were going to rape me! I didn't keep another man from touching me, and I fucking deserve to be punished for letting it happen!" Tears were streaming down my face as I continued screaming at Callen. A rush of pent up emotions spilled out of me. Emotions I hadn't even realized I had locked inside.

"Oh, come off it, Lacey! Who are you really mad at? Admit it!"

"You know what? Fine. I'm mad at you, Callen! I'm mad at you for so many goddamn reasons it doesn't even make sense! I'm angry you weren't there when they took me! I'm pissed that you found me, because C knows who you are now. Garrett only knew your first name. They never would've been able to locate you on that alone. After everything I did, everything I endured, you showed yourself to him!" I screamed as I strode to the kitchen counter, grabbed my water, and barrelled it at Callen's head.

He dodged to the side, never taking his eyes off of me.

"And then, somehow at the same time, I am furious that it took you so *fucking long* to find me! I was in hell, and it took you over a week to rescue me! Is that what you want to hear? That I want you to punish me because I blame myself? That I blame you just as much?" My chest heaved up and down with passion. There was such relief in letting all the frustration out, relief in acknowledging the turmoil that had built inside me. I stared at Callen, the handprint becoming more prominent on his face by the second.

"Finally," he breathed, "there's my mate."

We dove at each other and toppled to the floor in a heap of fervent emotions. Our kisses were rough and furious. Anger sparked with every touch of our lips. My hands shot to his waist and made quick work of his button and zipper. Callen rolled on top of me and pinned me to the ground.

"You should have let me scrub your identity years ago!"

"You should have vetted this company before they took me!" I spat back as I hooked his ankle and rolled us over.

I plunged my hand down his pants and fisted him as hard as I could. Callen grunted as I squeezed him between pumps. He was fully erect as I roughly throttled him. The feeling of his peeked desire spurred me on. He tossed me off of him onto the floor. Landing on my stomach with a thud, I pushed myself to my hands and knees. Callen slammed his body into mine, knocking me back down. His pants and boxers were pushed down his thighs. I could feel his skin against mine, causing my core to clench with wanting.

"You should have given them what they wanted," he hissed in my ear as he tore my panties from my hips and two thick fingers pushed inside me. I gasped at the intrusion, but they slid in easily with my dripping desire.

"You should have left me there!"

He pulled his fingers out and spanked me hard across the ass, the sound echoing through the room. "The hell I should have. You are mine!" he growled with another swat.

My backside stung from the force he used. I wiggled beneath him as he sat up, pressing a hand between my shoulder blades to keep me lying flat.

"This is mine!" he declared as he slammed his fingers back inside me. I moaned as he thrusted them in and out. "You let another man touch you. You sacrificed your body for mine. No one is ever to touch you but me. Do you understand?"

I found myself rocking backward onto his fingers, his possessiveness igniting the warmth inside my lower stomach. He removed his fingers and spanked me even harder when I didn't answer. "Do you understand?"

"Yes," I screamed breathlessly, "I understand!"

He flipped me over onto my back and positioned himself at my entrance. I tried to urge his hips forward with my heels, but he sat still, staring down at me. He grabbed my left wrist, brought it to his mouth, and sucked my soulmark between his teeth while caressing it with his tongue. My body bucked off the ground in pleasure as he abruptly thrust himself completely inside me.

"Who does this belong to?" he asked as I adjusted to him.

"You. It belongs to you," I answered. I pushed my hips upward to rock into him, but he refused to move with me.

"Who?"

"You, Callen. It belongs to you. Only you. I'm all yours. Now, please, please, I need you to move. I need you to take me," I begged him.

"You're damn right your mine," he said as he pulled out of me and slammed himself forward again. "All mine!"

He leaned over, and I dug my nails into his back as he violently thrusted into me. He bit my covered nipple, pulling it taunt. I gasped as he tugged, and I locked my fingers in his hair, snapping his head back. A growl ripped through his chest, and he wrapped his hand around my throat. There was no fear this time, only yearning. My body and mind needed Callen to dominate. I needed the reminder that I allowed him to do this, because I wanted it, not because it was forced. I wanted him to possess me just like I possessed him. He might be the dominant, but I held all the control.

I matched Callen thrust for thrust as he rutted into me. The tension was building in my core, and my walls clenched around him. His other hand found its way to my clit, and just the touch sent me over the edge. I screamed as my orgasm took me. Callen smashed his mouth to mine, swallowing the sound. His thrusts became more erratic and unorganized as he groaned out his own release. After he finished, he propped himself up to look at me while we caught our breath.

I gently grazed his cheek where I slapped him with my finger tips. "I'm sorry about your face."

"I'm sorry about your ass," he said, kneading the fleshy muscle.

"No, you're not," I giggled.

"No, I'm not," he answered with his own laugh.

The smile faded from my face as I stared into his eyes, "Thank you."

"For what?" he asked quizzically.

"For bringing me back in more ways than one," I replied with a soft kiss.

We left the safe house and headed back to the car from yesterday. Callen kept his arm wrapped around my waist as we walked. To the average onlooker, we appeared to be a typical couple out for the evening. We kept smiles plastered on our faces and lightly bantered back and forth as we passed other pedestrians. We came to the head of the alley where we parked the car and saw two men looking through the windows and pulling at the door handles. Callen inconspicuously steered me away and kept walking.

"How did they know that was our car?" I asked as I beat down the panic that was bubbling inside me.

"It might not be related. It could just be a couple guys looking to boost a car," Callen replied, but I could tell in his tone that even he didn't believe that.

"How far away is your truck?"

"Too far," he answered with a shake of his head.

He squeezed his arm tighter around me as we calmly walked. My anxiety grew as we headed for the main strip of the city. The music was blaring, and people littered the streets outside the bars and clubs. My eyes constantly scanned the crowd looking for anyone resembling the soldiers from the hospital.

Callen bent to whisper in my ear under the guise of an affectionate kiss, "We are going to have to snag a car from a dark lot."

He stood up straight, and I nodded with a smile. Before we could move any further, two additional men dressed in all black stepped onto the drag from a side road two streets up.

"Callen," I said, stopping in my tracks. My hand shot up to his arm in warning.

He turned to face me, putting his back to the men, "I see them. Do you recognize them?" His eyes were scanning the crowds behind us looking for additional threats.

"No. They don't look familiar, but their uniforms look like the ones the soldiers wore at the hospital. Minus the masks."

Callen stiffened, his eyes locked on the alley we had exited. "Shit, there are the ones from the car," he cussed.

Grabbing my hand, he pulled me into the closest bar. We slithered through the crowds toward the back of the building.

"Lacey, I want you to go out the back door and run. Don't stop. Run as far as you can, get in a cab, and go to my truck. It's at the store down the road from our apartment. The keys are in the visor. Then, go to the safe house. Nick will come and get you. I'll go back outside and draw them away in the opposite direction."

"No! I'm not going anywhere without you. You've lost

your mind."

"Lacey—"

"No," I said again, crossing my arms over my chest as I stopped to argue, "We are staying together. No matter what happens."

"Now is not the time for you to be stubborn," he hissed as he grabbed my arm and pulled me toward the exit.

"You're one to talk. You're as stubborn as I am!"

Callen glanced over his shoulder and groaned, "Ah, fuck, here they come. Let's go."

I quit resisting and quickly headed for the exit. Pushing the door open, we tumbled into the back alley and took off in a sprint. As we rounded the end corner, the bar door flung open, and gunshots ripped through the air. A man stepped into the alley to light a cigarette, and Callen pulled me into the building he exited. Pusheing our way through the crowd, we made it back to the main strip.

"Get across the road and into another building," Callen yelled in my ear so I could hear him over the raving music blaring through the street.

I nodded my head and jogged across the road to a hole-in-the-wall, dive bar. A few heads snapped in our direction as we passed straight to the rear exit. This alley was empty minus several dumpsters scattered up and down the walls. Unfortunately, I didn't see any other doors for us to dive into if the need arose.

"This way," Callen said as he took my hand.

We made it to the end of the alley and turned left into another. Voices shouted from behind us, followed by more gunfire. They were gaining on us. Callen sprinted a few feet in front of me, ripping through the alley. A soldier stepped out from the shadow of a dumpster, and Callen tackled him.

They rolled on the ground as they wrestled and fought. Callen was able to pin the soldier down and slam his head into the pavement.

Another soldier, however, stood in the shadows. He stepped forward aiming a gun at Callen, who put his hands in the air and slowly stood. The soldier moved closer to Callen, putting me - the lesser threat - to his back. My heart hammered in my chest as I desperately looked around the alley for help. My eyes landed on a metal pipe sticking up out of the dumpster. I quietly shifted the pipe and grasped it in my hands like a bat. I cleared my throat, and as the soldier turned around, I slammed the pipe into his temple. He dropped to the ground in a heap. Discarding the pipe, Callen and I resumed our flight.

They were quickly closing in all around us, and we were running out of options. At the end of the alley, three soldiers stepped out from around the corner, effectively blocking our path. Callen dodged to the left into an open door. I hurdled in after him with a side glance to the end of the alley. The soldiers were rushing to follow our diverted route. The door opened into a honky tonk bar with heavily intoxicated patrons filling the room, all eyes snapping to us as we entered.

"Quick, out the front!" Callen yelled at me.

Frantically, I rushed through the crowd with Callen on my heels. I was within a few feet of the door when a large man stepped out in front of me, grabbing me by the arm.

"Now, what's your hurry, honey?" he asked while pulling me close to him.

Before I could answer, the man's head snapped to the side as Callen's fist drove into his left temple. The man collapsed to the floor, knocked out cold. As I turned toward Callen, I saw the soldiers entering from the alley, but before I had time to yell a warning, another man tackled Callen to the floor. By instinct, I grabbed the man by his collar and yanked him backward.

From the corner of my eye, I caught the movement of a third man coming at us. I ducked and stuck my leg out, tripping him. He went flying into the table ahead and crashed to the ground. Callen regained his footing as the man who attacked him returned for a second round. Ready this time, Callen grabbed his swinging fist with his left hand and twisted the man's arm behind his back, a loud crack erupting as his arm fractured. The man screamed in pain, and Callen shoved him forward into our pursuers.

"Go! Now!" Callen barked at me.

These drunk idiots cost us precious seconds, seconds we didn't have. I launched myself toward the door through the sea of people parting to avoid the mayhem of the brawl. I scrambled into the road and saw a second group of men coming down the hill from the left, so I turned right and resumed my sprint. I looked behind me to ensure Callen was following. He caught up to me quickly and matched my stride.

"The bridge! Get to the bridge!" he yelled.

I could see it up ahead, extending over the Cumberland River. If we could make it, a quick dive into the water could lose them. It's over a seventy foot drop, but our options for escape were slimming by the second. A stitch was forming in my side, cramping with every breath, every step. I pushed forward as we closed in on the bridge. Only one hundred yards until we were there. As we neared our destination, a group of vehicles emerged at the other end of the bridge, barreling toward us.

"Oh, shit," I breathed heavily, halting abruptly.

Callen stood next to me turning in circles looking for our next move. He grabbed my arm and pulled me up a side street. We made it halfway down the road when another group of vehicles blocked the intersection above. Looking behind us, we saw the two groups of pursuers mesh into one.

"Goddammit," Callen cursed in exasperation, "They've herded us!"

"No, we have to be able to go somewhere," I replied, but I knew this was it. There was nowhere else to run, nowhere to hide. Soldiers poured out of the vehicles and headed toward us on both sides. All of them now wore masks with their black uniforms, aiming a mix of rifles and pistols forward as they approached.

Callen pulled me to his chest, embracing me tightly in his arms. He kissed my hair as he rested his chin on my head. The smell of him flooded my senses as I wrapped my arms around him. His scent made my heart flutter as a tear trickled down my cheek. Callen put a hand on each side of my face and lifted my head to look at him. In that moment, a million emotions passed between us. It was as if time stopped. He took my left hand in his and turned it over so my palm faced the sky. His fingers grazed the crescent moon shaped soulmark on my wrist. Tingles ran up my arm at his touch, lighting a fire inside me. This wonderful man was meant to be mine forever, and our forever was running out.

"When they get here, I'll distract them, and you have to run," Callen said.

"I told you, I won't leave you behind."

"Yes, you will. I'll keep them busy."

"No! We will do this together, one way or another," I insisted.

"There's no time to argue. I'll find you. I swear I will. I will find you again," Callen promised.

I prepared to protest, but before I could utter a word, Callen pulled me in for one last, long, passionate kiss. His mouth crushed mine in urgency, his tongue parting my lips to find its way to mine. The soldiers had just about reached us when Callen pulled back. He winked at me before turning around, grabbed the barrel of the closest soldier's rifle, and yanked. The soldier was tugged forward and down as Callen brought his knee up to collide with his stomach. He hoisted the soldier up and flung him into the next ones approaching, knocking two to the ground.

We were surrounded on all sides. Callen and I moved back to back, turning in circles looking for a break, but they were tightening in, closing their ranks. He grasped my hand and squeezed it. When he let go, we both charged forward into the wall of bodies. I tackled the man in front of me to the ground, but another instantly pulled me off. I tore his hand from my arm and snapped his wrist backward. He hollered as the joints hyperextended, and I shoved him away.

Another man grabbed me from behind and lifted me in the air. I kicked hard and connected with his shin. He grunted but wrapped his arms around me tighter. He turned, and I saw Callen. He was moving like lightning as he fought. Multiple bodies were scattered across the ground. His face was contorted in anger, his shirt drenched in sweat, clinging to his body. All his muscles were flexed and standing with effort.

A soldier stepped in front of me blocking my view. He grabbed at my legs, but my right foot made contact with his head, sending him to the ground. I reached my hands over my head and dug my thumbs into my captor's eyes. His grip around me loosened, and I darted away from him before he could recover.

"Run! Now!" Callen yelled to me as he threw a soldier whole bodily into a shop's glass window.

I started down an alley when I heard a shot ring out. Terror flooded my body as Callen flashed through my mind. Without thinking, I turned back toward the street and ran as fast as I could. Callen was down on one knee, blood seeping across the thigh of his jeans. Five soldiers were surrounding him. I launched myself toward them and knocked one over, drawing the attention of the others. Callen used my distraction to grab the rifle of another and rip it from his hands, slamming the butt back into his face.

In the same moment, I felt the barrel of a gun press into the back of my head, and I froze. Another shot rang out into the night air. For a second, I thought I was dead, but I took another breath as Callen stood and whipped around. The man holding me had fired into the air with a second pistol.

"Enough!" he yelled.

Callen stilled, taking in the scene. The man pulled me off the ground to a standing position. "Drop the gun, or I'll shoot her. Your choice."

For the first time ever, I saw true fear in Callen's eyes. I'd know that sickening voice anywhere, and I hated him.

"Callen, don't listen to him! He won't do it," I begged.

Callen tightened his grip on the rifle weighing the odds.

"On the contrary, my dear, I only need one of you. Ideally, you'd both be there, but I can make due with just your mate."

Callen glared at him, his knuckles white from his deafening grip on the gun.

"Shoot him, Callen," I commanded. "Do it." But, I knew he wouldn't, not while I was standing in harm's way.

C wrapped his fist in my hair and snatched my head backward, making me wince. He pushed the pistol's barrel up and under my chin, burying it in my skin. "Sweetheart, do shut your trap. The men are talking."

I set my jaw and went to speak, but I saw Callen move to set the rifle on the ground.

"Good decision," C said with a chuckle. "Now, on your knees and place your hands behind your back."

Callen did as he was told; however, his sharp jawline protruded as he clenched his teeth in anger. Two soldiers approached Callen, cuffed his hands in place, and flanked him on either side.

"It'll be okay," Callen said as tears stung my eyes.

Two more soldiers came and took me by each arm. C walked toward Callen, grabbed him by the shirt and slammed his fist into his face, delivering multiple consecutive blows. Callen's head whipped to the side, but he remained upright. He didn't move a muscle to defend himself, blood running from his nose as he stoically took the beating.

"Stop it!" I shrieked as I aggressively thrashed; but, the soldiers' fingers dug into my arms, holding me in place.

C sauntered back over to me and roughly pinched my cheeks in one hand. "I have had enough of you. Load her up while I finish," he ordered the soldiers restraining me.

I tried to pull free as they drug me toward the vehicles. "Just take me, and let Callen go. You never have to see him again. I swear I'll tell you everything you want to know," I pleaded.

Callen locked eyes with me and said, "I promise, Lacey," a reiteration of his vow to find me again.

A laugh of pure evil filled the street. "You shouldn't make promises you can't keep," C said as he raised his pistol and fired two shots at Callen. Both hit home in his chest, and Callen dropped to the ground.

A manic scream exploded from my chest, "You fucking bastard!" Chaos erupted inside me. I felt like I transformed into an animal as Callen laid lifeless on the ground before me. More soldiers came and grappled with my flying limbs. I swung my fists frantically as they tried in vain to restrain me.

Suddenly, I felt a crack to the back of my head as the butt

of a rifle slammed into me. I dropped to my knees in pain, my vision faltering. I tried to stand as a second blow connected with my temple. I crumpled to the ground, and the world went black.

## End of Book One

# A NOTE FROM
# THE AUTHOR

Thank you so much for reading. I hope you enjoyed *Soulmark*, and I look forward to sharing more work with you in the future.

If you could take a minute of your time to leave a rating or review for *Soulmark*, I would greatly appreciate it. I absolutely read all reviews and feedback left on Amazon and Goodreads, and I can't wait to hear all of your thoughts.

From the bottom of my heart, thank you again!

Follow this link to be taken to my Amazon Author Page where you can select your title for review:

https://www.amazon.com/author/blake.m.isles

# ACKNOWLEDGEMENTS

First, I would like to thank my husband for his support in this endeavor. My entire life I have written off and on, especially in my high school years. Back then, it was mostly for school projects and occasional poems I wrote for self-expression. Before *Soulmark* I hadn't written in over a decade. I've always been one to encourage make-believe, so I decided to give it a shot. Once I had written about half of the book, it dawned on me, like "Hey, I'm actually doing this!" He has been uplifting in this incredible journey, and I am so grateful.

Secondly, I would like to thank my parents. No matter what avenue I ventured down in my life, they have always been in my corner. While I have explicitly banned either of them from ever reading this book (Come on…I would utterly die of mortification if my parents read some of these sex scenes), they never failed to ask me how it was going or if I was going to publish it or not. I had told them I was really just interested to see "if" I could write a book (which they were completely supportive of), but they did encourage me to put it out there for others to enjoy - especially if it was a work that I was proud of. My dad, bless him, refers to it as my "dirty book". Well, their encouragement and support paid off, because I am proud of *Soulmark*. Also, I am excited to share it with the world - under my pen name, of course!

Lastly, I would like to thank you, my readers. As I have said, this was my first undertaking to write an actual novel. The cover design, epigraph, and content were all produced and created by me, and I am incredibly blessed to be able to share it with all of you. Thank you for taking the time to dive into this world with me, and I hope you enjoyed the reading as much as I enjoyed the writing.

# ABOUT THE AUTHOR

## Blake M. Isles

Blake M. Isles is an adult fiction author. A registered Nurse turned writer, she spends her days raising her two sons with her husband, and her nights writing smutty fiction for all those who need a little kink in their life. She is a lover of wine and coffee - both of which she enjoys during her writing escapades. In lieu of her own photo, below is a picture of her dogs, Cooper and Deaken (They're cuter anyway!).

# STAY CONNECTED

You can find all of Blake's published works on Amzon. For a one stop list, go to her Amazon Author Page to browse and follow along to receive notifications about new releases.

https://www.amazon.com/author/blake.m.isles

You can also go to her website for more information on her current Works In Progress and available releases.

https://blakemisles.my.canva.site/about-the-author

Follow Blake on Social Media for the freshest content from teaser reels to book excerpts, cover reveals, and more!

Facebook: Blake M. Isles - Author

Instagram and Threads: @blake_m_isles_author

TikTok: @blake_m_isles_author

# BOOKS BY THIS AUTHOR

**Soulmark: Trepidation**

Book Two of the Soulmark Duet

Coming Soon to Amazon and Kindle Unlimited